She Runs with Wolves, He Sits with Kittens

T. G. Reynolds

cometcatcher press

First Edition: 2023

Cover Images: iStock by Getty Images: credits: "maystra" and "laski"

Cover Design: Cometcatcher Press

Library and Archives Canada Cataloguing in Publication

Reynolds, Timothy G. M. 1960 -

She Runs With Wolves, He Sits With Kittens

Romantic Comedy/Timothy G. M. Reynolds

ISBN: Paperback print: 978-1-7380328-0-8

ISBN: eBook: 978-1-7380328-1-5

1.Fiction 2.Romantic Comedy I. Title II.

Title: She Runs With Wolves, He Sits With Kittens

Cometcatcher Press

Calgary, Alberta, Canada.

Stacey made me do it.

For Argaw, a kind, gentle soul and friend... gone from us far too soon.

For V and K and L and A and S.

For Calliope and Kerouac.

Special Thanks to

Stacey Kondla

Virginia O'Dine

Dave Bidini

Morgonn Ewen

Laura Resnick

Kevin Jepson

Ann Cooney

Barb Galler-Smith

Suzy Vadori

Stephanie Rozek

Deborah Easson

Derek Trask

Chapter 1

I PUSHED THE SHOVEL down into the hard, dry soil. Toronto hadn't seen rain in a couple of weeks and apparently, the grave hadn't seen a sprinkler in a while either. Throwing some weight onto the spade I got it to dig in just as a cute teen couple came around the corner, hand-in-hand and so in love that they didn't have their cell phones out. They slowed when they saw me and the girl edged a little closer to the boy. I smiled my best "Here's Johnny!" Jack Nicholson smile and nodded toward the grave.

"I'm just taking them home for the week. It's Mom's birthday on Tuesday."

Don't ever let anyone tell you that boys can run faster than girls. Her man bolted after her, but she left him in the dust, glancing back wide-eyed to see if I was following. I wanted to raise the shovel and make growling noises, but I'd probably done enough damage to their young psyches already.

I could clearly hear Mom's voice in my head, even though her ashes were six feet down in the grave at my feet. "Maxwell Aldous Walden, why do you have to say such things?"

"Well, Mom, maybe it's because I'm digging down into your and Dad's graves and I'm not happy about it. Sure, this little evergreen is dead and needs replacing, but this wasn't my idea, it was Lizanne's, who didn't show up to help me like she said she was going to. Besides, you know I say stupid shit when I'm freaked out."

"Don't swear. It's uncalled for."

"Yes, Mom." Ignoring the voice that wasn't really there, I finished the job at hand, reverently removing the tree and placing it in the nearby garbage can as instructed. I cleaned up around the hole, then bent over the grave marker next to Mom and Dad's, brushing away the leaves and using the scissors on the little knife on my key chain to cut back the grass that was encroaching on twenty-five-year-old Edward Kurasawa's final resting place. I was going to say that I don't know Edward from a hole in the ground, but considering where I was, that would be in even poorer taste than my crack about digging up Mom and Dad. His grave was simply the one next to theirs. Anyway, I finished up, and said a quiet prayer over the three graves.

On my walk back up to the street to begin the trek home, I texted Liz. *All done. Let me know if you need help with the new tree.* I wasn't happy with my sister for not bothering to show up and at least supervise the digging, but anger wasn't going to get me anywhere. It's not like she was the type to be sitting at home doing nothing while I pretended to be a gravedigger who scared the crap out of young lovers. At least, she better not have been.

Ten minutes later her text found me as I was boarding the bus home. *Chk ur messages, goofball. NEXT weekend we r doing the tree. Thx 4 getting it done, tho. I can handle planting new 1.*

Next weekend? I checked my phone's calendar. Yup. Sure enough. *Next* weekend. That's what I get for trying to rely on my crap memory. It really *is* crap. I'm not just some absent-minded, self-absorbed dude who can't remember shit because I don't care. There were a few blows to my head when I was younger that my doctor suspects might be why I can remember I have an appointment, but not always where or when. There was a head-to-the-goalpost incident, a tumble off a small bluff incident at Cub Scout camp, an accidental golf-club-to-the-base-of-my-skull incident on a tricky par three in high school, and the more recent standing-up-into-the-open-cupboard-door incident requiring six stitches. There may have been others, like baseballs to the head or tumbles off my bike, but they aren't in the brain files I have ready access to.

I take Omegas which seem to help keep my cognitive functions in good shape, and I use the usual digital reminders and sticky notes to make sure I don't forget big stuff like appointments or deadlines or clandestine grave-digging sessions.

I'm usually pretty good, but when I get stressed or distracted, things slip past me. I've definitely been more than a little distracted since I proposed to Michelle and she laughed at me.

oOo

Maybe the Hilton Toronto Airport has nice rooms, but as I dropped down onto one knee, took Michelle's hand, and stammered out "Will you marry me, Mish?" I didn't see the colour of the bedspread, the fullness of the minibar, and whether the painting over the bed was a pastoral sunrise, a relaxing seascape, or moose fornicating under a full moon. I barely even noticed her four shocked besties snapping pictures and live-tweeting the moment.

For her answer, Mish grabbed me by the arm, hauled me to my feet, and dragged me stumbling into the bathroom, away from Mandy, Amy, Cheryl, Stephanie, Instagram, and Facebook Live.

"Are you *joking*, Max? I'm about to fly home to have one of my kidneys cut out and put into my dying mother and you ask me *now,* in front of my friends and Instagram where I look like a complete *bitch* if I say no?"

"I didn't want you to leave without showing you how much I love you." Yes, I actually spouted those lame words.

Mish managed to simultaneously sigh, chuckle, and shake her head in her most perfect pityingly judgmental manner. Then she strolled out of the bathroom, calmly took hold of her wheeled gold aluminum suitcase's telescoping handle, and smiled sweetly at her baffled friends. "I have a plane to catch." Out the door she went, suitcase and friends obediently in tow. Her friends filed past me, standing numb in the bathroom doorway.

Mandy snarled, Amy wouldn't meet what I suspect was a stupidly stunned gaze, Cheryl squeezed my arm in sympathy, and Stephanie leaned in, kissed me gently on my bearded cheek, and whispered "True love doesn't run away."

Down at the gate, Mish gave me a convincing hug and simply said "I'll call you when I land."

Her going home to Ottawa to help her Mom was a big deal to me, mostly because no matter how many ways in the last few weeks I'd phrased the question "Will you be gone a while?" "When are you coming home?" "What's your ETA back to T-Dot?"—she never gave me a straight answer. Maybe I should have seen that as a sign.

oOo

A month later Michelle was still in Ottawa, her mother's kidneys had miraculously recovered without surgery now that her only daughter was back home, and that only daughter's dentist ex-fiancé was somehow back in her life. *No, I didn't know she had an ex-fiancé back there, let alone that he was a dentist. What's that expression? We can't control what happens to us, we can only control how we react?* Michelle had abandoned me and I reacted the only way I knew how... I cancelled my next appointment with my dentist and got on with my life.

Over the years I've learned that people leave and don't come back. That's why I'm now comfortably alone in my little red brick in-fill, spooning moist cat food into little dishes and mixing in medications or vitamins for Kerouac the tuxedo kitty, Ginsberg and Burroughs the short-haired gingers, Zwerling the Persian, and Calliope the Torby—the five kittens Michelle and I were fostering when she decided she needed to return to Ottawa for her mother.

To the kittens, I'm simply the two-legged slave who feeds them and scoops their poop, but in the human world, I'm the manager of the one and only *Long & Lat Maps* shop around the corner from the house. I'm also a more-mellow-than-cynical Spoken Word hobbyist with a Chinese tat on my forearm that translates as "beef and broccoli special", although I tell everyone it says "strength and courage", or "love and linguini", depending on the level of silly I'm feeling at the time.

oOo

"Wow. She's..."

"Yes. Her *ki* is so out of whack it makes me crazy."

The person Missy Wakabayashi and I were discussing was a sweaty but pretty mid-twenties blonde in black yoga pants, a bright yellow tank top, and a dark grey hoodie beating the hell out of the heavy bag hanging in the corner of Missy's karate school. The woman had no martial arts skill I could discern from my 'expert' hours of watching Jessica Henwick, Rhonda Rousey, and Lucy Liu; but what she did have was fury. She was punching, kicking—a lot of groin-area-kicking!—and even backhanding the bag in pure rage, her glasses askew, and her thick, shoulder-blade-length blonde braid flailing and slapping like Lara Croft as she grunted and attacked. I reflexively covered my groin, not envying whoever got this Rage Grrl so riled up.

I'd stopped by Sterling Wakabayashi's Karate School to drop off a map for Missy, or *Kyoshi*, as both her students and most of Bloorcourt call her. I'd studied karate for about three months when I was twelve, but that was long enough to know a Kyoshi was a serious ass-kicker with at least seven Dans of black belts, and maybe a Fred or Bob, too. I joke, but it's with affection and respect for Kyoshi. At nearly fifty, she looks younger than my thirty-five and moves like she's twenty. She's lived in the area all her life, pretty much raised on the mats in her father's school, which she now owns and runs with her son, Sensei Jake.

Kyoshi had commissioned me to make a big hand-drawn map of Japan and Korea on parchment as a gift for her father, Sterling's, eightieth birthday on Thanksgiving in October. It took me the better part of the last month, measured twenty-by-thirty inches, and was now carefully rolled up in the tube currently tucked under her arm. Her plan was to have her mother hand-calligraphy all of the family names and locations of importance onto it, then frame it, and present it to her father from the entire family. To have been part of such a project was not just a fun use of my education as a Cartographic Specialist, but it was also a great honour.

I have no idea how long Rage Grrl had been murdering both the heavy bag and her body, but she was sweat-soaked, red-faced, and slowing down even as I watched out of the corner of my eye. There was something both arousing and terrifying about her energy. Kyoshi tugged on my elbow and drew me towards her office behind us. "Come on, Max. She's not your type. I suspect she eats men for breakfast."

I took one last look over my shoulder to see the woman collapse on the mat. Whatever she ate for breakfast kept her in great shape. "She's a lesbian?"

"No, just angry. She's an old friend of Jake's from The Keg Steakhouse. She needed a place to work off some steam. Something about a flooded condo and 'expletive deleted contractors'."

"That's a lot of steam."

"Most definitely. I think she needs some serious Zen principles in her life."

She closed the door behind us to get some privacy before she gently removed the map from the tube and unrolled it on her pristine desk. She was quiet for so long that I was afraid I'd got something wrong, but when she turned to look up at me, her eyes were moist. "This is wonderful. You are truly a *renshi*—a polished master. Father will be moved. It will take some convincing to get Mother to put a brush to this wondrous work and add the names."

"Your mother has written books on traditional calligraphy and teaches masters classes, Kyoshi... I think she'll do just fine."

"Of course, she will, but you know Mother. She wears her humility like a badge of honour." She handed me a cheque for my work and I bowed thanks.

"It was my pleasure." I'd worked hard to emulate the style of the centuries-old maps Kyoshi had given me samples of, even down to using brushes instead of pens wherever I could. It was one of my best pieces.

There was some energetic noise out in the training hall and Kyoshi returned to the area to silence the enthusiastic arrival of the next class with a simple look. The entire group of fifteen or so teens snapped to attention and bowed respectfully. She returned their bows and smiled. While she calmly gave instructions to the students in Japanese, I returned to the dojo's entrance and retrieved my shoes, noticing Rage Grrl was gone, probably to shower and change. That woman needed either some serious therapy or less caffeine.

o0o

I had to get home to the kittens, so I hustled over to my best friend Aba's restaurant, *The Nigerian Prince*, to pick up my take-out order. Aba and Lydia's oldest son, David, was at the podium when I walked into the warm, aromatic, half-full restaurant. The name of the place was a tongue-in-cheek tease of the multiple famous Nigerian Prince email scams, but Aba, Lydia, and their Uncle Argaw treated their African roots very seriously with respect to both the ambiance of their award-winning restaurant and the exquisite menu. Lanky, goofy, fifteen-year-old David greeted me with the lopsided grin of a teen who thinks he's the wisest dude in the room and loped off to get my order of *ugali*, cabbage, and *kitcha fit-fit* with yogurt and *berbere*. Aba waved from the kitchen and held up his index finger, which was his way of saying "Wait! I'll be right out, Brother!" David returned with my order, and his father arrived a moment later.

"Max! I have something for you. Come into the office." He turned on his heel and led the way to the back of the restaurant, avoiding seated patrons with a quick step and a practised swing of his hips.

I followed along, less adroit and a bit slower. We went through the IN door to the service area, skirted the area of the garde-manger, and into the tiny, jam-packed, but well-organized office. He waved me over to his side of the desk while he poked two-fingered at the keyboard.

"I know you're not a wild and crazy party guy anymore, and I know Michelle broke your heart, but I also know you're too busy to go out looking for your perfect mate, so I have created a profile for you on eRomance-dot-ca. My late birthday gift to you." He handed me a 2x2 yellow sticky note. "That's your username and password."

I was stunned on a couple of levels. Firstly, that he thought my being single for a few weeks was tragic enough to need an intervention; secondly that he'd taken time from his busy life as a restaurateur, husband, and father to set this up for me. I was both moved and disturbed, but I leaned in and examined the profile.

"That picture is five years old! And I'm five-nine, not five-eleven. At least you've got my education right and didn't give me a Ph.D. in Particle Physics or some such." I kept reading. "'A perfect evening is soft music, delightful African cuisine, dancing, and a fun Zinfandel'? Hardly. I'm a merlot man, or Spanish Garnacha when it's available."

"I *know* that. We've been drinking together since we were teens. But as Lydia pointed out—"

"You got *Lydia* involved in this insanity?"

"Of course. David helped, too. And Genette."

"The *staff* helped?"

"David was the first to give me feedback, and then I realized if you were going to meet and keep a woman we were going to need help from actual women."

"I suppose." I'm amazed he didn't post it on Facebook for feedback from all his friends.

"Hey, Lydia wanted to sign you up for speed dating. *This* is a compromise. She pointed out that most women she knows prefer white wine, specifically Zinfandel."

"She needs to get out more. I'd rather meet a woman who drinks beer. Less pretentious."

"Since when is Zinfandel pretentious? You can buy it in a box with a spigot."

"Fine. We'll leave it. I appreciate all you've done with this, Brother, but Michelle's side of the bed is barely cold." It was actually quite cold, but it had been for a while before she left.

"Michelle *who*? It's time to move on. You deserve to be happy in love. *Everyone* does."

"If you say so." I didn't expect the dating profile to actually get any attention, so no harm, no foul. I know my Kenyan best friend meant well and I almost said *the Internet is no way to find love*, but Aba and Lydia actually met online in a Canada-Kenya Facebook group. She'd immigrated to Canada as a pre-teen with her family twenty-five years ago and Aba had been here since our last year of high school together. They had four children now and owned the restaurant with Aba's uncle, and all three had been trying to get me to settle down and 'produce many babies with a good woman' since even before I met Michelle six years ago.

"I *do* say so. I also say you should get home to your kittens and eat that spectacular dinner I cooked you."

"Good idea. I had six years to make the relationship work with Michelle. I'm just not 'dentist' enough for modern women."

He put his palm on my chest. "Then we will find an old-fashioned woman who is looking for a poet with a big heart."

"Who likes cats."

"Exactly, Brother."

As I walked the meal home five minutes away a runner blurred past on the sidewalk, white earbuds in, and looking a lot like Rage Grrl. I watched her pound down the sidewalk, dodging an elderly dog walker and making a quick right at the next corner. When I finally unlocked the front door and got inside, thoughts of her and my growling stomach were drowned out by the plaintiff cries of five tragically starving kittens. It was only four hours since they'd seen me for their last feeding, but that didn't dull their cries.

What in many older homes would be a salon or sitting room off the entrance, Michelle and I had converted to The Kitten Room with two carpeted cat trees, three litter boxes, five little cat beds, and a newspaper-covered custom rubber mat to protect the hardwood floor. I'd replaced the original door with a really nice matching Dutch door so we could leave the top open while keeping the bottom closed. We also set aside the small back bedroom upstairs to isolate sick or misbehaving kittens.

Slipping off my shoes, I sock-skated to the kitchen to put my dinner out of their reach, then hustled back to release the beasts into the rest of the first floor. Their little mews of hunger, despair, and absolute, abject agony filled the house as soon as they were released from their 'prisons'. To ease their mock pain I lay down on the area rug and sacrificed myself to the kitten gods, mauled by a Torby, two gingers, and a white/grey Persian. Kerouac hooked onto the scent of culinary Africa and raced in his clumsy kitten way to the kitchen.

For five delightful minutes, I was smothered in raspy-tongued kisses, sharp baby-toothed nips, and more purring head-butts than any person deserves. When Michelle decided she wanted to foster kittens, I balked, but she insisted and I caved. This group was the fourth batch we'd hosted in this house. When she left on her kidney-forfeiting adventure, I'd just kept the ball rolling with these five. The first three batches were litters that came with their mothers, so we only had to care for each mom and she did the rest. When this fourth batch of orphans arrived they were all malnourished, Ginsberg and Calliope had eye infections, and Kerouac tended to gorge himself on any food around him, then puke it up. He still does, so I'm trying a special diet with him for a few weeks before the vet decides whether or not to try medication. For the first week Michelle was gone, I took them all to work with me to monitor them, feed them, and ensure they kept warm. Our sales tripled that week, so even now I occasionally take one in with me and keep them on a harness in a carrier on my chest. They love the warmth and attention, especially cuddly, talkative Calliope.

With care and love, foster kittens thrive and eventually move on to loving homes. We lost two little ones early on through no fault of our own, but Michelle's training and experience as a vet tech made all the difference in the world. I'd watched her closely, though, and took plenty of notes to compensate for my wobbly memory, so I think I've gotten pretty good at it. The kittens might eventually get adopted out, but at least none of them have left me for their dentist not-so-ex.

Unable to get at my dinner up on the stovetop, Kerouac eventually joined the others for 'maul the human' time, head butting me and vocalizing like a helium-sucking jaguar determined to get what he wants.

"Yo, K-Cat! I'll feed you, I promise!" I scooped the determined little guy up and plopped him on my chest, where he immediately started kneading me, which was a pretty good indicator he'd been weaned too soon. That often happened with rescues. I let him knead and purr away while the others settled down on any part of me that was warm and comforting. Calliope nestled herself right into the small gap between my legs, and I was trapped. It was delightful and wonderful and a little frustrating, but only a little. How could I get mad at this kind of unconditional love? Every new batch became my favourite, and these five were no different. With the representative from the foster agency coming soon to do an inspection and chat, I was thankful the little fur-balls were all hail and hardy. I'd heard there were one or two people at the Hogtown Cat Rescue who had their doubts I could fill Michelle's shoes alone, but I had it all under control and the inspection was going to be a breeze. Probably.

An incoming text and my own hunger eventually broke up the love-fest. Careful not to move too quickly and spook or crush them, I got to my feet and shuffled to the kitchen, making my way around the scrambling kittens and their half-dozen empty cardboard boxes on the floor while reading the missive from my sister, Lizanne. *Thx again for digging up that tree. Wasn't sure I was going to be able 2 do it.*

I texted her back. *No problem. I love rooting around with a shovel in a cemetery. But next time I'll wait until it's dark, to avoid witnesses.* God, I hope not! I hated cemeteries at night. In college, I used to shortcut through the one next to campus to get to my girlfriend's residence building. I never saw anyone else, but I *always* felt like I was being followed.

Did you have any trouble? The groundskeepers didn't hassle u did they?

No. Just some curious teens. I might have told them I was digging up the bodies.

Damn! I can't believe I missed that?!!

I replied with a sad face emoji and got back to the task at hand.

Kerouac got his food on the kitchen island with me while the other four got their dishes on the floor, warm water mixed in with their kibble to stave off dehydration. Once they were all distracted with their dinners, I extracted my own meal from the compostable boxes and set it out on plates. It was still nice and hot, so I grabbed a wheat ale from the fridge and pulled up a stool at the counter, where I could both eat and keep an eye on Kerouac to ensure he didn't jump down and bully his step-sibs away from their food.

I ended up spending as much time keeping Kerouac out of my *kitcha fit-fit* as I did eating it, but at least he wasn't shoving his way into dishes I couldn't defend. Eventually, he head-butted me one last time and curled up in the shoebox placed on the island expressly for his comfort.

oOo

I lifted Kerouac and placed him on the floor, where he immediately licked any and all residue from the other four dishes. I led the little bouncing and mewing five-cat parade out into the hall and up the stairs to the room that doubled as my office/studio. The room was simple, with my yellow-sticky-note-reminders-ringed drafting table, drawing supplies, iPad, speakers, and computer at my level, and cardboard boxes, cat toys, and a small litter box on the floor. My old Yamaha acoustic guitar hung on the wall, but I hadn't played in ages and I was pretty sure it was as out of tune as my memory was. For the most part, the wee beasties slept or tussled with each other while I worked, with one or two occasionally climbing my pant legs to get into my lap. If they lay down and behaved, they got to stay. If they got rambunctious up there—like Ginsberg and Kerouac often did—they got plunked back on the floor. I closed the door behind us to keep them safely contained while I worked.

"Hey, Siri." *Beep.* "Please continue playing the audiobook *The Alchemist.*" It was the amazing book by Paulo Coelho, narrated by wonderfully sonorous Jeremy Irons. I picked up my mechanical pencil and returned to work on the coastline of Lake Ontario on a map for my buddy, Kevin. He lived in Alberta but had sailed tall ships all through the Great Lakes, so his wife Jayne thought a hand-drawn selected shipwrecks and lighthouses map would be a perfect gift for Christmas, five months away.

I was lost in the detail around Deseronto, Ontario when my iPad chimed with an incoming message. Slowly swivelling the chair around, I glanced down at the message summary on the screen. It was from Michelle.

Hey Max. Just checking in to see how you and the kittens are doing. We need to discuss the house. Miss you...

Shit. The house. Her name was on both the title and the mortgage. If she wanted me to buy her out, I was screwed. She put a little money into decorating the place, but the down payment came from my inheritance after Mom died, and the mortgage payments all came from my account. Besides, *she* left. She's the one playing doctor with the dentist and she can keep doing that. I suppose

I missed her, but people leave and don't come back. It's their default setting. I put a digital reminder in my phone to call my lawyer tomorrow.

Damn. The house. Was she going to make me sell it?

My phone chimed again, this time with a reminder that I needed to pick up milk, bananas, a lottery ticket, and toilet paper, and a reminder to take posters around to the shops advertising my basement suite for rent. I checked my watch. It was 6:45. I had fifteen minutes to get to the mini-market. I picked up a copy of the simple poster I'd made. "Hey, Siri." *Beep.* "Pause audiobook."

"Audiobook paused."

It would only take fifteen minutes, tops, to walk the half-block, get what I needed, and get home, so I scooped up Calliope and Burroughs and left the other three to play, slipping out while they were distracted with a bell ball I kicked into the corner away from the door. Calliope and Burroughs went into the kitten room downstairs while I grabbed my light jacket, keys, wallet, and phone, but the phone's battery was dead, so I stuck it on the entry table's charger. I then retrieved the kitten chest carrier off the hooks and two mini harnesses. I had plenty of practice with the next step, so the kittens were both up, harnessed, and in the carrier with their mewing heads peeking out in no time at all. Leaving them behind would have been faster, and legally I wasn't supposed to take non-service animals into the mini-market, but the fresh summer air would do them good.

I was out the door with ten minutes to spare to walk about a hundred yards. Up to the corner, cross at the light, cross again, then a few doors down to the market. Unfortunately, any time I carried a kitten with me, it took soooo much longer to get anywhere.

"Oh, my gawd! They're so cute!"

"Barbra! Look at the kitties!"

"Yousef, you must see kitty! *Two* kitties!"

"Douā? Minunat! Wunnerful! Such beauties!"

"Goyang-i! Kit Katties!"

"Can I touch?"

"Sorry, no. They're still babies." They wouldn't be getting their first shots until next week and I didn't want to risk it. I suppose I shouldn't have brought them out of the house at all, but they were safe in the carrier. It's hard to catch fleas or an infection up there. The bell over the door dinged as I entered the narrow shop, and my dear friend Kalani looked up from her senior university physics textbook laid open on the counter. Her smile was covered in braces, but that didn't stop her slender, dark face from lighting the place up.

"Max!" She glanced at her watch. "You have two minutes. QuikPik? Or your numbers?"

"LottoMax quick one, please." The lottery draw was only for $5 million, so I went with random numbers. Last week it was up to $60 million and I went with both random and picked numbers. Someone won, but it wasn't me. My tickets were now just bookmarks, as usual.

"Wanna play the Extra?"

I didn't usually, but with the kittens in the carrier, I felt lucky. "Yes, please." She pressed the buttons and printed out the ticket. "I'll just grab a few things and be right back."

"Okay. Wanna leave the kittens here? They can play with me while you shop. Hint, hint."

"Nice try, Kalani. The second I put them down you'll drop a silk cloth over them, wave your wand, and make them disappear faster than I can call Animal Services. I'll bring them up to say 'hi' in a minute." She wasn't just a cat lover, she was a budding magician.

"Okay... spoilsport. Then I'll show you my new trick."

"Cool."

I grabbed a basket and gathered what I needed before returning to the counter.

After she bagged everything up and handed my purchases over, she retrieved a deck of cards from the counter beneath the cigarette cabinet. "Check it out, Max." Holding the deck with the backs toward me, she snapped her fingers and wiggle-waggled her fingers in a magic sign probably intended to distract me. A moment later the six-of-clubs rose slowly from the deck. Halfway up, it tipped over and fell onto the counter. "Damn."

"I'm guessing that wasn't part of the trick."

"Hardly." She shoved the deck into her back pocket and squeezed a big dollop of anti-bacterial gel on her hands from the dispenser behind the display of Bic lighters. "So, who did you bring to tease me with tonight?" She rubbed the gel all over her hands, making sure they were as sterile as they could get.

"Calliope and Burroughs."

"My favourites!" She fanned her hands in the air to dry them. "How are the others doing? I know it's only been a week since I saw them last, but, you know..."

"I know. They're all great, thanks. Except for Kerouac. If you believe a word he says, I never feed him and I beat him just for fun."

"Silly cat. How about you? How are *you* doing?" Kalani and her wife Shannon were two of the handful of friends who came over to the house for potluck supper once or twice a month, so they were well aware of Michelle's absence. She reached out and gave the kittens purr-and-wiggle-inducing scritches.

"It's all good. Work, kittens, sleep, eat, kittens, work, sell the house..."

"What? You're *not*? Is she making you do it?"

"Not yet. Right now she just wants to talk about—" A raging car horn, a brief screech of brakes, a scream, and the metallic/plastic crash-thump of an accident in front of the store cut me off.

Chapter 2

I RUSHED OUTSIDE TO make sure everyone was okay, but it was only a fender-bender and no one appeared hurt so I left the two drivers to yell at each other while actual witnesses gathered. Back inside, Kalani was more angry than alarmed. I tucked my shaking hands into my pockets. I'm not a fan of car accidents. One killed my friend, Tracy.

"One of these days someone is going to get seriously hurt there, Max. The pedestrian signal is too short and everyone rushes to get across, but the drivers just zip around the corner. Dad almost got hit last week."

"Me too. It's worse when the sun is straight down Bloor. Westbound drivers can't see a damned thing but they barely slow down at all."

Kalani rubbed the heads of the vocally appreciative kittens. "We can't have anything happen to these little sweeties—or to you—so cross carefully."

"Always. You, too. Say hi to Shannon and your folks for me. I'd better get this stuff home before the other kittens tear up the house." I almost forgot the ad for the suite! I pulled it out of my pocket and unfolded it. "Would you mind sticking this up on the Community News Board? My cousin and her husband finally got possession of their place in Oakville, so I need to find a tenant for the basement suite."

"Of course." She accepted the paper, giving it a quick read-through. "Good ad. See a lawyer about the house."

"Thanks. That's the plan."

"Good." She blew kisses to the kittens and winked at me.

"Later, Amazing Kalanirini."

"Later, Cat-Man-Do."

The sidewalks were filling with people and I heard sirens approaching, so I squeezed through the growing gallery of camera-phone-raising gawkers and crossed cautiously at the next green light. I had my lottery ticket bookmark, my supplies, my kittens, and an itch to get back at the map waiting with the little furry mischief-makers.

o0o

I spent another two hours on the map, pencilling in the outline based on the satellite images I'd printed off. The kittens eventually settled into their boxes, on their perches, or on the high, wide top of the back of my chair. Kerouac and Zwerling's purring right behind my ears threatened to put me to sleep, but I soldiered on. Michelle always had a way of making me feel guilty for the time I spent on maps while she was crashed on the couch binge-watching TV shows from her childhood, so it was refreshing to be able to work straight through. I just wondered how long I was going to be able to keep this new normal before she swept it away. I could survive in some one-bedroom condo if I had to, but it would make fostering kittens a lot tougher.

By the time I was too tired to focus on the heavy linen paper, the kittens were out cold. I scooped them all up into one big cat bed and carried them downstairs. There was a little fussing as I deposited their drowsy butts into their own beds, but they quickly settled down. I topped up the water dishes and cleaned the litter boxes before calling it a night myself. It wasn't particularly late, but I had to get to the shop early to start month-end inventory.

o0o

The one and only Bloorcourt Village *Long & Lat Map Store* was owned by Leona Montagne, a local realtor with a killer track record for sales of both residential and business properties. Even though she owned the shop, she didn't have much to do with the day-to-day business except to approve the larger bills I presented her with. I've never seen her do a shift and she leaves all of the ordering and accounting up to me, which means I'm fully aware the shop is almost always hovering in the red by a little and she's probably using it as a tax write-off.

I've never worked for anyone as laid back about profit and loss as Leona. She pays me a decent salary and her only shop concerns are a clean, professional appearance, and a solid community reputation. When I showed her a map I'd playfully sketched out of the neighbourhood with the shops all labelled and colour-coded, she handed me a hundred bucks and said "Polish it up, print off a few, and give them away. Just make sure to put the shop logo, domain name, and address on it, as well as creative credit to yourself." That first map was so popular Leona asked me to propose a few other local maps we might actually sell.

The tiny brass bell hanging over the door rang as I was inventorying the Routemaster map books with Kerouac in the chest holder while Ginsberg was napping in his harness and short leash on a little blanket on the counter next to the debit machine. Lord Huron's *The Night We Met* was playing softly over the shop's speakers. I stood up, expecting one of the many locals who often dropped by before a vacation looking for a map of their destination, but it was a stranger, a confused-looking professor type in a corduroy jacket with actual elbow patches and crisp, newish blue jeans. His glasses were smudged but he didn't seem to notice as he rubbed his thick red hair and looked around the shop.

"Good morning. Welcome to Long & Lat. What can I help you find?"

"Um...mandolin strings?"

"Oops. This is a map store. You want the music store a few doors down." I pointed west, where the big chain store was. Confusion about the two places was a common occurrence since the names both started with 'Long'. "But while you're here, are there any maps I can help you with? Maybe for your next vacation?" He turned and was almost out the door. "Or maybe to the Heritage Music Festival in Shelburne in a few weeks?"

He stopped mid-step, the sound of the door's bell still tinkling in the air. "I don't know that festival. I'm visiting from Moncton, here for the rest of the summer."

"It's a great festival! It's home to the Canadian Open Old Time Fiddle Championship. When you get to the music store, they can tell you all about the festival, but I've got the best map. You won't get lost or miss a single performance."

He adjusted his glasses with a long finger and smiled. "That would be lovely. Thank you."

Before he continued on his way, I sold him the map of South Western Ontario, a map of Toronto tourist attractions, spent fifteen minutes explaining how to get to Shelburne, and talked cats and music with him. I knew a few chords on my guitar and didn't dare try the narrow-stringed mandolin, but it was always nice to chat with a fellow pluck-and-strummer. Kerouac kept trying to get out of the chest holder to get his due affection from the stranger, but Ginsberg was content to just lie in his bed and accept head scratches from me. After the gentleman continued on his quest to find mandolin strings, I got back to the inventory. To some, it was boring, detail-oriented work, but I enjoyed the simple, pressure-free pace.

The alarm on my phone chimed. *Call lawyer about house*. I'd completely forgotten. What would I do without my phone? I called my lawyer, Juergen. The welcome recording said he was away on vacation for another two weeks but to Press 1 to speak to his assistant to make an appointment or Press 2 to speak to his partner if it was a legal emergency and couldn't wait until Juergen returned. I pressed 1 and grabbed the first available appointment... three weeks away. It wasn't an emergency, but a lot could happen in three weeks, especially with Michelle involved.

I returned to the inventory. An hour later I took a break to check the online orders. We had a simple website with a basic catalogue and an online store. When I came on board three years ago to replace Leona's son, Forrest, when he was diagnosed with skin cancer, there wasn't even a website. Forrest beat the cancer and moved his family to Halifax to follow his dream of living by the ocean, and I started the slow process of bringing the shop into the 21st century.

There were three orders, so I pulled the maps, packed them up, and dropped them in my out-basket, to be taken to the post office when I went home in an hour to feed the other three kittens. This was a pretty typical day. A few maps were sold in person, a few orders were filled online, and efforts to keep the window display clean and fresh. With breaks to walk home around the corner for kitty feedings—every few hours when they were younger, but once a day now—the days went by at a leisurely pace. Every so often I got an idea for a custom map for the shop and spent time sketching out the idea. Some of them had flopped, but my two most popular maps were *Runaway Grooms: Toronto's Best Places for LGBTQ+ Weddings* and *Brinkley's Map of West End Dog Parks.*

After I took over for Forrest, the shop had two employees, me being one of them, but when the part-timer, Nikolette, quit to go to Teacher's College, Leona decided if I was okay with doing it all, then maybe we should just make it a one-person operation. I'd been on my own here for four months now, and although it got busier on weekends as foot traffic increased up and down Bloor, I could probably handle it myself until the Christmas holidays started to roll around. For most of December, though, I couldn't stock vintage map replicas or globes of all sizes fast enough to keep up with the demand, and at least one part-time staff member was going to be a must.

By the time I mailed the packages and got home to feed the fur-balls, Kerouac and Ginsberg had had enough of me and just wanted to hang out with their siblings and eat. I grabbed a quick tuna sandwich, fought off the inevitable tuna-scent-catching feline love train, and once they were all fed and back in the kitten room, I returned to the shop. Inventory waited for no grunt.

o0o

Half an hour into the count of Collins Touring Maps, my phone chimed with an incoming text from Michelle. Holy crap. More about how she missed me but was never coming back? Or more about the house she hadn't sunk a dime into for a couple of years? In the few days after she left, her notes were affection and hopeful, but after she'd been back in the nation's capital for a week, the tone of her texts changed subtly and by the end of week two all hints, suggestions, or promises she'd be returning to our "home" faded away. She never once mentioned my proposal. At first, I was wounded and Skyped her to actually talk face-to-face, but it didn't take an empathic savant to read the distance in her tone and the coolness of her expressions. She'd moved on—or back or whatever—and so, I guess, had I. It wasn't my style to be so obsessed about my ex that I jumped when she snapped her fingers, but I should probably see what she had to say.

It was simply *Are you ignoring me, Max?*

What? Yes, I probably was. I swiped the texting app and went into my calendar where I placed an actual digital reminder to call the lawyer, or at least talk to Leona for advice. Then I went back to the inventory, both wanting to talk to Mish about what we were going to do about the house, and *not* wanting to talk about it. We'd done a lot of work on the place to fix it up and it was worth quite a bit more than we paid, but I didn't want to sell it. If she wanted a lot of money, though, it's what I would have to do because I really didn't have the cash to buy her out. Right now, though, I didn't have the energy to deal with the future dentist's wife face-to-face.

o0o

After an hour of barely concentrating on the inventory, I gave in and texted Mish back. *Sure. Good idea to talk about the house.* It *wasn't* a good idea, but I had to say something. God forbid I appear to be ignoring the woman who abandoned her nice life with me for a nicer one with cleaner teeth. There are always greener pastures, I suppose. I just happened to like my pasture just fine. I was finally comfortable.

Although I was distracted by my gut twisting in this fresh stress about the house, I got the inventory done. With forty-five minutes to spare, I had everything counted, entered into the spreadsheet, and saved in the cloud. Tomorrow I will look at the payables, receivables, and revenues and make it all balance. I reflexively checked my phone for a reply from Michelle but there was nothing and I was relieved. Then the phone buzzed and my Batman TV show theme song alarm startled me and I nearly dropped it. *Spoken Word night... 7 pm (read ...Women)*

Right! It was Thursday. The poem I'd picked was one of my newer ones, heavily inspired by recent developments in my life. It was also one of my shorter ones, but I still hadn't memorized it. I pulled it up on my phone and read it aloud to the maps and globes, for practice.

"WHAT I KNOW ABOUT WOMEN
Socrates spoke out and pointed out that
'All I know is that I know nothing',
and some days nothing is so much more than I could ever know.
I know no answer will be sufficient.
Insufficience reigns down in torrents.
I know no apology will cover my sin.
Sin is not in... not in style, indeed.
I know no reason will be reason enough.
Quite unreasonable,
I reason.

I know that I know not what I should know about that which we are discussing.
Discussed ignorance, mine.
But day in and day out I know, irrevocably, unconditionally, without recourse,
That before I even utter any words... I am wrong.
And that is all that I know, about women."

Okay, maybe it was more than a little cynical, but imagine how bad it would have been if the house crap had come up *before* I wrote it. Yeah. Exactly.

At five o'clock my phone chimed with my daily five-minute warning to shut up the shop. I went through my routine, checking the door and window latches, turning off the pedestal fans that made the place tolerable in Toronto's intolerable mid-summer heat and humidity, and locking the modest float in the cheap safe in the back office.

On the stroll home for a quick dinner and to feed the beasts before going to the club, I wondered if *All I Know About Women* was the right poem for this evening. Maybe I should go with something longer. *All I Know...* was the perfect length, though, if they drew my name for the competition part of the night. But they'd yet to draw my name. I suppose this poem would do for either the competition or the showcase. Maybe.

Back home all five fur-kids cranked up their poor-poor-pitiful-me acts before I even got my key out of the lock and back in my pocket. I peeked through the open top of their door. "Hello, my little demon furry terrorists! Yes, yes, it's me! Your jailer, your chef, your manservant." They tried to climb the door, mewing madly to get at me. "Come to Papa!" I opened the door carefully and knelt down for the love fest to begin. Whatever else was on my mind vanished in a puff of kitty cuddles.

oOo

The club lights were dimmed halfway when I finally arrived, thirty minutes before host and organizer Benny Love took to the stage and got the ball rolling. A few of the two dozen or so people looked toward the entrance and waved at me or smiled and nodded. They knew I'd sit in the back, get settled, order a drink, and then do the rounds of greetings before the show. We each had our pre-show routines.

A lot of people aren't quite sure what 'spoken word' is all about, so it's not as popular as stand-up or improv. The events are also known as *Poetry Slams*, and although it *is* poetry, it's also so much more. The 21st-century version grew out of hip-hop music, emphasizing wordplay and the actual performance in the reading or reciting. Cadence, intonation, and inflection are all important. *I'm* of the school of thought that firmly believes it has its roots in the Beat Generation writers of the forties and fifties, with the likes of Jack Kerouac, Allen Ginsberg, and William S. Burroughs. Ginsberg's poem, *Howl,* particularly inspired me, though it was the subject of a famous obscenity trial at the end of the fifties. I even have *My Own Howl*, a straight riff off the original, but it's too long for events like this. Maybe it'll make it into the book I'll write someday.

In the meantime, I was here in the club amongst fellow poets and howlers. I opened the Notebook app on my phone and pulled up the name list for the club. Most of the names I could remember, most of the time, but every so often I drew a complete blank on someone I should know. Most of them knew my memory sucked, but I liked to at least make an effort. From where I sat I could see the club's owner, Tio, at the bar, chatting with tonight's lone server, Dionne. Host Benny—looking like a cross-clone of Chris Rock and Denzel Washington—was off to the side shooting the shit with two dudes I'd only ever seen on television... Ziggy-something and Jimmy Jones...no, Jimmy *James,* of the National Spoken Word Team. Yes, we have a National Team, and if Ziggy and Jimmy were the showcasers tonight, it promised to be a great show. Rumour had it Benny was trying to get Moncton's Sammy Lefevre to come and speak some words with us when he rolled through town in the fall. I've heard the Slam Champ could get a room so lit it would burn all night with the energy.

Spread out amongst the tables I recognized regulars J'Neece, Patty, Normal, KC Chuck, and Trey, each sitting with friends or family. Dionne came by, I ordered my Jack and Coke. We were a small large community, if that makes sense. Only Normal and I actually lived in the area, while the others travelled from elsewhere in the city to get some stage time and hone their craft. There were probably two dozen spoken word events across Toronto. Some were monthly and some weekly, so there was always something happening somewhere in the city on almost every night of the week. I'd attended a few others for fun and inspiration, but this is the only one I came to regularly, prepared to get up on stage at. Truth be told, even though I was 'prepared', I've never actually stood up in front of the room and read a single damn word.

It scares the shit out of me. I can write the poems and I can read them aloud to the kittens or the empty shop, but once the microphone is in front of my face, I freaking freeze in the spotlight like a raccoon in the headlights. I'm stubborn, though. I still get ready most Thursdays, come out to participate and cheer on my friends, but I stay stuck to my seat during the show, hoping that the nerves I'm lacking will magically manifest and carry me up on stage.

"Thanks, Dionne." She handed me my drink with a big smile and continued on her rounds. I took my never-enough liquid courage in hand and started my own way around the room. I got three steps before J'Neece waved me over to her table.

"Max!" She stood and gave me a big hug as I joined them. She was nearly as tall as my five-nine, so we were a good hugging fit. Her waist-long box braids smelled wonderfully of olive oil and her skin had a citrusy scent that was so refreshing after my litter boxes and the stuffy shop. "How are the kitties, Max?" Speaking of which...

"Keeping me busy, of course. They're growing so fast. Soon they'll be off to their forever homes. How are the kids and Sammy?"

"Like the kittens, the kids are growing. Sammy has them out to the movies tonight. Some free pass to a preview of the latest Star Wars or Star Trek. They're such nerds, I love it." She turned to face the three people at the table, none of whom I had any recollection whatsoever of meeting, ever. "Max, these are my cousins from Montreal: Fabienne, Ricardo, and Chedeline."

I shook each of their hands. Some people just nod and greet, but I'm a hand-shaker. The strength of their grip, the texture of their skin, and the temperature of their hand all help me to make a connection with a person, to help me remember their name, maybe. "Salut. C'est un plaisir de vous rencontrer. Bienvenue à Toronto." My French was limited, but I could scrounge up the basic 'nice to meet you, welcome to Toronto'. What a mistake! They immediately started speaking to me as if I was fluent, and although I caught bits and pieces, I was lost damn fast. "Whoa! Sorry. You just heard my only comprehensible French, other than 'Je m'appelle Maxwell. Donnez-moi deux whiskies, s'il vous plaît'."

Ricardo roared a wonderful, rich laugh. "Mon ami, that is *all* you need to know!" He raised his bottle of beer in salute and I laughed and tipped my glass back at him.

J'Neece nudged me gently with her shoulder. "What have you got tonight,

Max?"

"A totally new one. The kittens give it four stars." I pulled the printed and folded copy of the poem out of my back pocket. I had trouble getting up on stage, but I had no problem sharing the poems for people to read. J'Neece opened the paper and read it. Her eyes narrowed, then widened, and finally crinkled with her big smile.

"*That* is a daring piece. At first, it smacks of misogyny, but a closer look reveals it's about the power struggle in a relationship and how the man is not always the one with the power. I'll bet Michelle would be pissed at it." She handed the sheet back and I returned it to my pocket.

"Probably. How about you? What are you treating us with?" J'Neece was one of the most powerful poetry slammers I've ever seen. Passion, humour, pathos… the works.

"I'm polishing up *Never Loud Enough*, for the regionals in the fall."

"Great choice!" And it was. A powerful blend of hip-hop, anger, prayer, and a plea for support, the poem brings tears to the room every time. It's a showstopper and the reason why J'Neece is a rising star.

"Thanks. I have a couple of timing issues I want to clear up, then I'll put it away and slam a couple of others in the weeks leading up to the regionals, just to keep the competition off balance."

"Smart thinking." I wanted to say 'hi' to the other poets before we got started. "I'll leave you to get psyched while I chat with Benny." I smiled at her cousins but didn't dare to butcher any more French. "It was nice to meet you. Enjoy the show."

"Merci. Au revoir."

"Later, Max."

"A bientôt, cher."

J'Neece and I hugged again and I moved on. I quickly checked my watch. Fifteen minutes to finish saying hi to everyone. It may sound like I was making the rounds like King Shit or Frank Sinatra, but I don't get out much and these were friends I actually had something in common with other than just being neighbours. I didn't like interrupting conversations in progress, so I quickly said my hi-howyoudoins to couple Normal and Patty, then finally six-foot-three, black-leather-clad, heavy metal guitarist, DJ, and finally poet KC Chuck. Normal, Patty, and DJ said quick 'hellos' while KC nodded and smiled, deep in a phone conversation.

"I'll be home by eleven and give the babysitter a ride wherever she needs to go... of course..."

We knuckle-bumped and I left him to sort out his post-show night. By the time I got around the room to Benny, he, Ziggy, and Jimmy were chilling with beers, and I was feeling an energy around the room I was personally lacking tonight.

"Max! Meet Ziggy 'Zig-Zag' Mitchell, and Jimmy James, tonight's showcasers! Sit, man."

I greeted the two guests and pulled up a chair. We chatted for five minutes about all and sundry, and then Ziggy asked the inevitable question.

"Max, brah. Are you up tonight?" He smiled warmly.

I glanced at Benny, who smiled patiently, which I appreciated. "I was. But I think tonight I'll just watch and learn."

"You have something you were going to slam, no?"

"I do." I tilted in my seat, tugged the sheet out of my back pocket again and handed it to him. I tried to keep my hand from shaking. I wasn't afraid, but I was definitely nervous. Here were two members of the National Team taking a look at one of my poems! Ziggy held it up and the three of them positioned themselves so they could each read it. Beneath the table, my fingers drummed a fast beat on my thigh as I watched their expressions closely. Eyebrows rose, half-smiles twitched, and when they were done, all three gave me the only reward I could ever ask for... they laughed.

Ziggy handed me the sheet back, but it was Jimmy who spoke first. "You have a good universal voice, Max. That speaks to *all* men. Women probably won't be impressed, but you have to speak your truth, and the truth is, sometimes no matter how hard we try, we men don't have a goddamned clue what women are all about. Nice work."

"Thank you."

Benny checked his watch and excused himself to get ready to start the show. Ziggy exchanged a vertical fist pound with him and turned back to me. "Jimmy nailed it. You've got a sweet rhythm and a dope way with words. You obviously have fun with the language. When I started out, I read the old white Beat Generation dudes, to see what else was out there. You've got their style, their flavour. I love it. If you could do this while playing bongos, you'd have a fun act. It's not slam style but could be a fun performance piece with wide appeal. Thanks for sharing that." He reached into his shirt pocket and pulled out a stylish gold-on-black business card. "If you've got others, I'd love to read them. Just email them to me."

Ziggy 'Zig-Zag' Mitchell wanted to read *my* poems? Holy shit! I tried to stay calm and cool. I accepted the card from him and read it, knowing to never accept a card and just slip it straight into a pocket. "Thank you. I appreciate that. I will." The lights dimmed and Benny took to the stage. It might only be an informal open-mic night, but Benny liked to keep a professional touch to both show respect for the art and to add gravitas to even the newbies' performances. While Benny did his intro, I took out my phone, and quickly inputted Zig-Zag's contact info and a reminder for the weekend to send him some stuff.

The remainder of the evening was spent laughing, hooting, pounding the table, and snapping our fingers enthusiastically, as is done instead of applauding at poetry slams. Everyone brought their A-game, and I got to hang out at the heart of it. As I strolled happily home along Bloor, past dark shops and a few folks walking their way to McDonald's or the pub, I spotted what Dad would have called 'a real looker' waiting to cross at the light. There was something familiar about her, but with my crappy memory that happens all the time. Her expensive, tailored, dove-grey skirt and suit jacket were decidedly out of place on someone sober at this hour, then the light changed and as she crossed and stepped into better lighting I recognized Rage Grrl, looking all so serious in a kick-ass power suit, midnight-black heels, and a thin, expensive-looking leather briefcase matching her shoes. While glancing down at the glowing phone in her hand, she strode across the intersection and turned left on the other side, going in the opposite direction from my house. The light changed before I got to the corner, so I just admired the confidence with which she moved through the night.

By the time I got home to my kindle of kitties, I was so tired it took me a couple of long slow blinks to realize something was seriously wrong. Kerouac didn't rush to the bottom of the door, begging to be freed. From where I stood, I couldn't see him in the room at all. The other kittens mewed at me like tattletales narking out their criminal sibling.

"Kerouac! *Where the hell are you?*" He could be anywhere in the house. It was 99% kitten-proof, but there were still little corners he could get into and maybe not get out of.

Mew.

The sound came from behind me. I turned, sliding my feet rather than stepping, as anyone with small animals knows to do, and there was my adventurous little tuxedo boy, curled up on the afghan on the couch like he was waiting for me to come home. He uncurled himself slowly, stood up, stretched, shivered, and yawned all at once, then leaped down onto the floor and padded over to me as if he hadn't just given me a freaking heart attack.

Mrow.

I picked him up and he head-butted my chin. "How the hell did you get out, bad boy?" I carried him over to the kitten room and kept a tight grip on him while I released his kindle-mates. I was impressed with his Houdini routine but was also concerned. Unfortunately, I couldn't fix the problem until I knew how he was doing it. With the playful kitten train tagging along behind me, I retrieved the dust-covered little motion-sensor-activated security camera that pointed out the kitchen window and put it on the charging cord.

It was nearly midnight when I finally got the furballs medicated, fed, cuddled, and back to bed. I was so knackered I didn't even bother checking my email or Facebook and Twitter feeds. It could all wait until tomorrow. The second I pulled the quilt up to my chin, I was out. Bing, bang, boom, snore.

Once the security camera was fully charged and installed in the kitten room facing the door, I was off to work. Friday's air was a bit cooler than the earlier part of the week, so foot traffic picked up and the shop was busy enough that I barely had time to look at the accounting books before it was time to get home for lunch and kitten care. I was in such a rush that although I saw the gold Lexus parked across from the house with one of those magnetic signs on the driver's door for a local realtor, I didn't take the time to go speak with the woman sitting in its air-conditioned splendour looking at her phone. *Maybe* it was because I was in a hurry or maybe it was because it was I was sure it was Michelle's disapproving friend, Mandy. Rather than stroll over for uncomfortable small talk punctuated with her growls of disapproval, I went in and tended to the herd of my heart.

Kerouac was still with his siblings, so I wondered if the camera was a bit of an overreaction. Lunch was uneventful, with not even a text from Michelle to stir my nerves. On the way back to the shop my phone chimed a reminder that tomorrow, Saturday, was potluck night at my place with Argaw, Aba, Lydia, Kalani and Shannon, and Rose, the widow down the street whose daughter and family moved two hours west to London last year. Rose's potluck specialty was the most amazing pies and a wicked sense of humour. Everyone was welcome to bring a guest, just so long as they gave the others twelve hours' notice and the guest wasn't allergic to cats. I sure couldn't keep my little ones penned up when I had familiar company that needed to scratch them behind the ears and rub their bellies, so on potluck nights the little monsters were let loose to share their love and fur with everyone there.

I hosted these dinners every two weeks on average, mostly on Saturdays and sometimes on Sundays, depending on consensus. We were all fairly flexible and it didn't start until eight, just to give everyone a chance to finish work. Since I closed the shop up at five on Saturdays, it gave me a couple of hours to clean up and burn a little incense to get the worst of the litter box tang out of the air. On Sundays, the shop was closed, so I didn't have to worry about over-imbibing should a bottle of wine or two show up in someone's basket.

Like Rose with her pies, we each had our specialties. Argaw was the salad man, bringing together different variations from around the world every time. He had a knack for finding just the right fruit, vegetables, or nuts to go with his homemade dressing of the week. Aba and Lydia were the Instant Pot slow cooker wizards, sharing the savoury stews of Africa and the Mediterranean with some of our less experienced palates, while Kalani and Shannon always tried to surprise us with some funky appetizer they learned to make from Instagram or YouTube. Me, I'm the unimaginative king of veggie dip platters, so I double-checked that I had a reminder set for noon tomorrow to pick up a platter during my break.

Between two and four traffic flow into the shop was slow enough that I was able to enter the last of the month's receipts and email a list of invoices to Leona we needed to pay. At 4:30 a courier dropped off a package for me from Indigo Books. Between the kittens and the shop, I rarely had time to get out and shop for anything but groceries, so online it was. This package contained a hardcover edition of Mark Manson's *The Subtle Art of Not Giving a F*ck*, which Aba had suggested I read. Also in the order was a how-to for drawing maps for fantasy gamers and fans. It was recommended by one of my former classmates for ideas to spice up my custom maps and I was always open to learning a new technique or style. I leafed through it and was excited to see some really cool illustrated step-by-step instructions.

My phone chimed right at five with a reminder to pick up tomatoes and cucumbers for my salad tonight. I'd forgotten all about them. I snoozed the alarm, scribbled a note, and stuck it in my shirt pocket. My memory required multiple redundant back-ups, especially on Fridays.

Some small shops will close a few minutes early on a slow day, not expecting anyone to rush in at the last minute. Our shop wasn't a bustling enterprise, but I never flipped the sign to CLOSED or locked the door until five minutes *after* closing, mostly because I shut it for lunch in order to get home to the kittens. Now that they were getting big and almost ready to go out for adoption, I could probably leave them all day, but they were a nice break and a sandwich and soup at home was always fresher than ones eaten in the store at the sad little table in the back room, surrounded by maps. Usually, I sat alone for those extra five minutes, but on this summer Friday I was rewarded with a customer darting in with thirty seconds to spare.

She nearly tripped over the sill on her way in, the brass bell ringing madly as she swung the door open with urgency. Her Loblaw's uniform was a pretty good hint she'd just come from work at the grocery chain.

Chapter 3

"THANK GOD YOU'RE STILL open. The subway was delayed and then the sidewalk was packed with strollers and walkers like it was a marathon for tortoises."

"Hi. Welcome to Long & Lat. Take a deep breath, and tell me how I can help. I'll stay as open as long as you need me to."

She took a breath, smiled, then "Thank you. A map of the U.S. Please."

"Folded or book form?"

"Um, folded, please. It'll be going up on a corkboard."

I had a dozen choices for her and quickly pulled the three best from their racks. "Do you need geographic features like mountains?"

"No. Just states and capitals. It's for my nine-year-old."

I pushed one of the maps aside since it had a lot of land feature details she didn't need. "School project?"

"Sort of. He's teaching his thirteen-year-old brother the states and their capitals."

"Your nine-year-old is teaching your thirteen-year-old?"

"Yes. The youngest one is actually going into his first year at York University. He's a math prodigy but likes to help his brother in every subject."

"Wow." That was amazing. "Nine?"

"And a half."

"Well, that makes *all* the difference in the world." I smiled my best goofy smile at her. "That extra six months is *huge*." I opened the two maps to show her the details. I knew which one I'd pick, but it wasn't for *my* little Einstein, it was for *hers.*

She laughed. "You joke, but with Cho, it really does. In the spring he taught his brother the periodic table, and for the last three weeks he's been coaching his father and me on the policy positions of the three main parties in the upcoming Federal election." She quickly looked over the two maps and picked the same one I would have, with the state names and major cities all labelled with larger, bolder fonts than the other one.

"He sounds like a good kid, despite the big brain."

"His heart is even bigger. You hear people talk about 'old souls' but Cho truly is one. He's like a hundred-year-old man in a boy's body. He reads to Seniors two Sundays a month, plays clarinet in the school band, and in his spare time is writing a novel about some world he invented in a dream one night. We don't even try to keep up anymore. He's amazing and we feel blessed he picked our family to be born into."

That was a weird way to phrase it, but I got what she was saying. "Does he have a good globe?" I gestured at the tops of the shelves around the shop, showing our various choices.

"He has a wonderful one he made himself for a science project when he was six. He also has one of Mars and one of the moon he made out of paper maché. But thank you."

I rang up the order, she paid, I handed her the map and the receipt, and she was gone out into the summer evening with a quick thank you and a look at two messages that chirped on her phone as she left.

Nine-and-a-half years old at York U. Holy crap. I hope poor Cho doesn't burn out like a couple of prodigies I'd known over the years. One of my English classmates in high school was so far beyond the rest of us that he was like an alien just faking it in our society. Then he took his own life the next semester and left his suicide note addressed to his favourite teacher. Two weeks later the teacher—an odd duck but a brilliant light in his own right—took *his* own life. When I think back to those two kind but screwed-up geniuses battling depression and whatever else, it makes me thankful I'm just Joe Slightly-Above-Average.

The shop remained quiet for the next five minutes so I closed up and then swung by the market for the vegetables. A text from Rose while I was touching the tomatoes in an almost improper manner asked if she could bring a friend, Joe, who was in town for the weekend and was a wizard with absinthe. I replied *Sounds great, bring him!* and moved on to the cucumbers, trying not to look like a pervert. I'd never had absinthe, but I'd heard some interesting stories about how it sharpens the mind but messes with the body. Since everyone was walking to and from my place tomorrow evening, it might be a fun experience. We needed to have as many of those as we could before I had to sell the place. As I walked home I texted the group to let them know that Absinthe Joe would be joining us.

Again, Kerouac was right where I'd left him. After the usual you've-been-gone-forever welcome, they ate, I ate, and I opted for a break from maps and went straight to the couch for some movie streaming and iced tea. The cats alternated between climbing on me and licking any exposed sweaty skin they found—which in summer was considerable since I mostly wore shorts and golf shirts, especially around the house—and chasing each other or one of the various noisy cat toys around my feet. That was my world, in a beige, no-spark nutshell. Then a text notification from eRomance.ca alerted me to a waiting message. I clicked the link and signed in to my account using the login information Aba had given me.

Hi CatDude416. I like your profile. I'm in T-Dot, too. Would you like to have coffee? Maybe Sunday evening? The website says we're 88% match. Must be our love of animals. Lol.

Let me know.

RayRay420

A date? For coffee? I suppose I could do that. I checked my phone's calendar to make sure I didn't have anything planned on Sunday. Nope. Just the grave-digging I'd already done. I deleted that event and clicked on RayRay420's profile to check her out. Her picture was of a pale-skinned redhead with her coppery curls pinned up, deep red lips, big blue-grey eyes, high cheekbones, and a Chihuahua held up next to her face. Hmm... She was pretty, and obviously really close to her dog. But looks were only one small facet. I read over her profile. She was a writer who loved to travel but hadn't in a while since she rescued her dog Rupert from Mexico. Her profile background was faint leaves that on my phone's small screen looked a lot like marijuana. Not my scene, but it was as legal as booze, so who cared? Her interests included bookstores, long walks, sunsets, World of Warcraft, and reality television. I'm not sure how the dating algorithms put us at 88%, but going for coffee might be the break I needed from my routine. I replied to her message. I really didn't want to meet a complete stranger right down the street from my home, or even in my neighbourhood, so I suggested a coffee shop I used to take Mom to, around the corner from her condo. I suggested 6 pm. Not too early, not too late, and if we hit it off, maybe we could walk up the street for dinner at a café and keep the conversation going.

Oh shit.

I'd made a date.

oOo

Saturday started off with a leisurely walk to the shop, travel mug of iced coffee in hand, but I only had time to turn on the lights and boot up the computer before the customers began streaming in with their lists of wants and needs. With the August long weekend rolling up on us and many folks heading off on summer travelling vacations, maps of Ontario, Quebec, and nearby New York State were the most popular requests. My eventual one-hour lunch was trimmed back to a running twenty-minute sandwich-inhaling while the kittens pawed at my feet and protested my lack of attention.

On my way back to the shop I rounded the corner to see half a dozen locals waiting for me to tell them where to go, or at least how to get there. As I closed the distance, my phone chimed with a reminder to pick up a veggie platter for tonight, but I snoozed it, definitely not having time at that time.

"Max! Right on time!" How timely.

"Hey, Stu. Sorry about this. Had to feed the kittens." They all stepped aside to let me through to unlock the door.

"How are they?"

"Growing fast and almost ready for college. Except Ginsberg, who starts writing for the West End Phoenix next week." I held the door for them and they filed past, greeting me with a smile, a nod, or a friendly "Hey, Max". Five minutes later I was alone and once again restocking the Ontario and New York map slots on various racks. When done, I logged onto the Bloorcourt Village/Christie Pits Facebook page and posted a quick blurb about how Long & Lat had the maps everyone needed for their summer road trips. Then I placed a rush order for more stock of the most popular maps.

Sales remained steady for the rest of the day, coming in at fifty percent higher than the same Saturday last year, so I emailed Leona the numbers, restocked the racks for a *third* time that day, and closed up. I had a niggling feeling I was forgetting something, so I checked my phone and saw the veggie platter reminder. On the way home I picked one up at the deli, snapped up a bottle of red wine at the liquor store, and got home with two-and-a-half hours to spare to give the house one final cat hair vacuuming, grab a nap, and take a shower. A reminder popped up to email poems to Zig-Zag so I quickly fired off three of my favourites.

Still no further word from Michelle. I think I was relieved. Sometimes it's hard to tell.

oOo

Aba sat on the couch, letting Ginsberg lick a spoon clean of gravy from Lydia's God-sent Moroccan lamb stew. "Your worst date Max. The *one* date that has convinced you to never, ever ask a woman out again."

My belly was full, my wine glass was half so, and Calliope and Zwerling purred happily and possessively on my lap. "Ha ha! I didn't say *never*, Aba. As a matter of fact, I have a date tomorrow night. Direct from eRomance."

"Really?"

"Max has a date?"

"That's wonderful!"

My friends were nothing if not supportive.

"So Michelle didn't break you?"

Almost. "No. And I'm not broken, just reluctant. This lady contacted me."

"What's her name?" Lydia was all about names. She found them to be a fascinating insight into people's personalities.

"I don't know."

"You don't..."

"Her online name is *RayRay420*."

"Hmm... An interesting choice. She sounds like a petite pot smoker."

"At five-two she's definitely the first, and judging by some images on her profile, she very well could be the second."

Aba asked his inevitable question. "But is she beautiful?"

"She's definitely pretty. As for beautiful, I'll have to get back to you after coffee tomorrow when I chat with her and see what her personality is like. Beauty is as much her ideas and words as it is what she captures in selfies."

"True enough."

"How many dates have you had since Michelle told you she's not coming back? One? What was wrong with that lady?"

"Nothing. She was terrific." Actually, she was smart, pretty, and funny.

"Too tall?"

"Nope."

"Too short, then?"

"No. Just right. About five-six, which is my ideal."

Kalani leaned in. "You have an ideal date height?"

Joe stood up slowly, his sixty-year-old frame a little creaky, judging from the frustrated expression on his face. "Who's up for some absinthe while Max defends himself?"

I definitely needed something stronger than the Shiraz if I was going to be getting the third degree, and absinthe should just about do the trick. "Me, please."

Everyone but Argaw and Shannon raised their hands. Argaw hadn't had alcohol since his divorce ten years ago, and Shannon claimed health reasons for passing on a 'green fairy' experience. Joe quickly assembled his fancy set-up on the sideboard with what he called an absinthe fountain, while Burroughs-kitty mewed at his stocking feet, wondering what the new human was doing. The fountain was a fancy glass candy-jar-looking bowl on a glass pedestal with two spouts. Joe said the fountain was filled with ice water chilled to near freezing and the water was dripped over special dense sugar cubes into the absinthe, with a ratio of 3:1 water to absinthe. It was fascinating to watch.

Shannon rapped my knee lightly with her knuckles. "Never mind the height limits, tell us about this date that nearly finished the demolition job Michelle started."

"I'm hardly demolished, I've just realigned my priorities. Work, kittens, maps, poetry... and an actual date tomorrow evening."

Kerouac tumbled from the back of the couch to Shannon's lap, as if to make my point for me. She gently rubbed his head while he kneaded her stomach. "Not fair, K-Cat! Let your papa win his own arguments!"

They wanted the story, so I gave it to them. "I think it was the eye patch that did it."

"Eye patch?" they asked in unplanned unison.

I had their attention. "I'll get to that. I first met her over the phone when she called to ask some questions about some maps she was thinking of ordering. We had a nice chat about the weather, the Blue Jays, and where she was travelling to. At the end of it, she asked if I'd like to meet for coffee. I was surprised, but said 'sure'. We set a place and time and exchanged descriptions of ourselves.

"She said she was slender, had shoulder-length blonde hair, and would be wearing a navy-blue-and-white dress. I said I'd be wearing an eye patch, and walking with a cane and a limp. She laughed and said I wouldn't dare. I said of course I wouldn't."

Rose saw right through me. "But you dared, didn't you?"

I smiled wickedly.

"Why, Max? What kind of first impression would that make?"

"I suppose I wasn't exactly taking the dating scene seriously. Sorry, Aba." I flashed him a sheepish look but he just shook his head in resignation. "I wore a scruffy old coat, a baseball cap, a black pirate-type eye patch, and walked into the coffee shop with a heavy limp, using an old cane of my mom's, and carrying a fully stuffed plastic grocery bag like a homeless person. The place was pretty full, so I took a seat at the counter and ordered a coffee. Two minutes later, in walked Cheryl, sitting two seats down from me. She glanced around, but she looked right past the scruffy-dressed guy with the eye patch.

"Five minutes after I was due to arrive, I hobbled into the men's room, peeled off the sweatshirt hiding my button-down Hilfiger, pulled my classy trench coat out of the bag, stuffed the old coat in the bag with the hat, hung the cane inside my trench coat, gave my hair a quick finger-combing, and returned to the counter. 'Hi, Cheryl.' 'Hi, Max. I was watching for you but didn't see you come in.' 'I was already here. Eye patch, cane... two seats down...' I dangled the eye patch and opened my coat to reveal the cane. 'No way!' 'Way!' She laughed, I laughed, we sat, drank coffee, and chatted for almost an hour."

Kalani sniffled. "That's so adorable! If you did that to me and I was single, I'd have had the barista marry us right then and there!" She looked at her wife. "Sorry, Love."

Shannon laughed. "No worries, Hon. I'd have done the same... if I liked boys at all." She looked at me, eyes twinkling.

"There was no wedding. She's already engaged. She just liked the sound of my voice and wondered what the map dude was like in person."

"So *not* cool! She led you on!"

"Not at all. She asked me for coffee. At no time did we suggest it was a date. Besides, Michelle's side of the bed is barely cold and I was meeting a strange woman for coffee. Once we both confirmed that it wasn't a date, we relaxed, chatted some more, and then went our separate ways."

"That's sad," Lydia opined.

"I guess."

"But he did the eye patch!" The Amazing Kalanirini appreciated the illusion and misdirection of the situation. "That takes balls, Max. I love it! And that was your only date since Mish left?"

"The one and only. But since we're exposing my soul to my dating faux pas, I should probably tell you about the time I had a blind date with a deaf girl, before I met Michelle."

If mention of the eye patch got their attention, 'blind date with the deaf girl' took their breath away and froze the room into this bizarre tableau where only the kittens moved. Joe finally broke the silence.

"The absinthe is ready. I promise it'll take the tale to a whole new level. And maybe when Max's done I'll tell you about the time I got kicked out of a whore house." Mic drop. Boom! In one sentence, Joe earned himself a place at the potluck dinners for as long as he wanted. Holy shit.

I needed to stand up and let that wondrous dinner settle a bit. "How about we all take a break and stretch our legs? I'll feed the kittens and then we can settle back down and let the absinthe make our hearts grow fonder."

Rose slapped my arm. "Oh no, you didn't just say that!"

"My bad."

"Bad? That was horrific. Joe, Max gets a double shot for that one."

"Yes ma'am. But let's wait until he's fed the kitties because a double shot is going to knock his legs right out from under him." He flashed a wicked grin like he knew a secret he wasn't going to share with me until it was far too late for me to do anything about it.

Some of the group got air on the porch, I fed my fur brats, Argaw put on a fresh pot of coffee for himself and Shannon, and we eventually settled back into our spots, absinthe or coffee in hand. I held my glass up. "May the roof above us never fall in, and may we friends gathered below never fall out." We all sipped, as per Joe's instructions. Apparently one simply did not 'chug' sweet, potent, licoricey absinthe.

Rose raised her glass. "May your home always be too small to hold all your friends." We sipped.

Shannon lifted her mug. "May you have a world of wishes at your command, God and his angels close at hand, friends and their family love impart, and an

Irish blessing in your heart."

"Here here!"

"Cheers!"

"To friends!"

"To loved ones!"

"To deaf blind dates!"

Oh crap. The story. I reached out to put my glass on the table, but my hand was already feeling a little fuzzy. Of course, having a couple of glasses of wine before starting in on the 'green fairy' probably wasn't the best idea, but what the hell. I was in the safety of my own home. The strange thing was although my body was starting to feel numby-fuzzy, my mind was sharp as a tack. "Anyone else feel totally effed up?"

Lydia and Rose both giggled and Kalani stage-whispered, "Not yet, but I feel the F-Train roaring down the tracks." Aba tried to stand up but fell back into his seat. We all snickered like twelve-year-olds. The kittens on various laps didn't seem to care.

It was story time. "Okay. The deaf blind date... This is a short one. About eight years ago I took a course and got my American Sign Language Level One. I knew the alphabet and about a dozen signs, mostly for food, and I was so certain I was fluent enough to date a hearing-impaired lady that I swiped right. I went out on a couple of dates with Beth but quickly learned that my fluency was greatly overestimated.

"When not out together, we often communicated through Skype and texts, but Beth was a little old school and still liked to use the TTY system because it didn't save the messages. She typed her message and a special operator read it to me. Then I spoke my reply and the TTY operator typed it back to Beth. I knew things weren't going too well in the relationship, but I thought we should at least meet over coffee and decide what to do. I called to set it up and that day the TTY operator was a dude named Michael. Although I suggested coffee, Beth had something else in mind, which Michael read to me. 'Max, I think you're a really nice guy, but I don't think we should see each other anymore.'"

Shannon spit her mouthful of coffee back into her mug. "Oh shit. He *didn't*."

"He did. Michael broke up with me."

"Sucks to be you, you cis het dude." She blew me a kiss.

Aba stared at me for a long moment, then finally said, "Maybe you shouldn't be dating. At all. *Ever.*"

"Forget about me. I want to hear how Joe got kicked out of a brothel." I turned my floppy head to grin at our absinthe king.

Joe brought his glass over and sat next to Rose on the loveseat. It was obvious the two of them were more than just friends.

Lydia put her glass on the coffee table with exaggerated care and stared at her hand as she sat back into Aba's arm. "Was this before or after meeting Rose?"

"After."

"So, recently?"

"No, about twenty-five years ago." He smiled, and then he and Rose both sipped, all mysterious-like.

Shannon asked what we were all wondering. "How long have you two known each other?"

Rose looked at Joe and blinked as if she was doing a mental calculation. "Forty years, give or take. We were college sweethearts at Queen's."

"OMG! That is soooo sweet! Why can't I feel my feet?" Kalani wiggled her feet.

"The brothel, Joe?"

He laughed. "It's actually a boring story, but here you go. In the mid-nineties, I fancied myself a science fiction writer and went to Las Vegas for the first time. Some guy on a street corner handed me a little guidebook to the escorts and rent-a-dates Nevada is famous for, and in there was a map to The Berry Patch Ranch in Crystal, about sixty miles outside of the city. In my novel I wanted the sex trade to be legal in the future so I thought I should interview a legal sex trade worker."

Argaw softly asked, "Is 'interview' a euphemism for..."

"*No.* Interview. Talk. *Pay to have a conversation with.*"

"Why couldn't you interview prostitutes here in Toronto? Sadly, there's no shortage of them." Shannon had a good point.

"Because a street prostitute here lives in fear. Fear of johns, fear of her pimp, fear of other girls, fear of arrest, fear of diseases. In a legal brothel, the ladies are licensed, get medical coverage, have security to protect them, and don't fear being arrested for discussing oral sex, let alone performing it. I believed the mindset of a legal prostitute would be completely different."

That made sense. "So how did you get kicked out?"

"I asked for the one thing you can't buy in a brothel.... *information*." He took a long sip and let the wicked stuff slide down his throat before continuing. "The place was creepy as Hell, literally. The main building, The Berry Patch, was closed for renovations and probably a much-needed cleaning. A sign directed customers around back to a bunch of joined box trailers under the name of *Martha's House of Prostitution* and *Madame Ladybug's Bath & Massage Salon*. Parked next to the scruffy, black, wrought iron fence and locked gate were a couple of dusty pickup trucks, and—no word of a lie—an old, pale metallic blue Cadillac Eldorado convertible with six-foot-wide longhorns bolted to the hood like something out the old show, *Dallas*."

The room was silent, caught up in the telling, so Joe continued.

"I went up to the gate and rang the bell, just like the little official-looking sign said to do. About twenty feet away, up the pathway, was a heavy steel door with a mirrored window in it. I'm pretty sure I was given the once over, deemed to be no threat whatsoever, and the gate buzzed and swung open. Up to the door, I went, nervous as crap. It was one in the afternoon, I was out in the desert in the middle of Buttscratch, Nevada, and no one I knew had a clue where the hell I was. For all I knew I was going to be tossed into the back of one of the trucks and taken out to some arroyo where I'd learn to squeal like a pig.

"Anyway, the madam opened the door and let me into a dimly lit, black-and-red-velvet-and-lace Spanish Bordello of Blood reception area with a little cashier's window and office off to the left. Now, when I say 'madam', please don't think curvy honeysuckle-sweet Dolly Parton or toothy, friendly, cute Heidi Fleiss. I'm sure this lady was really sweet away from the job, but in the low come-hither-and-be-killed light, all I saw was her square-jawed face, hair looking like it was styled by a half-blind chainsaw-wielding lumberjack, and a solid brick-wall frame that probably could have snapped me in two if I stepped out of line."

I took a sip, my mind focused tight on Joe's every word while my hand struggled with the concept of 'glass of liquid'.

"I laughed, nervous, and said 'In a place where I'm sure you're used to getting strange requests, I have a strange request. I'm a writer and I'd like to interview one of the girls. I'm willing to pay—'.

Joe's voice got rough like he gargled battery acid. "'Nope. Can't help you. You'll have to talk to the manager and he won't be back until later, and even then he probably won't be able to help you.' Did I mention her gravelly, smokes-a-pack-of-Marlies-an-hour voice? She opened the door and motioned me out.

"'Um. Okay. Thank you.' I scooted out, the door closed firmly behind me with a thump and the shot of the bolt being thrown. Down the walk of shame to the gate, out and back to the rental car. I have never, in all my life, been so glad to be turned away and denied what I wanted. Putting *Martha's House of Prostitution* in my rear-view, I drove away pretty sure I could write the necessary scenes without actually talking to a prostitute."

I was almost disappointed. "So, no hand on the collar or boot on the ass, just a scary woman pointing the way out?" Calliope stirred on my lap and I looked down. For a second or two I thought she was counting her toes in French, but I'm pretty sure it was the absinthe messing with my head. I wasn't completely sure, but mostly. I *did* know I was a mess.

"Exactly. I told you. Boring."

Aba reached for his glass, stopped, looked at his hand, looked up at Joe, blinked, and whispered "Holy shit. That was *so* cool, brother. You got kicked out of a brothel!"

Lydia nodded. "Wow. We just won't tell our sons that story. Attitudes towards women in the sex trade have evolved, thank God."

Sober Argaw was nonplussed by the adventure. "Did you ever finish the novel?"

Joe chuckled. "I did. I published it last fall. And none of the sex dealer scenes got past the final edits. It was a cool concept, but it really wasn't necessary for the plot."

"You were college sweethearts?" Kalani wiggled her fingers now, looking a little confused by the sensations, but after a moment she smiled back up at Rose and Joe.

Rose grinned. "Yes."

"Did you stay friends all this time?"

"No. We lost touch for a long time. I found Joe on Facebook about ten years ago and we reconnected. Then my husband of twenty years, Scott, died, but Joe was still in his marriage."

Joe nodded along with Rose's telling of their story then picked up where she stopped. "Shortly after my wife and I split up five years ago, I was in town to visit family and took Rose out to dinner. It was like we'd never been apart. Now, I try to get back from Vancouver at least twice a year to see her. I'm here all summer, but next year, when I retire..."

"When you retire, we'll talk about it then," Rose finished for him like everything hadn't already been decided.

"You got kicked out of a brothel." Aba giggled and the rest of us joined him. The absinthe was definitely a hit.

We spent another hour talking about Rose's two adult daughters, the youngest one actually named Joanne, after Joe, and Rose asked Aba and Lydia for an update about their brood, and the conversation eventually evolved into an in-depth analysis of the current state of Canadian education and university admission requirements.

I needed something to counteract the strangeness of the absinthe. "Who's up for coffee or tea?"

"Me, please."

"Please."

"God, yes."

I tried to lever myself up off the couch, but failed miserably, flopping back down when my arms decided to not work together to give me leverage. This was bizarre. My mind was fine, but my damned limbs were made of rubber.

Shannon set a hand on my shoulder and gently pushed me back. "Stay put, Max. Uncle Argaw and I can handle this."

Argaw nodded and smiled kindly. I'm sure he saw the humour in the situation, but as always, he took the high road and wore his empathy on his sleeve. "We certainly can, brother. Stay put. We don't need you hurting yourself." He followed Shannon to the kitchen with all five kittens trailing after them, yawning, stretching, and mewing for food.

Five minutes later we each had a mug of coffee or tea cupped in our hands, cross-eyed concentrating on not dropping them. We looked around at each other and the sight was so ridiculous I couldn't help snickering. The snicker became a chuckle, then Aba and Lydia joined in, and within seconds, everyone was howling at the absurdity of grownups as messed up as teens with their first joint. In the middle of it all, Shannon pulled out her phone and started recording us, which got us laughing even harder.

Somewhere around midnight, the effects of the absinthe had worn off enough for everyone to get up and try walking again. More coffee and tea were consumed, then serving dishes were carefully gathered up and covered in foil or plastic wrap. Hugs and cheek-kisses were exchanged back and forth and forth and back and we all agreed Joe was welcome any time, with or without the mind-messing absinthe and stories of brothels visited.

The sun rose on Sunday with me a little hungover and a lot not wanting to leave the house, but I had a coffee date with a complete stranger. Before that, though, I needed to clear my head. The weather was cloudy and cooler, and a walk was in order to shake off the clinging oddness of the absinthe high. It was just outside McDonald's life took a wee bit of a jog to the left.

Chapter 4

CHRISTIE PITS PARK WAS just three short blocks from the house so I harnessed up Kerouac and Ginsberg and put them in the chest carrier. I envy dog walkers who can have six or seven of their charges on leashes, all obediently walking along, sniffing and chilling. Just the *thought* of trying to wrangle five kittens on leashes and harnesses made me want to stay home and hide in the shadows. Two in the carrier was my max, and only if those particular two were getting along and not violating a feline peace treaty by lobbing claw and teeth attacks at each other while they were strapped to my chest. Before I even got out the door, though, Kerouac started in on Ginsberg, so out he came and back into the kitten room. Burroughs willingly replaced him, and the little guy nuzzled right up to Ginsy as if to apologize for their idiot foster brother's misbehaviour.

The stroll east along Bloor was nice, but progress was slow with the sheer number of people out and about. Since the fresh air and walk were the point of the whole excursion, I wove our way through, sauntering along, stopping periodically for people to say hi to the ginger feline symbiotes growing out of my torso. Christie Pits Park isn't huge by Toronto standards, probably three small blocks square, but it is a unique bowl shape with a playground, basketball and volleyball courts, multiple pools for splashing or wading or swimming lengths, one with a long curving yellow slide, three ball diamonds of varying sizes, and my favourite part, the community garden where, when my timing was right, I could find a friend or two there harvesting their zucchinis, tomatoes, or asparaguses. Asparagi? Anyway, there was also an improvised skateboard park, long pathways meandering amongst the moss-coated trees, and the history of a 10,000-person, six-hour Nazi riot in 1933. Sort of a park-of-all-trades. Michelle and I used to walk here all the time. Even without her, I was going to miss the place if she forced me to sell and move. I took a breath and shoved those thoughts out of my head. As I pointed out, everyone eventually leaves and I had to suck it up and move on, leaving the anger behind.

We three meandered amongst the joggers, the strollers, the dawdlers, the phone-obsessed stumblers, and others like myself, looking like they needed fresh air after a night of overindulgence. The three of us took breaks in the shade on benches conveniently placed for kitten walkers, and we generally unwound and cleared our heads of green fairy fog. Or at least *I* did. Ginsberg and Burroughs were hardly ever uptight, except when they got a little too much attention from dogs being walked past, so for the most part they curled up at the bottom of the cat-sack.

Despite the clouds, it was still late July in Toronto and the light breeze didn't do much to dispel the humidity or the trace of smoke from forest fires somewhere to the north or west. I watched flushed, sweaty joggers and inline skaters zip up and down the sloped paths, but the idea of exercise in the heat made my head spin, especially today. The kittens periodically poked their heads up for the free rubs they knew I always had ready for them, so we relaxed—people-watching, head-scratching, finger-licking, and absinthe-fog-shaking.

I rubbed my bearded chin on Ginsberg's head and he pushed back, purring. "When you kids grow up, I want you to say no to absinthe. That stuff'll melt your brain and turn you into dogs. *Dogs*, I tell ya." They stared at me, pretending they had no idea what I was saying and was only valuable to them as a source of food and shelter, which, to be honest, was pretty much on the money. I heard and felt the rumble of a subway train rolling through its tunnel beneath the south rim of the park, then I caught the scent of cooking meat wafting up from one of the park's public grills. My stomach growled like a Chihuahua with a bone, but I knew it was right. I needed some grease in my belly to counteract the alcohol. The sad thing is I only had four—no *five*—drinks last night. There's no way I should be feeling this grizzly the day after five drinks, but at thirty-five, I guess I was now officially a lightweight. No more chugging bottles of ice-cold Mateus rosé, no more knocking back eleven shots of schnapps in eleven minutes, no more eating raw eggs with shells and chasing them with tequila... no more absinthe. *Ever*. Once was enough. Once was cool, but once was definitely enough. Until next time.

The clouds thinned out and drifted off, and the day heated up quickly, so it was time to get the kittens home before they cooked. We strolled back toward the house, the sidewalks a bit less congested now that the heat was rising again. As we got near McDonald's the scent of fries riding the moist city air like the junk food of the apocalypse slapped me twice in the face and once on the ass, telling me resistance was futile. I couldn't very well go in there with the kittens, so I picked up my pace, got them home and into the kitten room with their litter boxes, water dishes, and crying siblings, then I was back out the door and headed back the half-block to McDonald's. Sure, I could have started up my own grill on the little deck out back, but that would have taken time I didn't want to spend when I was famished, and it still wouldn't have given me McDonald's fries. Or a strawberry shake. Or a Big Mac. Or...

There were two self-order kiosks open, so I stepped up to the nearest one, placed my order like a pro, and waited for my number to be called. It took mere moments for my order to be filled and another two for me to get it to a quiet corner away from the play area. I won't bore you with the details of me chewing delightedly on my Big Mac or McNuggets, or the soft slurping of the cold, thick, perfect-for-the-day strawberry shake, but needless to say (although I will still say it), it was fast food heaven. As much as Mickey Ds gets a bad rap from all sorts of health bloggers and tweeters and documentary filmmakers, I just can't help myself. I worked only five shifts at McDonald's when I was a teen, but I became addicted to Big Macs. I don't eat them a lot, but probably indulge myself once every week or two. Of course, I could hardly have a Mac without fries, so I always got the meal. Today, the burger, the nuggets, and the small shake went down easily, targeting the absinthe with military strike precision. As always, I saved the fries for last, taking them with me for the walk home. I *had* to. What if I got lost on those hundred yards of moss-cracked sidewalks and was at risk of starvation?

Those fries might be all that saved my life and gave me the strength to find my way back to my fur-kids. It was survival instinct at its most bullshitty.

I stepped out of the air-conditioned restaurant and back into the heat—burger, shake, and nuggets in my belly, fries in hand. I considered dropping by the grocery store to see how Kalani was doing after our little gathering last night, but it was Sunday and her day off, I think. I hardly wanted to ask her father/boss how she was feeling after drinking at my house, so I turned toward home...and nearly bowled over Rage Grrl walking past in shorts, a tank top, runners, and a cigarette in hand. We both jerked to a stop.

Full of grease and feeling cocky, I pointed a fry at her, just as she gestured with her cigarette at me, and we both said, "Those things'll kill you, you know."

"Ha! Jinx!" We both snapped back. I laughed at the childish absurdity of the moment.

She smiled. No sign of rage at all. "But I'll bet yours taste better."

I held the fries up. "Help yourself." I don't like sharing food with people I know, let alone a stranger on the street corner, but I felt like she'd just *dared* me to offer her some, and I'm nothing if not a fool for a harmless dare from an attractive woman.

She plucked a couple of fries and ate them in two bites, and I saw her wedding and engagement rings. Oh well. "Perfect. Thanks!" The light changed so I started to cross west, but she stayed put. When I looked back at her, my eyebrows arched in an unasked question, she pointed north with her cigarette. "I'm headed *that* way." She finger-waggle-waved at me and turned her attention to the light in her direction. I got dragged along with the other pedestrians, my fries forgotten for the moment. Then I was across and she was gone, having forgotten me already, I'm sure. That's me, just a strange dude on the street who willingly gives French fries to fit, pretty, married smokers prone to nut-kicking sparring dummies.

o0o

Being the bearer of all things edible, I was welcomed home with enthusiasm by the brood, but since I'm a cold, heartless bastard, I left them in their prison, immune to their pitiful, desperate wails while I relaxed on the couch and finished my fries.

o0o

Once the katkraakens were released and fed, I set the alarm on my phone, stretched myself again out on the couch, and let them climb aboard for a short nap to recharge my battery. It might have taken them a while to settle in, but I didn't know because I tripped quickly into somnambulance, the last conscious thought in my head being shorts, a tank top, a cigarette, and a smile I just couldn't shake.

An hour later the alarm on my phone woke me. None of the kittens moved even an inch when I woke up, so I had to do it the hard way, gently yet firmly plucking them off and placing them on the floor. The two girls, Calliope and Zwerling, hopped right back up on the warm spot I vacated, vocalizing their displeasure. Kerouac made a beeline for the kitchen, assuming there would be food in it for any kitten smart enough to be available. Burroughs scampered back to the kitten room where I could hear him scratching in a litter box, and Ginsberg sat and waited for me to make my move. When I stood, stretched, and shuffled off to the kitchen, he followed along at my side. Kittens are good for the soul.

o0o

Arriving fifteen minutes early to meet RayRay420, I bought an iced coffee, found a table for two facing the door, and watched people come and go. Couples, seniors, teens, and one or two solo women who could have been my eRomance date, but simply took their drinks and left. After half an hour of this, I checked my phone for messages and found one from RayRay herself. A quick look confirmed that I'd forgotten to turn on the phone's ringer. Shit. Then I read the message and counted my blessings.

CatDude416. Can't make it. Ex-roomie dropped by with some fine herb she owed me & we got a little—no A LOT—baked. So sorry. Text me back. We'll try again.

Abandoned. I took a couple of long, slow breaths, picked up my cup, got a muffin to go, and left. Why do I even bother? Women just let me down. I'm sure there's some karmic shit in there, something I did in the past that keeps screwing up my relationships with women in the here and now. Did I break some girl's heart that I don't remember? Or was there some past-life crap that keeps getting dredged up? I don't exactly believe in that mumbo jumbo, but I buy lottery tickets because I believe in luck and if I believe in *good* luck, I should probably believe in *bad* luck. Since I seemed to be falling victim to bad luck, I suppose I should just live my life and stop stressing about women and relationships.

Back home eventually, I fed the kittens and myself and retired to the couch with five bundles of love who would never stand me up, let me down, or tell me what I can or can't watch on Netflix. Just before I called it a night a text came in from RayRay.

I'm sorry about coffee. My head is finally clearing. That was some dope dope. How about a mulligan or a do-over one night this week? Cheers. Rachel.

Ah, 'Rachel'. I thought that might be her name. I was really hoping it wasn't 'Raymond'. It hardly mattered, though, because dating a forgetful chronic pot smoker wasn't really a step up from living alone after being abandoned by a chronic dentist-lover. I thought hard about it and drafted about six versions of what I wanted to text back and decided that simple was best. *No problem about coffee, Rachel. You seem really sweet, but I'm not really in a dating place right now.* Maybe the too-high-to-drink-coffee thing was a one-off and maybe I was having a knee-jerk reaction because I got ghosted while trying to make an effort, but I didn't have the energy to create a new relationship when the old one was still haunting me.

Her reply was quick. *OK. Text me if you get to that place. ~R.* She was so chill about it I started to second guess my decision. Then again, maybe she didn't stuff her emotions into texts and emails like Michelle did. Either way, it was a relief to keep it all simple and done.

oOo

The shop was open for about an hour on Monday when the door's bell called me from the back room where I was shuffling stock between half-full boxes, trying to make room for the new maps due to arrive the next day.

He took two steps into the shop—just far enough for the door to close behind him. He looked the place over, right to left, left back to right, as if he'd just entered a party he didn't want to be at where he knew only one person and was ready to turn on his heel and run away if he didn't see them in the two passes. I slowed down, not wanting to spook him. Short and round, wearing a baggy red golf shirt and black shorts with sandals, he looked like a robin, alert and easy to startle. At least he wasn't wearing black socks like Dad used to do with his sandals.

"Hi. Welcome to *Long & Lat Maps*. Is there anything, in particular, you're looking for?" No sudden moves, no loud sounds.

He relaxed, just a shade. "A model of the Earth."

"You mean a globe?" I gestured slowly at the display behind the counter.

"Globes are round. I want a *true* model—a Chris Pontius model, not some fake NASA thing."

Damn. A Flat Earther. I wish they were as rare as people thought they were, but the shop attracted them like a sucking whirlpool of stupid. "Finally! A customer who knows his science! I'm sorry about the globes. The owner makes me keep them on hand to throw off the government stooges. They have an office three blocks over and wander by once a week or so, ever since they caught me with a Pontius model in the window and traced a Bedford Level Experiment support website to the shop's IP address."

"Bastards!" Got him! Hook, line, and sinker.

"I *know*, right?" I lowered my voice to the kind of conspiratorial whisper they used in cheesy comedies and he leaned in while I went on. "I mean, it's obvious Rowbotham's experiment showing no curvature of the Earth on a six-mile strip of river was definitive." It wasn't at all, having been debunked repeatedly.

"Yes!" He smiled, big and toothy. Like, really creepy toothy, with bad veneers that made his mouth almost glow, they were so unnaturally white. "And the experiments since then have all been conducted by government shills."

"You know it, brother. And NASA is the worst. Kennedy needed to beat the Russians in the space race and the Russians couldn't stand to lose to the West, so both sides started faking data and images."

He whispered back. "I have a copy of the documentary, *In Search of the Edge*, and I've seen the model NASA used for the first fake photos. It's kept in a warehouse in Florida, exactly twenty-six miles, three-hundred-and-eighty-five yards from the Mercury Redstone Pads on the Banana River."

"That's the Kennedy Space Center." It was on my bucket list of places to visit, and the documentary was actually a government-made mockumentary made to promote critical thinking in children!

"Down there they call it the Kennedy Fakery Bakery."

I laughed, honestly. "Where they 'cook up' their fake evidence? That's hilarious!" It was about the only funny thing about these anti-science wingnuts. "What else have they got in the warehouse?"

"They have Rowbotham's telescope and a movie of his 1838 experiment."

A movie from 1838? Obviously a fake. I studied cinema in freshman year and the first moving pictures of people were later in the nineteenth century. I can't remember the exact year, but it sure as hell wasn't as early as 1838. "That's *so* cool!" My phone chimed and I slid it out to see the five-minute warning reminder to get home for lunch. Playtime was almost over. "Shit. It's the shop's security system, alerting me the round-Earth stooges are trying to access our computer records. I don't have the model you're looking for—they're too risky to have in stock—but I have The Photo."

His eyes went wide, at first probably from fear of the over-watchers I hinted at, and then likely with excitement at a copy of The Photo. "With the Antarctic ice wall ringing the disk, keeping the oceans from flowing off? I have a postcard I got from eBay, but it's poor quality and I didn't dare risk ordering anything bigger online."

"This one is a thirty-by-thirty-inch poster titled *Azimuthal Equidistant Pro-*

jection." It was labelled that because that's exactly what it was. It's a projection with the North Pole at the centre and all points on the map are proportionally correct distances from the pole, and in the right direction, or azimuth. But because it's a two-dimensional projection showing correct distances, the Antarctic looks like an ice wall surrounding everything else, like the gold rim of a big dinner plate. It was the Holy Grail of Flat Earth proof, at least for some of them. There's some serious math behind the projection and an example of it is on the United Nations flag, so I always have a few on hand. "We've got maybe five minutes before one of the stooges wanders in to harass me and ID you. Do you want it? With tax, it's exactly $40. But it's not some cheap reproduction. This is a quality photo on heavy archival-quality paper."

"Yes," he whispered. No word of a lie, he rubbed his stubby hands together in glee and I thought he was going to wet himself with excitement right there in the store. I trotted into the back, grabbed a copy of the projection off the shelves of high-end maps, and snatched up a matching tube. I returned to the retail area and carefully laid the photo out on the display table in the middle of the shop.

"It's *beautiful.*" And it was, made by National Geographic with rich colours and wonderful detail. If a person didn't know the Earth was in fact a sphere, this image made a good argument for the Disk Earth. "I'll take it. Do you take cash?"

"For *this,* I *only* take cash. There can be no record of its sale. They can't know we have copies on-site or they'll shut us down."

He pulled out his wallet and handed me two twenties. I tucked them into my shirt pocket and would put them in the till and ring in the sale after lunch. I gently rolled the map up and reverently slid it into the tube. With him staring at it hungrily, I felt really, really dirty, like I was selling contraband porn or something.

"I'll tell my friends about this place, that you have The Photo."

Oh shit! "No. Thank you, but you can't. You can't tell *anyone* where you got it." The last thing I needed was for the shop to become known for promoting the freaking Flat Earth Society! "Our supply is limited and I can only get copies through, um, *three* numbered corporations and four anonymous mailboxes in Detroit. That's our...ah...second last copy. Until I can get to the US. Tell no one. Post absolutely *nothing* on social media. Nothing on the net. Not even in an email. Enjoy this beautiful proof of the truth in the privacy of your home." My phone chimed a final time. Lunch waited. "Swear on the soul of Samuel Rowbotham you'll tell no one. They're almost here!" I grabbed the door handle but stood between him and the exit.

"Yes! I swear! I swear!"

"Then go in peace, Flat Earth Brother." I held the door open and he bolted, thankfully to the west, away from the direction I was off home.

o0o

There was definitely a bounce in my step as I walked home for lunch. Was it wrong of me to get so much joy and satisfaction from messing with Red Red Robin Flat-Earther? He was just a sad, misguided nut job, hurting no one. It's not like he was dangerous, like an anti-vaxxer.

Distracted by the memory of Robin's glee as he scooted off with his treasure-in-a-tube, it took me a moment or two to notice Kerouac was missing from the kitten room, again. Dammit.

"Kerouac, you little shit! Where are you?" I could hunt over the whole house and never find him, but he loved the attention and was a vocal little brat, so calling him usually worked. I left the other four in the kitten room, using my foot to scoot them all back from the door as I closed it. Their cries for attention were so loud I closed the top half of the door as well so I could concentrate and listen for their errant sibling.

I started with a circuit of the first floor, living room first. "Kerouac, where are you, Fat Boy? Kare-oo-ak..." I peeked and poked as I went. He wasn't behind the curtains, under or on any of the furniture, or in any of the cardboard boxes. On to the sparsely-furnished dining room and... the same results. "Come on, Kerouac! Out you come! Lunchtime!"

I was worried. He was always hungrier than the other four together. I moved from the dining room to the bathroom. No Kerouac. It was in the kitchen where I heard a faint *mew*.

"Come on out Kerouac. I'm home. Time for lunch."

"Mew."

"Hey, buddy. Stop messing around. Come out, come out, wherever you are."

"Mew." His cry came from somewhere near the stove and my first terrified thought was he got stuck behind it or the fridge. I stood in front of the stove, trying to figure out exactly how I was going to pull it out without either scratching the tile or more importantly, crushing Kerouac.

"Mew."

That's when I knew *exactly* where he was. I opened the narrow cupboard door where I stored the plastic container of kitty kibble to the left of the stove, but no Kerouac. The kibble container lid was up, though. I pulled the four-litre plastic bin out and it wiggled in my hands, a little heavier than usual. I set it down on the granite-topped island but before I could peek inside, Kerouac leaped out and landed on my chest with his entire armament of mini claws in full extension. The tiny needles sunk straight into my chest. *I* screamed and *he* puked... half-digested kibble straight down the front of my shirt. "Ow! Holy shit! Ow! Kerouac! Oh shit!" I quickly but carefully plucked him off my now blood-spotted and puke-covered shirt and placed him on the countertop. The pain in my chest was ridiculous, but the little adventurer head-butted my hands and began purring. I rubbed his head. "You're a little shit, K-Cat."

I put him back into the kitten room where the other four mauled him like he was the hero of all kittens and was going to inspire them to rise up in rebellion. I set a reminder in my phone to check the video to see how the little monster got out then went upstairs to clean up. Time was short, but I didn't have much choice except to shed my fouled clothes and step into the shower. I tried to catch as much of the puke in my shirt as I could, while also trying to keep the same puke from getting into the dozen or more bleeding, stinging, tiny claw holes.

Once in the shower, I ground my teeth and rode out the pain as I washed away the kibble remains and the blood, making sure to get each wound clean. For tiny punctures, they sure bled a lot. Eventually, I had to be done. I was still bleeding, but it slowed after I towelled off and tossed the now-blooded towel into the tub. The ruined shirt followed it, then I set about applying antiseptic cream and little Band-Aids to each wound. The pain subsided, but I knew it was going to hurt even more when I removed the Band-Aids and probably half the hair on my chest.

I ran out of time and although I made a couple of sandwiches, I had to take them with me, to eat when I could. The day was going from 'hot' to 'yuck', so once I was back at the shop I turned the fans on high, ate, and wondered how the hell Kerouac was escaping the kitten room. Eventually, I got down to work, planning the new window display. I changed it at least once a month, sometimes twice. Just because your revenues got dusty didn't mean the merchandise had to.

An hour into the task my personal phone rang in my back pocket while I was on my knees laying out maps like shelf-lining paper. I answered it while I clambered out of the display space. "Hello."

"Hi. My name is Tori McLeod, and I'm calling about the apartment. Is it still available?"

That was quick. "It is."

"Perfect. Would you be willing to rent it month to month? I'll pay $500 more than you're asking."

"Um..." Month to month wasn't what I had in mind.

"My place is unlivable for at least a month and I hate hotels for more than a few days."

An extra $500 would be nice, and last time the place sat empty for three months before my cousin moved in. "How about you come to see the place, and we can talk about it. Do you have references?"

"Would talking to my condo board be enough?"

There was something familiar about her voice, but I couldn't place it. "A call would be fine. I'm home after six this evening if you want to drop by."

"Unfortunately tonight I have a class. How about tomorrow?"

"Tomorrow is good, too."

"Perfect."

I gave her the address and my name, and she said she'd swing by after six-thirty tomorrow.

The afternoon was quiet and I was able to lock the doors right at 5:05. I detoured past the liquor store to see if they carried absinthe and discovered they sold a kit that included the absinthe, the silver spoon-thing, and a six-pack of the fancy sugar. Although Joe was always welcome back with Rose, the absinthe experience had been so popular I wanted a small supply on hand. Of course, at some point, I might have to actually test the product and see if I can get it right before sharing it with company. My resolve to never try absinthe again was fading fast.

Kit in hand, my first thought while unlocking the front door of the house was where would I find Kerouac this time.

"Mew." A call came from the kitten room.

"Mew mew mew mew mew!" the chorus joined in. I peeked over the half-door on my way past to the kitchen and Kerouac was in the middle of the mob waiting for me. I started breathing again. I hadn't realized how stressed I was at his escapism. There wasn't much trouble he could get into in the house, but he was as fearless as he was, he was still a kitten and I didn't want him spraining or breaking anything before I returned them all to the adoption center in a few weeks. I put the absinthe kit away, returned to the kitten room, and released the kindle.

Ten minutes into our communal dinner, my phone alarm chimed to remind me to check the video to see how Houdini-cat was getting out. I snoozed the alarm and finished my chicken-loaded chef salad. Sated, one by one, the kittens wandered around, sniffing, exploring, or pawing my bare legs to inquire into my general health and make sure I was eating properly.

I finished the salad and retired to the couch with kittens and Netflix when the alarm sounded again. Phone in hand, I switched from data to WiFi, opened the alarm app, and paused the current recording session. It was one big file, going back three days, so I scrolled back to just before I left for work first thing this morning. The camera was pointed at the Dutch door so I watched myself scoot the kittens back with my foot. Video Burroughs ran up and leaped on my errant shoelace.

"Alright, Lace-chaser, I have to go to work." I watched as I picked up the little ginger and placed him on the cat tree, part of which was on the left side of the screen. I managed to escape on my second attempt. "See you later, kids. Stay out of the liquor cabinet!" The front door closed with a gentle thump and I could even hear the bolt being thrown as Past Me locked up. The sound recording was as clear as a bell. I was impressed.

Kerouac's head appeared on the second-highest platform of the cat tree. He stared out the door where I had just left, then he backed out of view. A second later he charged into view, leaped semi-gracefully through the air and landed on the four-inch-wide shelf capping the bottom half of the door. Unfortunately, he had nothing to grip or dig his claws into and his momentum took him right off the other side, landing with a soft thump and a surprised mrow in the living room. Dammit!

I could now see that the giant six-foot-tall cat tree was too close to the door. It hadn't always been, but now the kittens were bigger and it was definitely too close. It was also a three-and-a-half-foot drop. I stopped the recording and the camera went live again, continuing its monitoring/recording. I put the phone down and picked Kerouac off my lap where he was kneading my thigh. "Let's take a look at you, stunt-cat." Holding him in one hand, I turned him over and carefully examined his paws and legs, gently squeezing them and checking for injuries. I'm no expert, so I was relying on him reacting to pain if I hit a sensitive spot. He struggled but didn't seem to mind what I was doing. He probably thought I was playing. He appeared unhurt. The resilience of the kitten acrobat, I suppose.

I placed him on the couch and then went to their room to move the cat tree to the far side of the window, away from the door. All five kittens followed me. The thing had to weigh well over a hundred pounds, so it took some pushing. It didn't help that all five kittens raced up the tree to see what I was doing. As soon as it moved, though, Calliope ran down and raced over to the smaller, knee-high tree in the corner and hid behind it. She didn't like sudden movements, unlike the other four who clung to the carpeted behemoth and rode out whatever it was their human slave was doing for their entertainment.

Once I was done and happy with the tree's placement, I returned to the couch and Netflix, feline parade bounding and chattering along behind me. The mystery of Kerouac's escape was solved, but now I was wondering how long it would be before he could simply leap straight up and over the half door.

Chapter 5

WEDNESDAY STARTED OUT HOT and got stickier by the minute as the humidity climbed. I went around the house and closed all of the blinds and curtains, then turned the ceiling fan in the kitten room to 'high'. As I stepped out into the heat radiating off of Ossington threatening to melt the soles of my Sketchers, I remembered my first date with my university sweetheart Leah, in the snow on a February 15th, two days after her birthday and one after Valentine's Day. Sure, I missed Leah, but right then I missed that snow even more.

Snow falls, big as coins, light as wishes,
Blanketing the warm suburban night with white,
  For the two wannabe lovers.
Teasing other, each and one,
With contradictory arguments
About blue parrots and fjords,
Singing of Sharks and Jets, and music in living hills.
  Making angels of snow,
Him, heart growing, falling into... something.
Her, smile showing, confessing to having... someone.
Else.

Facing north, the store remained fairly cool with all its pedestal fans blowing, but when I locked up for lunch and braved the searing sidewalk I was sweat-soaked within fifty feet. I'm not a big fan of extreme heat and humidity, having fainted once in third grade while standing at the teacher's desk to say I wasn't feeling well and felt like I was going to faint, but I can usually stand it for short periods of time. I don't really tan well, either, but I do burn like a pro and am usually okay with SPF 300 lotion and drinking lots of water.

Before I even released the kittens and filled their bowls, I drained half of the jug of water I always keep in the fridge. I then went upstairs and got a clean, dry shirt, which I hung on the front door knob—I'd change once I got back to work and towelled off. I let my babies loose. Kerouac must have discovered he could no longer reach the door from the tree because he ignored me and marched past, straight to the kitchen.

"Tough luck, Papillon. Your days of escaping Devil's Island are *done*. Nobody gets out of Kitten Hell without my express written approval, and a payment of at least five francs." As expected, Prisoner 24601 ignored me. He stopped in front of the kibble cupboard door and pawed at it, knowing damn well where the food was. The door didn't budge. He stared at it, but his narrow experience with rubber bands didn't let him figure out what was holding the door closed now when it had so easily opened before. "We've spared no expense on security, Papillon. Your access is denied."

I scooped him up, placed him on the countertop, retrieved everyone's food and dishes, and doled out their servings. As hot and sweaty as I was, it didn't stop the kittens from mauling me and licking my salty skin when I took my salad to the couch. Their ministrations and purrs relaxed me and I dozed off until my phone chimed and reminded me to get back to the store. My memory was bad, but it wasn't so bad I would forget to go back to work, I just sometimes got distracted and lost track of the time.

Back out on the streets on fire, Mandy-the-unfriendly-realtor was gone, but as I sweated my way to the shop I suspected I'd see her again.

I sold a foldout map of the Kawartha Lakes District and two Dog Park maps, but that was it for the muggy afternoon. I guess I wasn't the only one being beaten down by the heat. Before closing up, I called *The Nigerian Prince* and ordered one of Aba's exquisite cold fish dishes. The only cold food I had left at home were frozen chicken fingers, or cereal with milk, and my volatile blood sugar wouldn't let me subsist on cereal for very long.

"How was your date, Brother?" Aba held my take-out order, looking like he wasn't going to give it up until I fed him the juicy details of my date with RayRay.

"You're holding my dinner hostage?"

"Until I get the whole unedited, steamy version of the truth. Did you get lucky?"

I reached out for the box. "Then hand it over, because she didn't show up."

He reluctantly handed over my meal. "At all? Not even a text?"

"She sent a text. She got high with a friend and forgot. I consider myself *quite* lucky."

"Ouch. What now?"

"Now? Now I go home, eat, and relax instead of running around the city meeting for coffee and tiramisu or whatever."

"Then go. Do. Enjoy."

So I did.

My feline Mod Squad and I were halfway through our second episode in a row of Jerry Seinfeld's *Comedians in Cars Getting Coffee* when the doorbell rang. The episodes were brief, funny, and didn't really require me to use much of my heat-baked brain so it took me a moment to figure out what the bell sound was. No one ever rang the bell. The antique brass lion's head knocker invited everyone to get my attention with a couple of short, sonorous raps. As I stood slowly enough to give the kittens time to react and hop off my lap or shoulders, I checked my watch. 6:25. My potential new tenant. I opened the door six inches, using my feet to keep the Curious Five back and would have looked like a distrustful loon doing a shuffling dance in his bare feet . . . if she hadn't been looking back at the street.

"Hi Tori? Sorry, I have kittens."

She turned back. It was Rage Grrl! She looked over her sunglasses at me. "Is that like shingles? Is there a vaccine?"

"More like herpes...there's always more where they came from." *Herpes?* What the hell was I talking about? "Give me a second to corral them and I'll be right out." If she didn't run away in the meantime. Herpes? Nice icebreaker, Walden! You *idiot*!

"Sure."

"Thanks." I closed the door without trapping any kitten heads and immediately started scooping them up and depositing them carefully over the half-door into the kitten room. I got four of them quickly, but Kerouac did a runner, bounding upstairs. "Stay up there, you little booger! I'm not chasing you." I slipped into my sandals and scooped the keys off the table just inside and behind the front door.

"Mew." He was creeping down the stairs.

"No. I'm not playing Catch-the-Kitty right now." I slipped out quickly, and joined Rage Grrl, aka Tori, on the front porch. I locked the door behind me.

"You're the French fry guy." She smiled. Her blonde hair was tied back in a ponytail, probably because of the heat, and she was dressed in a beige summer-weight ladies suit-type outfit. I don't know women's fashions worth a shit, but I knew the look of a professional when I saw one. When she wasn't working out, she took her look seriously.

"And you're the—" I almost said 'angry smoking chick' but managed to instead say "I saw you at the dojo, working out." It wasn't much better than what I *almost* said, but it sounded less judgmental.

She laughed that warm, rich laugh. "Oh shit. You saw that? I was just working off a little steam."

"That's a good way to do it. Better than heroin or crack, I suppose." First herpes and now crack? My inner idiot was shining through in all his glory. It's a damned good thing she's married, though why was she here alone? "Let's go take a look at the place." I led the way off the porch to the side walkway and through the gate to the backyard. "The deck isn't big, but you're welcome to use it and the BBQ if you want. As you can feel, it gets a little hot back here in the afternoon, and there's no denying the proximity of a dumpster or two."

She took off her jacket and hung it over her arm. "Hot is okay. I like the sun. I'm most comfortable outdoors. I was pretty much raised outside." She sniffed. "I can live with the smell, just so long as it's not as bad inside."

"No, the suite is fine, smell-wise." I unlocked the door to the suite, turned on the stairwell light, and led her down into the cool basement.

"Wow. Is it air-conditioned?"

"No, just a well-insulated basement. Upstairs the heat can sometimes be oppressive, but down here it's never bad." We walked along the narrow boot/coat area and through the door into the apartment proper. I stepped aside to let her in.

"Wow. It's lovely. Minimalistic, but with that Scandinavian style IKEA does so well. I like it."

"If you need anything more, I'll buy it—"

"Thank you. Now, why is a nice place like this vacant? Was the previous tenant a serial killer?" She winked. She *did* have a wicked sense of humour. Nice!

"No, the previous tenant was my cousin, Sondra. But before her was a wicked stepmother who buried her stepchildren in the floor. They've since been removed and the concrete is good as new."

"Well, that's important. Wouldn't want shoddy concrete." She moved around the space, looking up and down and around. "Do you allow pets?"

"I don't, but there's an extra deposit required. You have a dog?"

"No. I occasionally look after my brother's bonobo chimp. He's quite tame and usually just plays Jenga and keeps to himself."

She was a risk taker, taking a chance on me finding her funny rather than being freaked out by her comments. That was refreshing. "As long as he doesn't listen to Justin Bieber or Taylor Swift until all hours of the night, it should be good."

"God, no. He's a Barenaked Ladies fan."

"Haha. Aren't we all?" Oops! Sexual innuendo. Too far.

She turned and looked at me, taking my measure, then grinned. "Only in art class." She stepped into the kitchen and inspected the cupboards and appliances.

"You've done nice work here. It doesn't feel like a typical basement suite."

"Thank you. I believe a home should be a sanctuary, a place to get away from the craziness of the world outside."

"Agreed. Nice and quiet."

"Except for Wednesday nights." I couldn't resist.

"What's Wednesdays? Violin lessons?"

"Clog dancing." I was on a roll, and why not? I missed reparté.

"Oh, is *that* all? At least it's not Morris dancing with all the bells and sticks."

"Never! It's a bells-and-sticks-free zone."

"Clogs only."

"Just on Wednesdays."

"Of course." She wandered out into the living room and began checking out the other doors. The bathroom raised her eyebrows. "A jet tub for two *and* a shower. This is unexpectedly lovely."

"We like clean tenants. We also got the tub on sale and my plumber cousin did the work for free."

"Lucky you. Shared laundry?"

"No, you have your own over-under machines, as do I upstairs."

"I? Not '*we*'?"

"It was 'we' but is now 'I', unless you count the kittens, then it would be 'we'."

"How many?"

"Five fosters. They were my ex's project, but she left them behind when she..."

"Found greener pastures?"

"Sure, if a dentist could be called a greener pasture."

"Maybe to some." She found the bedroom. "I like this! Lots of room, and even though it's in the basement, you've lit it up nicely, with a dimmer and everything."

"My grandmother used to say if your bedroom doesn't welcome you in for a good night's sleep, then the rest of your day will be ruined."

"Wise woman."

"She was." I knew I was forgetting something. Something important. Her wedding rings twinkled in the light. Oh yeah. "Is it just you? Not your husband?" Or your wife?

"What? No. Just me."

She didn't elaborate, so I didn't ask.

"I like a sanctuary, too. My days and many evenings are spent in pubs and restaurants, so I like quiet at home."

"For work or play?"

"I'm the full-time Training Coordinator and occasional Marketing Manager for *Montgomery's 1837 Taverns*, so mostly work. It keeps me busy."

Wow. There were Montgomerys all across southern Ontario. "That *would* keep you busy." I led the way to the couch and chair facing the coffee table, where I'd placed the rental agreement when I came down earlier to turn on the lights and air the place out. "All kidding aside, I do host a dinner party every two weeks or so. Just a quiet event with six or seven people from the neighbourhood. It's a simple potluck, but you're welcome to join us. We avoid conversations about politics and religion, but everything else is pretty much fair game."

"Like the dinner parties in the movies?"

"Exactly, but without corpses or terrorists or divorce battles."

"That doesn't sound like much fun. What kind of potluck can it be without at least one terrorist attack?"

"We can arrange for one next time if you'd like--just for you. Or a Purge."

"God no. No Purge. Those movies make me lose all hope in mankind. I think a simple potluck and conversation would be good for the soul. Does that mean you'll rent me the place for a month? If I need a second month I promise to give you at least a week's notice. I know it's not ideal. I'm sorry."

It would be nice to have someone else in the building, even if she was down in the basement. "A week's notice will be fine."

Tension seemed to drain right out of her as she leaned forward and picked up the rental agreement. "Thank you. And I promise not to smoke down here. Is the back deck okay?"

That's what I was forgetting! She's a *smoker*! "The back deck is okay." I'd have to keep the kitchen window closed, though. "There are even chairs out on the lawn next to the fire pit, if you prefer."

"Better still! I'm trying to quit."

"Me, too."

"Cigarettes?"

"No, *fries*."

She laughed. "Of course! Those things'll kill you." She began reading the document and I gave her quiet to do so. She had a nice energy and I was looking forward to having her here, even if it was only for a month, maybe two. I couldn't help but wonder of course if her husband was going to show up in the middle of the night. Would he know she's here? Was she running from him? Or was he stationed somewhere exotic and she was just holding down the fort until he got home? All questions that were none of my damned business, of course.

She was okay with the rental agreement terms and gave me the condo board's number. I agreed to give her condo board a call and get back to her ASAP. She expressed a desire to move in by the weekend, as the couch she'd been staying on was being loaned out to her friend's brother who was arriving unexpectedly from Vancouver on Saturday morning. I didn't foresee any trouble, so we shook on it and I led her back outside. Under the suit, the humour, and the confidence, I sensed a hint of vulnerability in her. I think her current living situation had her a little off-balance and she was palpably relieved I was willing to rent the suite to her. To that end, after she left and I was back in with the kittens, I looked up her condo board online, confirmed the number she gave me was legitimate, and called it.

"Hello." A woman. A little older, by the sound of her voice.

"Hi. Mrs. Konrad? My name is Max Walden, and I was given this number for Tori McLeod's condo board."

"Tori? Yes! Of course! She said you'd be calling. Terrible thing about the flooding in those three units. She is a wonderful resident and we've never had a speck of trouble from her, Mr. Walden. I think you'll be very pleased to have her there, even for a short time."

"Thank you, Mrs. Konrad. I appreciate your candour."

"My pleasure."

So, that settled it. Tori was a good choice. Still no mention of her husband, but if he wasn't staying here for the month, he was no business of mine. I texted her the good news and told her she could drop off the signed agreement and a check here tomorrow evening or any time at the store. Five minutes later she rang my bell again and handed me the check and signed agreement. I grabbed a pen and the keys to the apartment and stepped out onto the porch to sign as well.

"Thank you. I couldn't wait." Behind her sunglasses, I thought I saw a tear or two.

"Of course." I handed her the keys. "Here you go, just in case you want to sleep here tonight, er *there*, tonight." Oops. "That Sealy mattress is probably ten times more comfortable than any couch you've been sleeping on."

"Thank you. I just might. Good night, Max."

"Goodnight, Tori."

She left, off with a purposeful stride, despite the heat of the evening. She looked like whatever she was dealing with, she needed a bit of a break, and I was glad to be able to help. Mom and Dad would have approved. Of course, Mom had approved of Michelle, too, and we all know how *that* turned out.

Back inside, the kittens demanded to know why I wasn't hanging out with them at their beck and call, so I made some iced tea for myself, freshened their water dishes, and all six of us went back to watching comedians driving in cars and drinking coffee.

o0o

Wednesday: Kittens to vet for 8 a.m. The reminder popped up on my phone just as I was bundling them off to bed. The little furkids weren't going to enjoy the experience, but I was actually looking forward to them getting their shots. A vaccinated pet is a safe pet and usually a healthier pet. The shots were also mandated and paid for by the rescue agency.

Before calling it quits for the night, I set an early alarm to get me up at seven, moved the pet carrier from the spare room down to the front hall, and booked a taxi for 7:40. The clinic was only a ten-minute drive away, but better early than late.

o0o

The alarm went off, I dragged myself up and out of bed, started the kettle for coffee, and threw into the toaster a couple of pieces of pretentious artesian, free-range, keto-friendly, sugar-free bread-like substance Kalani had challenged me to try. It was actually pretty good, but without the usual overload of sugar found in commercial breads, it didn't brown up as prettily as I liked. Lathered in marmalade, though, browning didn't matter a whit.

High-pitched pleas for freedom hammered at me from the Alkittentraz, but the kettle popped in readiness and the French press with dark, Kenyan roast was much more urgent than the five not-so-starving, hardly-tortured-at-all love brats.

o0o

The hardest part of any vet visit was corralling my babies in the first place, but since I did it all in the kitten room, they were all quickly captured and contained in the carrier, with a fluffy old towel for comfort. This may have been my first visit back with all five of these little ones, but it wasn't my first rodeo with kittens to the vet.

o0o

I'll spare you the details, but the kids took their shots like troopers, Kerouac strutted and purred and won hearts, the vet was happy with the condition of all of them, and they were worm-free. If she'd seen any symptoms or signs she would have had me isolate the patient at home and bring stool or vomit samples. It was easily fixed with medications, but dangerous in young kittens if not caught in time.

The five were all super-clingy after their shots, but once we were home to their food, water, and treats, I was left in the dust.

And that was the excitement for the day. Back at the shop I made some sales, did some dusting, jotted down some map ideas, and that was it. It was so quiet I almost texted Rachel to suggest another attempt at a coffee date, but I held off. I was bored, I wasn't crazy. Why set myself up for more disappointment?

The kittens were fine when I went home for lunch and all lovey-dovey when I wandered back in at 5:10. It was far too hot to cook, so I munched on the last of a macaroni salad while the beasts crunched kibble and gobbled vitamin-supplemented soft food. Still hungry when the salad was gone, I had two bowls of Raisin Bran and gave a couple tablespoons of milk to each of my mewling charges.

o0o

I'm not certain exactly when Tori moved in, but on Thursday night around midnight, while I was sitting with the kittens after another quiet night of watching everyone else slam their poems at the club, I heard her voice through the open kitchen window, then heard her door open and close with a soft thump. Tempted as I was to go ask her how she was settling in, and maybe see who she was talking to, it was none of my damned business. She was just my tenant and nothing in the lease forbade overnight company, whether she was married or not. I'd never cheated on Michelle, but my dating record prior to Mish was hardly spotless. Once, in university, I snuck through a graveyard at 2 a.m. and slipped into Leah's dorm room to spend the night with her while her other boyfriend was away.

o0o

The week at the shop finished off with a quiet day on Saturday as the heat was replaced by a thunderstorm and the tempest battered potential shoppers back to their homes. Even Kalani at the market acknowledged the rain was a relief but the pounding thunder and frequent flashes of lightning scared off all but her diehard regulars. By late evening the rain was gone and the heat was rolling back in, but I could still smell the loamy wet earth and comforting sharp tang of storm ozone in the air over the angry bite of dumpsters.

The weather app showed a roller coaster of hot and damn hot for the next week, with a humidex that made me want to swim in Toronto Harbour—and no one *I* know swims in the Harbour. Dad used to tell us stories about family swims at Hanlon Beach on the west end of the Toronto Islands back in the late sixties and early seventies. Back then he said the lake was so polluted they had to step over and around the fish skeletons and half-rotted corpses on the stony beach to get to the water. Blech. Yes, it was humid enough to make me want to brave the zombie perch in order to cool off.

oOo

I spent the entirety of Sunday sequestered in the house working on the shipwreck map while the kittens climbed all over me and critiqued my work, so I felt no guilt whatsoever in opening an after-dinner beer and sitting on the porch without them, just watching the world go past. With my bare feet up on the white wood rail and the beer on the wide arm of the bright red Adirondack chair, I must have dozed off because a soft, familiar voice reached down and tickled my slumber.

"All you need is a straw hat and a shotgun to complete the picture."

I opened my eyes and shook off the doze. "Hey there." I motioned to the other chair and Tori sat. Judging by her tights, Nikes, mesh runner's singlet, and water-bottle-equipped hip belt, she'd been out for a run. She was also sweat-soaked, but in the summer city heat that didn't take much more than walking home from Starbucks. "Are there a lot of straw hats and shotguns on the porches where you're from?"

"Thunder Bay has plenty of shotguns, but more Bass Pro and Cabella's ball caps than straw hats."

"T-Bay, eh? When did you move down here?" That would have been a helluva culture shock.

"Right after high school. I followed my boyfriend and his big dreams."

"Dream big or go home, they say." At least I think they do, and I'm never quite sure who 'they' are.

"Yeah, well his dreams were the only big thing about him."

Whoa! "That's a little more information than I was expecting."

She blushed and looked down. "Oh shit. That is *not* what I meant. He *dreamed* big, but he never followed through. Last I heard he's living a small life with a wife and twins somewhere near Woodstock."

Her rings flashed in the twilight. So, the big dreamer isn't who she married. Again, not my business. "And I'm guessing you don't wish you were still with him, twins and all?"

"Hell no." She shifted in the chair. "But my former romantic life isn't why I stopped to say hi. I have two tickets for Friday to see a hypnotist act, with five hundred credits for Head-to-Head Game Loungedown by the tower, and I wondered if you'd like to come catch the show and game for a few hours. Do you game?"

"Do I *game*? I'll let you know young lady I was the video game champion of my Grade Seven homeroom *two* months running."

"So you *did* game, back in the old days. That was what? Ms. PacMan? Or Pong?"

"Ouch! It was *Tomb Raider: The Last Revelation*, missy miss. Pong? I think that was my dad's game of choice. Or maybe it was Defender. He was seriously Old School."

"I'd say! At least he played, though. My dad found Mario Kart to be too complicated."

"He'd have got along fine with my mom, who never saw the point of any of it."

"So, Friday?"

"Sure. Just so long as you let me buy the first round."

"Just one round? So you *do* know the place and their prices."

"I can afford the games, but the beers and the booze-infused donuts nearly busted me last time."

"But the donuts are soooo good." She smiled at a memory.

"Mother of *God* they're sweet! I thought I was going to get diabetes from just one." I shivered at the memory.

"The first time I had one it took a whole beer to wash down the sugar and get the taste out of my mouth." She pushed herself up out of the chair. "I have a meeting until six at our restaurant on King Street. I can meet you at the Lounge shortly after, or come back here, get changed into something less boardroom and more Friday-on-the-town and we can head down together a bit later. The show doesn't start until nine."

"I work until five and have to tend to the kittens for a bit, so if it's not a pain, come back here and we can go down together?"

"Sure. Since we may have a drink or two, do you mind if we take the subway?"

"Let's see... Friday summer evening in downtown Toronto...drive or take the subway...? Um, transit, please. Oh, wait. Are the Jays in town?"

"No, they're in Boston for the weekend. I checked. And the Argos are in Calgary. BMO Field isn't close to the Lounge, but the traffic all flows that way. It shouldn't be busier than any other July Friday. At least the Ex isn't on."

"True. You can't pay me to go near the lakeshore during 'the world's largest county fair', or whatever they bill it as now. I worked there for four years and had my fill of Belgian Ice Cream Waffles and roller coasters."

"How can you *ever* have your fill of Belgian Ice Cream Waffles?"

"It's not the waffles that got me, it was the roller coaster ride with a belly full of ice cream and waffles. Not a pretty sight." I puffed my cheeks out as if I were going to puke. She laughed and my heart skipped a beat at the sound.

"Then no roller coasters. In the meantime, I need to shower and polish a presentation I'm giving tomorrow. It's amazing how much work goes into a lecture on respectful workplace behaviour. You'd think 'Don't be sexist, racist, insensitive little shits' would be all that's needed, but no."

"I feel your pain. I tried that with my staff but the blowback was insane. I got ignored for a week."

"Didn't you say you work in the map shop? How many staff do you have?"

"Just me. But I have a horrific attitude. I was going to suspend me, but then I'd only have to cover the shift myself."

"Well, you can't be doing that, can you?" She winked and smiled and I forgot my own name.

"I try to avoid pissing off the staff. They keep threatening to unionize."

"Bastards!"

"Damned straight!" I stood. It was time to get back inside to the little ones.

Tori stepped down off the porch. "I'll give you a call Thursday to confirm everything, Max."

"Please do. My memory is shit, so I need reminding, a lot." I planned to go in and put it in my phones calendar before I got distracted, but it would be good to have her remind me, too.

"Have a good night."

"You, too."

She jogged around the corner of the house. I heard the gate open and shut with a firm click, picked up my empty bottle, and went back inside to find my phone.

oOo

The one week I would have been ecstatic the weatherman was a lying jerk, he was dead-on with his meteorological prognostications. It was either grill hot or pizza oven damned hot all the way to Friday. It was so hot—*how hot was it?!*—it was so hot I stayed home from the club on Thursday evening, zombied out on the couch with the kittens and three pedestal fans keeping us as cool as they could.

I only saw Tori once, on Wednesday, from a distance as she jogged off at about ten o'clock that evening, but as promised she called Thursday to confirm our plans for Friday.

"Is the Game Lounge air conditioned, Tori?"

"It is. I called and asked. I can handle the heat, but this week has been crazy. It was thirty-seven today."

"Oh, is *that* all? It felt like it was well over forty with the humidity."

"The Weather Channel said the humidity did make it feel like forty-one, but yes, the Game Lounge has A/C."

"Thank God. I wonder if they'll let me bring the kittens."

"The heat's hard on them, too?"

"It's not *too* bad. They have plenty of water and fans continuously cooling the room off, but still, they could probably use a break from the sweatbox, too. How's the basement?"

"It's surprisingly cool, thanks. So, just to confirm, I'll come back to Bloorcourt, get changed, and we'll take the subway down together?"

"Roger that." A goofy thought occurred to me. "I wonder if they have a walk-in fridge we could hang out in." At this point, I was ready to go sit and read a book in the hospital Emergency waiting area, if they had A/C.

"I'll call and ask. Maybe if we tip the kitchen staff we can get our drinks served to us in there, too."

"Of course, that all depends on the fridge not being full already with management."

"True enough. Okay. I have to go, Max. I'll see you tomorrow between six-thirty and seven. I'll come up and knock."

"See you then."

o0o

Friday morning dawned as hot as it had been all week, and the shop was barely tolerable. I was standing in front of a fan when the doorbell rang and the shop's stylish, sixtyish owner, Leona, walked in. I don't know how she managed it, but it didn't look like the heat was bothering her in the least.

Chapter 6

"HEY, KID!" LEONA THRUST a large, plastic, sweating cup of beige something-er-other at me. "An ice cap for my favourite shop manager." She had a second, smaller cup in her other hand.

"You're a saint!" I accepted the drink, the cold intense but oh so welcoming in the heat. I put it straight to my forehead, rolling it back and forth to cool me off. "You've just saved me from melting like the white chocolate globes we carry at Easter."

"I'm sorry I can't air condition the place, but I have two more fans in the car for you."

"Two?" I took a long sip of the iced cappuccino and sighed. "You're officially my favourite boss of all time."

"Then my life is complete! Sweet Jee-sus can tayk me awayuh!"

We both laughed, as much as the heat let us.

"How are the kittens in this heat?"

"They're okay, but as I was telling my new tenant last night, it's starting to get to them, too."

"Then there's a gift for them out in the Audi's trunk."

I looked past her and could see her baby blue Audi parked at the curb. "A gift? I'm not sure I'm allowed to feed them ice cappuccinos."

"Haha. It's heavy, so we'll have to drive it over to your house. You're about to take lunch, aren't you?"

"I am. It's heavy *and* it's for the kittens?"

"And you, I suppose. It's an air conditioner. A window-mount one. My sister and her husband just got central air and I already have it, so I thought of the poor kittens."

I sipped the drink, afraid to say anything for a moment. Such unexpected kindness threatened to overwhelm me. After a moment I dared to look her in the eyes and whisper "Thank you. That's won—", and the brain freeze hit me, *hard*. I barely got the cup onto the counter before I had to let go of it. I slammed both palms to my temples. "Mother of God! Holy son-of-a..."

"Are you going to live? I didn't think I needed to tell you to drink it slowly."

The pain lanced through my skull but subsided quickly. It was just brain freeze after all, and not a tumor. I picked up the drink again and took a smaller, less energetic but equally appreciative sip. "You're too good to me, Leona. Thank you."

"It's my pleasure. You treat our little shop with respect and joy, and that makes all the difference in the world to me. Your love of maps is obvious."

If it wasn't already a million degrees out, I probably would have blushed. "I guess I'm a bit of a geek when it comes to cartography."

"And I'm grateful you are." She checked her Fitbit. "Shall we get that unit to your house?"

"Yes. Sure. Hopefully, it'll fit."

"It will. The sash window in your living room will accommodate it. Trust me. You do maps, I do houses."

"Then I'll take your word for it."

"Of course, you will, Kid."

o0o

Leona had an open house she had to set up for a client over near Christie Pits, so we first got the fans for the store out of the Audi, then we made the short, heavenly, air-conditioned luxury drive around the corner to the house. While she held open the house doors, I carried the unit inside and placed it on the scruffy carpet next to the front closet. We hugged, she handed me my quickly-melting drink, and she was gone. This unit looked a lot like the ones we had when I was growing up, so I didn't anticipate any trouble installing it, once I bought a short heavy-duty extension cord. But that could wait. The kittens and I all needed food, and they no doubt needed cool fresh water.

We had our lunch, though they were as listless as I was in the heat, so I set a reminder in my phone to swing by the market on the way home after closing the shop to see if they had an extension cord like the one I needed. I also emptied and refilled the ice trays in the freezer, then dropped cubes into their water dishes.

o0o

Clouds started to roll in just after four, cooling the day a tad, but when five-oh-five rolled around I was out the door and out of the shop on a mission. I wanted to get home, install the A/C unit, get a bite to eat, and be ready in plenty of time before Tori knocked on my door. I was just rounding the corner on the second and last leg of the short walk when my phone chimed at me. I stopped and checked the message. *Check the market for a cord*. Crap. Yes. Of course. I turned back and crossed the two lights to the market. Kalani's father, Noah, was behind the counter, assisting the first of three people lined up in front of him. I found the extension cords down the aisle with the light bulbs I'd needed a while back. There was a skinny three-meter cord with a multiple outlet head, and there were three heavy-duty two-meter cords. Perfect! I plucked one of the heavy ones off the display hook and joined the line at the front of the store.

It was Friday, and the lottery was up to thirty million dollars, so the line moved steadily as everyone bought lottery tickets and smokes. I got a ticket as well as the cord and left Noah with a quick thanks, not wanting to hold up the line that had formed quickly behind me. I don't know if the market made much money off of lottery ticket sales, but it probably did okay with the extra little stuff people picked up when they came in for tickets. I wondered if there was a way to make that work at the map shop, too.

Leona was right of course. The air conditioner fit right into the window. Once it was installed and running, I checked that the air coming out was cold, and released the kittens from their room. Four of them followed me to the kitchen, but Calliope went straight for the loud humming noise in the living room, chattering away, full of questions.

I whipped up and ate a toasted tuna melt, pouring the skipjack water over the kittens' food. When I was done, I grabbed a quick shower and changed into khakis, a t-shirt for the inevitable sweat, and my least-tacky Hawaiian shirt. I debated wearing my tackiest one, but it was a gift from Michelle and was covered in hearts and hibiscuses. It wasn't just tacky, it was nausea-inducing and I think it only got worn once before it found its way to a hanger at the back of my closet. It's not something I ever want to be seen wearing, for aesthetic reasons. I put a reminder in my phone for tomorrow morning to drop the shirt in the church next door's donation bin on my way to the shop. I'm sure there was *someone* somewhere who could look at it without gagging.

At six-thirty-six the brass lion rapped firmly and distinctly three times on the front door. I was in the midst of scooping up the kittens, so I answered it with the last two—Kerouac and Zwerling—wiggling in my arms.

"Holy crap! Max, they're adorable!"

"Thanks. Come on in while I put them to bed. It'll just take a second."

"Nice shirt. Very Thomas Magnum."

"Thanks. This was the least tacky one I have."

"That's the *least* tacky? I'd love to see the tackiest one."

"No, you really wouldn't. It hurts the eyes."

"I'll take your word for that."

I stepped back and let Tori into my home. As she stepped across the threshold my stomach did a bizarre twist-and-drop. I know in my heart Mish was never going to be here again, but the place still very much carried some fragment of her presence. It didn't help that Tori wore a loose, cream-coloured summer dress covered with a subtle pattern of greenery of some sort that failed to draw my eyes away from the semi-plunging V-neck. What *did* drag my gaze away were her blue eyes. They were a little grey, a little green, and sparkled behind her glasses even in the low light of the foyer.

Kerouac bit down briefly on my thumb and wound up to full wiggle in an attempt to escape, but as soon as Tori reached out to pet him, he calmed down and butted her fingertips with the white spot on his forehead. "This is Kerouac. Kerouac, this is Tori. And *this* little Persian cutie is Zwerling, one of the two girls." I walked over to the Dutch door, reached over with a kitten in each hand, and gently deposited them with their siblings. The mewling at the door was outrageous, and Tori squeezed in next to me to peer in. Her scent of shampoo, soap, cigarette smoke, and a subtle application of some perfume I recognized but couldn't name, was toxic.

"You really *do* have five kittens?"

"They're fosters. They're due to soon go back to the centre and be put up for adoption."

"Wow. So, who's who? Kerouac is the black and white one—"

"Yup, he's the tuxedo."

"You said Zwerling is the Persian fluff ball, so how about the two gingers and the tabby?"

I tried to focus, but stumbled. Her scent... "Um, Ginsberg and Burroughs are the gingers and Calliope's the gorgeous, er, a Torby—tabby/tortoise-shell combo."

All five scrambled and climbed all over each other to get the attention of the two humans staring down at them, but *this* human barely noticed them. I stepped back from the doorway. Since I wasn't taking them out to play and explore, I didn't want to taunt them. I also didn't want Tori to see the dorky flush I felt rising up my neck from my chest.

"Those are unusual names for cats." She, too, stepped back.

I grabbed my keys and phone off the entry table. "They're the Beat Generation. Jack Kerouac, Allen Ginsberg, William S. Burroughs, and Harriet Sohmers Zwerling."

"And Calliope?"

I held open the front door, and we exited. I locked up. "She's the Greek muse of eloquence and epic poetry. It wouldn't be a house full of writer cats without a muse, now would it?"

"Definitely not. Is she *your* muse, too?"

"They all are, if muses give unlimited love in addition to doubling as distractions and puking at random." We started the block-and-a-half walk to Ossington subway station. "If I work on something for more than twenty minutes in one place, though, they settle down and purr up five-part harmony."

"Nice. What do you work on? Music? Painting?"

"Maps. I make custom, hand-drawn maps. I just finished one of part of Asia for the owner of Sterling Wakabayashi's Karate School down the street."

"Jake's family?"

She knew them? Oh, shit. Yes. That's where I first saw her! "Exactly. It's a secret, but it's a birthday present for Jake's grandfather, commissioned by his mom."

"Fascinating." She wasn't just tossing the word out, she actually seemed fascinated.

"And fun. The research was the best part; trying to match the style of vintage maps from those countries. How about you? Music? Art? Maps?"

"I like to needlepoint the lyrics to Death Metal songs."

"No shit!"

"No, *total* bullshit. Sorry. I think it would be cool to do, but I can't needlepoint to save my life. Or knit. I sew, sort of. I enjoy music, art, and maps, but I'm more of a blogger, when I'm not busy with work. Every once in a while I do web design or put together marketing packages for small firms. I used to play a little drums and some piano, but they got rusty without practice."

"I mess around on the guitar, but to get rusty I'd have to improve."

We arrived at the station, where I retrieved my Presto card from my phone case and followed Tori through the little plexiglass entry gate that opened when we tapped our cards on the sensor. Down the stairs onto the platform we went, where we ended up next to a family of three. The little girl—who looked to be about six—smiled up at Tori and said in the straightforward way kids have, "Your dress is beautiful. Did your husband buy it for you?" She then shared that smile with me and I almost choked.

Tori saved the day without even a blink or a missed beat. "Why thank you, sweetie. I love your dress, too. I bought this for myself, to make me feel pretty when the summer gets too hot." Nice empowering save!

"I got my dress for my birthday. It's good for heat days, too."

"Then we're both pretty lucky girls to have cool summer dresses!"

The subway platform wasn't rush-hour-packed, but I was surprised at how busy it was. "Is it usually like this?" I wondered aloud.

Tori looked around as if to assess the size of the crowd. "This is about right for this station at this hour. I expect the train will have picked up a few on the way in from Kipling. It *is* Friday evening, after all, when the party lemmings make their way down to the liquor-serving cliffs to jump with their friends into the sea of wasted oblivion."

"I thought you made your living serving lemmings."

"I don't serve them anymore, I just try to find ways to entice them to the cliffs. Sorry. Sometimes I get a bit cynical. During my day-to-day, it's pretty straightforward, but at trade shows and out-of-town courses and meetings, alcohol flows freely and some guys just can't handle it. I had to break a couple of fingers of a European marketing asshole last month in Vegas. I nearly got fired, until the event coordinator stepped up and admitted that Mr. Eurotrash had been grabbing her on and off for years and she wished she'd had the balls to do what I'd done. He got kicked out and banned, and I got a little more respect from the men who witnessed it all."

Now *that* is the Rage Grrl I saw! "I'm sorry you have to put up with that shit."

"I'm used to it and I can handle myself, but thanks. Last year I actually dyed my hair brown to see if it made a difference and it did. When I stopped being blonde, the whistles and shoulder rubs slowed down."

"But why should you have to change how you look or dress or act in order to keep men from behaving badly toward you? *They're* the assholes, let *them* change."

She turned slowly and looked at me. *Really* looked at me. Right in my spotted hazel eyes, like she was seeing me for the first time. I mean, we'd only known each other a short time, but still. "You get it. Thank you." The sound of the train approaching and the change in air movement saved me from what looked like an incoming hug, as the people around us shifted to be ready to board and maybe grab a rare, lone seat.

The long silver snake arrived and it was at least half full, as Tori said it probably would be. We got jostled along once the exiting few were clear of the doors and the boarders made their moves. We were just two more lemmings. I've had a few jobs downtown over the years and struggled daily with the rush-hour crush, but now I wonder how I managed to do it. Living a block from work and coming home on lunches has spoiled me. I'm going to miss that if I can't find a way to keep Mish from forcing me to sell the house.

The train was too full for us to chat about anything serious without a dozen pairs of ears reaching for stories that weren't theirs, so Tori and I chatted about unimportant stuff, like whether either of us had ever seen a stage hypnotist before (we hadn't), what I liked best about Bloorcourt (the family-owned businesses), and what she liked least (the difficulty of renting a place for only a month or two), and dogs versus cats.

"I raise kittens, but I'm also very much a dog person. You?"

"I love them all, but I'm partial to horses. My condo has rules, though."

"Inconsiderate jerks."

"They *are*, too. I even tried to organize a goat yoga session in the common room, but got shut down so fast I hadn't even booked the goats."

"Wouldn't goat yoga be better outside?"

"I *was* going to book the rooftop garden, but goats jump and the wall isn't that high."

"No, I suppose falling goats would affect your standing with the condo board, and maybe the neighbours who like to walk past the building."

"My condo board are a bunch of old goats anyway, so they probably thought that's what 'goat yoga' was."

The train arrived at Spadina and got fuller still. St. George was the next stop and where we had to transfer to the University line. I started making my way to the door and felt a hand on the small of my back. "It's just me, Max. I didn't want to freak you out and grab your belt like I see parents do."

"Haha." I reached behind me and took her hand, then quickly looked back in a panic, hoping both that I had the right hand, and that she wasn't freaked out. I had the correct hand, though her raised eyebrows made me wonder if I'd screwed up. But she didn't let go until the train stopped and we were off, and that's when we *both* let go. I couldn't remember which way the stairs to the other level were, but Tori sensed my hesitation and stepped past me to lead the way. The crowd was a bit thinner than on the train, and it was easy to follow her, but she looked back to see if I was following, which was kind of sweet. Here I was, raised in T-Dot being led around by the T-Bay girl who knew my city better than I did. She didn't offer to take my hand this time, so I kept close on her heels without actually stepping on them.

"Still there, Max?"

"Still here. I can't remember the last time I was downtown on a Friday evening. I don't mind it so much, but Michelle would get freaked out by the crowds so we avoided it."

"That's too bad. It's a hopping place. When the weather is warm, there's so much to do down here. Even over on the islands, they have stuff happening. I've been to plenty of cities and one of the worst was Calgary. Where Toronto has pedestrian areas beneath the buildings, like a city under the city with shopping and connections to the subways, Calgary elevated the pedestrian crossing areas fifteen feet and more above the street level and most of the businesses now have banker's hours. It killed the nightlife in all but a few places. So sad."

"I've always felt if a person could afford to live in one of the condo towers above a subway station, and had a job in a building that was connected, too, they could spend all of winter and the heat of summer inside, not even needing a coat for like five months of the year." A train pulled up and I squeezed on with her. It was a tight fit. A nice, cozy one. Maybe too cozy for my sanity.

She nodded. "They made a movie about that, back in the late nineties or early 2000. I think Don McClain was in it. No, it was Don *McKellar*. A friend had it on DVD up at her cottage. Said it was to remind her why she had a cottage."

I worked my cell phone out of my back pocket without elbowing anyone in the gut and opened up IMDB. "Don McKellar, the writer?"

"Writer? I know him as an actor and director."

"He co-wrote the screenplay for *Thirty Two Short Films About Glenn Gould*."

"I've never heard of it."

"We studied it in film class in college. It was made in '92 or '93."

"Wow. You're old! That's when I was born."

I did the quick math in my head and came up with her being twenty-eight. Seven years younger than me. It would explain the extra energy she had. Well, that and the fact she runs and I sits. "Hey! Wait a minute! I didn't say I saw it when it came out! I saw it in class. 2005, maybe."

"You can remember a movie you saw that long ago? You've got a great memory."

"Not even close. Some things just stick. Names don't, but I did a major paper on the film and periodically listen to Gould's *Bach: Goldberg Variations* at work, so Gould sticks in my memory."

"You like classical?"

"I do. It's calming. My mom bought me a subscription to the Toronto Symphony when I was a kid, so I got exposed to live classical music early on."

"I could never sit still as a kid, let alone listen to classical music."

"I had my share of trouble sitting still, too. My buddy Andrew and I sat up in the top balcony and I remember one Saturday afternoon making a paper airplane out of the program and launching it from the balcony."

"Oh no."

"Oh yeah. That sucker floated all the way down in a straight line like a lazy cruise missile."

"Oh shit. Who'd you hit? Not the *conductor?*"

"No one. But it skidded to a landing right under the grand piano."

"Nice! Did you get caught? Thrown out?"

"Almost. They came looking for us, but we had moved seats and just played dumb."

"No one narced on you? That's what *my* friends would have done."

"On a Saturday afternoon, the few people in the nose-bleed seats had dozed off."

The train's automated announcement interrupted us. "UNION STATION."

"That's us." She edged her way to the door and I followed. Up into Union Station, which was the always-under-construction hub for the GO commuter train, VIA Rail passenger train, and the city's southernmost subway station. Over the crowd chatter, I could hear strains of a violin, playing an emotional piece that sounded a lot like Paganini. As we made our way to the Skywalk the music got louder until we finally came across an Asian man who looked to be about seventy, making magic on his beautifully-cared-for violin. I pulled all of my change out of my pants pocket, made sure there were no shopping cart tokens mixed in, and slipped it all into his open violin case next to three of his CDs.

"Thank you, kind sir."

"My pleasure. You play beautifully."

He smiled his thanks. Tori looked at me with that raised eyebrow thing she did. I did it back, as best as I could. "What? We artists have to stick together."

"I said nothing. Did I, Master Leung?"

Without missing a note, the violinist shook his head. "No, Miss Tori, you didn't say a thing. How do you like the new CD?"

What?

"It's wonderful, Master Leung. I especially like your take on the Aerosmith song."

"I thought you might." Others dropped coins as they passed by. One young girl carrying her own violin case dropped a five-dollar bill in the case and kept going.

"Have a good night, Master Leung."

"You, too, Miss Tori."

She blew him a kiss and we were off.

"I take it you come through this station a lot, to know each other so well."

"Not really. Master Leung is usually at College Station, and that's where I see him."

"He's amazing."

"He teaches at the Royal Conservatory."

"And plays in the subway?"

"He loves the acoustics. The tile in the stations bounces the notes around something fierce. The girl who dropped in the five was one of his students. I've seen them do duets that make the crowd stop and stare, no matter how much of a hurry they're in."

"But she dropped money in his case."

"It's *his* five. They do that to each other. Folks see a five in the case and they reach a little deeper. He donates everything he makes to the Food Bank."

"You know him well."

"I guess so. I like to talk to people, and he's one of the more interesting ones. Sometime over beers, I'll tell you the part of his story that's public knowledge. He was once a soldier and played in the Red Army Orchestra. Speaking of beers," she checked her Fitbit. "We still have a lot of time. Did you want to get something to eat at Head-to-Head or just grab a dog and a drink from a street vendor when we get down that way?"

"A street dog and drink sound good."

o0o

And that's when I discovered I had left my wallet at home. Shit. Shit. *Shit.* Upon finding their wallet missing, most people would jump to the assumption it was stolen, but the pocket my wallet fits into is just tight enough I'd notice someone slipping it out. I know everyone says they'd notice, but I used to be a pickpocket, so I know of what I speak. No, I wasn't an actual thief, just a light-fingered practical joker in high school, slipping wallets out of pockets, making textbooks vanish off of desks, or switching jackets on the backs of chairs. Silly, harmless stuff. No, my wallet was at home, and I knew exactly where it was, too. On the kitchen counter. The bigger problem was that I was out with Tori and I couldn't pay for a damned thing.

"Um, this may not be the most embarrassing thing that could happen to a person, but it definitely ranks up there for me. I... *forgotmywallet.*"

"Really?"

"As God as my witness. I grabbed my keys and phone off the table by the front door and would have grabbed my wallet, too, because that's where it's supposed to live, but it's on the kitchen counter, and I forgot it."

"No worries, Max. I've got it."

"Yeah, but—"

"Max, if you're going to throw out some medieval bullshit that a man can't let a woman pay, I might just have to hurt you and leave you for the street crew to pick up."

"Well, I've seen you hit, so that's a valid threat. You might not hit what you're aiming for, but you'll definitely hurt what you hit."

"Don't try to change the subject. I'll cover whatever food and drink we have this evening and if your delicate, antiquated masculinity needs to keep score and maintain balance, I'll respect that and let you buy me a burger and a beer or two at a pub back in Bloorcourt one night next week. Deal?"

I was embarrassed as shit, but she had a point. "Deal."

"Good. Let's eat."

o0o

We found a tree-shadowed bench beneath the nearby CN Tower and people-watched while we ate. Tori's comments about passersby tended to be more *Wow! Three kids under the age of four. That's gotta be a challenge!* than *What is she doing wearing that colour with that hair? It's all wrong!* that one or two of Michelle's friends might have lobbed out in front of us. Tori was a keen observer with a heart. I liked that.

Wiping the last of the mustard from her lips, she crumpled up the paper tray and napkin, took a swig of her iced tea, and sighed. "That was good. Hit the spot. I've been going all day and needed a little something before we head inside." She retrieved a pack of smokes from her little purse. "Do you mind if I have one? I'll stand over there." With the unlit cigarette, she pointed under the trees twenty feet away.

I *did* mind, but not for the reason most would. I minded because smoking was her only glaring fault. She was funny and smart and beautiful... but she smoked. She was also married, but that's hardly a fault. The fact that she smoked, though, was none of my business either. "Sure. Take your time."

"Thanks. I tell myself that it helps with my digestion." She stepped downwind and lit up.

Rather than watch her and either make her uncomfortable or make myself look like a creep, I took out my phone and checked my messages. The first one was a reminder of the potluck group dinner tomorrow. "Hey, Tori," I called over to her. "Have you got any plans tomorrow evening? It's our biweekly potluck. Last time we ended up trying absinthe and got a little messed up. It's not too wild and crazy, but it's good laughs with good people."

"That sounds great, Max, but I'm leaving for London first thing in the morning to lead a Code of Conduct workshop for the staff at our three Southwestern Ontario locations. I won't be back until late Sunday. Maybe next time. You said it's biweekly?"

"Every two weeks, usually."

"Cool." She returned to her cigarette and I returned to my messages. There was an email from a writer friend inquiring about getting a map done for his fantasy novel, and a last reminder to check my grocery list and pick up a half-dozen things. When Tori was done, she joined me back at the bench.

"Thanks. Do you want to go into the venue to get seats, or shall we do some gaming first and use up some of these credits before the show?"

I was flexible either way, enjoying her company and getting out and about, but I had the urge to play a few games before sitting back down for the show. "I'm up for shooting a few zombies or taking a few turns around the race track before having some charlatan make us bark like dogs when we hear the word 'Purina', or whatever it is he does."

"Ha! It should be interesting to see what he's really all about, but I'm up for starting with zombie hunting and NASCAR head-to-head, too." She stood and held her hand out for my garbage, which I handed to her. She was not a lady who needed looking after that's for sure. "Shall we?"

"We shall."

She dropped the garbage in the can on the way past.

Chapter 7

I DISCOVERED REALLY DAMN fast that Tori was not just a voracious competitor and gifted gamer, she was also an excellent loser when she was clearly bested. I was damned good with a video gun, but she kept right up with me in *Time Crisis 5* and *HALO*. It took both of us a couple turns to get used to the bowling game, but she kicked my ass hard on *X-Games Snowboarder*. It was on *Superbikes 2* where she went down in flames and grace.

"I'm guessing you've ridden a motorcycle before, Max." She almost had to shout to be heard over the noise of the machines and people in the massive, packed arcade.

"I was a passenger on one once but he took off and I was holding onto the bar behind me instead of his waist so I did a backward somersault off the bike and landed on my ass while my buddy drove away. If I hadn't been drunk, I probably would have held on tight to the bar and separated both of my shoulders. As it was, I bounced and was fine. So, yes, and no. You?"

"I used to own a Kawasaki sport bike."

"Ouch. So this should have been your game."

"I suppose. It's all in fun, though."

"True enough."

"So let's see how you are at hoops."

"Hoops?"

"*NBA Game Time*, my friend. Shooting real balls into real hoops. No simulation, no digital screen. No plastic guns."

I was great at Wii Sports hoops, but hadn't shot a real ball at a real hoop since

I was a kid. "Lead on, Kawhi!"

"This way, Map Man!"

She was kicking my ass fair and square, lobbing the smaller-than-regulation balls up into the not-much-bigger hoop as easily as throwing a golf ball through a soccer goal, when I heard my name called.

"Max!" I finished my throw and turned toward the voice. I didn't see anyone looking specifically at me, and then my thrown basketball bounced off the back of my head. I stumbled forward a step, but Tori grabbed my arm and kept me from plowing anyone over.

"Oh, crap! Max, are you okay? That was the strangest thing I've ever seen."

I shook my head to clear it. "That was the strangest? You need to get out more." I *had* to joke. I'd just hit myself in the head with a junior-sized arcade basketball.

"Okay, maybe not as strange as the giant tortoises mating at the zoo next to the picnic area, but strange for an arcade fail."

I glance up at the scores. Our time ran out and the final result was Beauty for the Win, Beast for the Ass-handing. "What's the saying? Fail hard or go home?"

"Yeah, *no*."

"There is no fail. Do or do not?"

"Wrong again. Obviously, you've got brain damage." She checked the time. "We've got twenty minutes before the show. Do you mind if we step out for a quick smoke?"

"Fresh air would be good. And maybe a little less noise."

"You're sure you're okay? No concussion?"

"Nothing bruised but my pride."

"Come on then, Shaq." She took me by the elbow and out we went into the heat and clinging humidity to a roped-off area with a half-dozen other smokers. After the cacophony of bings, bongs, whistles, and the shot to the head, the quiet outside was astounding. I could clearly hear my ears ringing.

As promised, it was a quick smoke and we were back inside before I reached my limit of second-hand airborne carcinogens.

"More games, or shall we find seats and beers and get settled in for the show?"

Option two, please. "A beer sounds good."

Pulling our show tickets out of her purse, she waved them over her head and shouted back as she started through the crowd. "Then keep up, slowpoke!" She led and I followed. Again.

o0o

It turned out that our special tickets came with reserved seats at a table near the stage, so we ordered a couple of pints and wound down from the energy of the gaming area. "So, Max... brothers, sisters, parents?"

"Um, one older sister, Lizanne. No brothers, both parents dead: Dad ten years ago, Mom four years later. And you?"

"Mom and Dad still alive and mostly getting along, up in Thunder Bay; older brother, Eddie, an hour-and-a-half away up in Collingwood and married with two kids."

"You're an aunt-times-two? I have three nephews."

"Are they here in town?"

"The two youngest are still here in high school and their big brother is studying The Philosophy of Underwater Basket Weaving or some such useful degree at Western."

"Nice. What does he want to be when he graduates?"

"In debt for the rest of his life for a degree that's the bare minimum for getting hired at Burger King, I suppose."

The lights dimmed suddenly and the MC took the stage, thankfully preventing me from getting into my rant about the nation's impossible debt-to-education ratio.

"How're you doing tonight, folks?"

"Woooooo!" was the response from most of the room. It sounded like we were all suffering from heat stroke and 'Woooo' was the best we could manage before we threw up and passed out. The MC got us riled up, then the opening act of a stand-up comic got us roaring or groaning with a raunchy ten minutes of 'my ex-wife' jokes. I'm guessing he was there to set the low-brow tone for the hypnotist, because when the MC introduced hypnotist 'Uncle Scooter', the first words out of mid-forties Scooter's mouth when he charged on stage and caught the mic tossed by the MC were "Hey assholes! Who wants to be humiliated?"

He asked for and quickly got ten volunteers up into the line of chairs on stage. Then he told everyone to turn off our phones, put them face down on our tables, and 'shut the hell up'. We did. He told us all to close our eyes and simply listen to the sound of his voice. We did that, too, and he started into his patter. He had a soothing voice, a relaxing, guiding-us-to-enlightenment kind of voice. My focus on it was so tight that soon it sounded like he wasn't on stage anymore but was standing right beside me, talking just to me. He told me to raise my right hand and I obeyed. Not doing so didn't even seem like a possibility.

He directed me to lower my hand to the table and I clearly heard someone nearby snicker. My hand touched down on the table, and I tipped forward, banging my forehead on the tabletop. I jerked upright and popped my eyes open, afraid I'd dozed off and distracted everyone when I banged my head. Uncle Scooter wasn't on the stage, though. He was standing on my left, close enough to poke me in the arm if he wanted to.

"Sorry, man. If I'd known you were going to tip forward I would have stopped you."

I rubbed my forehead. "Um, no problem." Confused, I looked at Tori, who had her fist to her mouth to keep herself mute, but tears of laughter rolled down her tanned cheeks.

Scooter returned to the stage and got on with the show, while Tori leaned in and whispered "Holy shit, Max! He had you under, just *sitting* there. They say that creative people are more susceptible to suggestion. I guess this proves it." She tipped her glass of beer to clink against mine, which I must have *just* missed when I face-planted on the table. "Here's to your artist's soul. First the basketball, and now the table."

I picked up my glass, clinked it to hers, and took a sip. "Yeah. I guess. That was the strangest feeling."

"Are you okay? My psych prof told me to never volunteer for one of these things because they're dangerous when the hypnotist isn't a trained medical professional. I didn't believe him because I didn't think hypnotism for entertainment was real."

"I wasn't so sure, either, but now I'm more of a believer." I couldn't shake off the odd feeling, and Tori picked up on that.

"We don't have to stay, you know. We can just go back down and fry our brains with video games. Hunt some dinosaurs, try the climbing wall."

"No. You got the passes and all. I don't want to spoil the show for you. I'm sure I'll be fine after a few minutes."

"Bullshit. Your eyes are having trouble focusing and your hand is shaking."

I looked down and she was right. My hand next to the glass had a steady, freaky tremor. "Okay. Sold. Shall we be obvious, or subtle?"

"Since I got the tickets from work, we'd better be subtle. I'll get up, go to the bar and settle the tab. After a minute or so, get up and go toward the bathroom. It's right near the exit and we can slip out from there while he's messing with *other* people's heads."

"That'll work."

Instead of going straight back to the game lounge on the first floor, we got the backs of our hands stamped and stepped out for more hot, semi-fresh air. Tori lit a cigarette, but held it down by her side, away from me, and when she took a drag she blew it up and into the light breeze.

"What was it like, being 'under' like that? Were you scared that you'd never come out of it?"

"Scared? Not really. To be honest, it wasn't some great, mystical experience. I was just really focused on his voice and other sounds sort of got pushed into the background where the volume was lower. When he told me to move my hand, it seemed like a totally reasonable thing to do. I wasn't even aware that I was under until after the fact. In hindsight, it was a little creepy, though. I'm not a fan of relinquishing control. I remember a school trip to a school environmental camp where one of my classmates, Kimmy, said she was a witch—" Tori's eyebrows shot up and she spit smoke. I put my hand on my chest. "True story.

Kimmy claimed to be a witch and offered to hypnotize someone. My buddy Ian volunteered to give it a try. He was one of the cooler jocks and had a big heart, willing to lend support where it was needed. Kimmy was just trying to fit in."

"By claiming to be a witch?"

"By being able to do something cool and earn some cred, I suppose. Anyway, she asked Ian what his least favourite colour was. It was beige. She counted him down and it looked like she got him into a trance, walking through beige hallways in a beige house. Pretty harmless stuff. We all thought he was faking it. Then she got beige monsters chasing after him and when he looked like he was going to have a full-blown meltdown, she snapped him out of it."

"That was kind of her, considering that she put him there in the first place. How did he take it?"

"He played along and laughed and said that it was cool, but when I got him alone later he gave up the truth. She *had* put him under and he was scared shitless when the monsters came for him. He wanted to snap out of it, but he couldn't break out of it until she did it for him."

"See! This is why my professor said not to do it. This Kimmy probably didn't mean ill, but she shouldn't have been screwing around with that stuff. I hope your friend had no residual effects."

"Not that I know of. I wouldn't be surprised if he had a nasty dream or two afterward, though. Just seeing the terror on his face when he thought beige monsters were going to get him gave *me* the chills."

"Then I guess we should be thankful you head-butted the table." She squinted up at my forehead. "You might have a bit of a bruise there, but you haven't got a bump, so I suspect it sounded harder than it was. Your head is a real bonk-magnet"

"That's why I have such a crap memory. I've had a few serious bonks over the years."

"Like serious head injuries?"

"I didn't think so at the time. Only one that needed stitches, and that was just two years ago."

"I hear that Omegas are good for memory and brain function. My mom swears by them."

"That's good to know. Thanks."

The fresh air helped a lot, so we went back inside to continue virtually thrashing each other. I gave her a rematch on *Superbikes 2* where she found her balance and left me in her dust. We teamed up on *Star Wars Battle Pod* and the fast Hoth ice planet action was like being right in the movie, but the controls were sluggish and sloppy so we quit after one round. The arcade was so full that there were line-ups for most of the cool games and those without lines were usually pretty lame. But the credits we had were free, so we even tried the lame games, like *Fishbowl Frenzy* and *Iceball FX*, both of which were over so fast that we wondered if we'd done something wrong.

We were just starting into the giant screen two-person shooter version of *Tomb Raider* when a loud "Hey Hot Stuff Tori!" made us both turn our heads, just enough to see three slightly-bigger-than-me dudes in their early twenties, each with a half-empty beer in hand, standing shoulder-to-shoulder. They clearly knew Tori, but she didn't look too pleased to see them, or at least their inebriated condition.

She addressed them, but her gaze went back to the game, shooting attacking wolves with shocking accuracy as she spoke. "Doug, Levon, and Skip. How are you doing, guys? Looks like you're having fun. You won the extra gaming credits at work?"

"Damn right! Having a blast! Doug fell off the climbing wall from three feet up!"

She glanced at them, then went back to the game. "I'm surprised they let you on the wall at all."

The taller one, obviously Doug, leaned in. "They didn't exactly let me. I sort of snuck on while Levon was flirting with the chick in charge. Got her all distracted until some twelve-year-old little shit narced on me. Said I was ruining his climb." He took a large gulp of his beer. "Maybe Levon should flirt with *you*. Would he get *you* all hot and bothered and distracted, Vic-tory-*ah*?"

One of the other two put a hand on Doug's shoulder and pulled him back.

"Come on, dude. Show some respect. She's *married*."

I saw Tori's knuckles whiten on the plastic gun, but she kept acquiring targets and finishing them off. "How about you show some respect *because I'm a woman*? Or show me some respect *because you're here as Montgomery employees*? Or maybe just maybe show some respect *because I'm someone who isn't going to put up with your drunken, frat boy, team-up-on-the-girl bullshit*?"

The three went silent, but by their looks of confusion, it wasn't because she got through to them, but rather because she used too many words at once and they were slow to process it all. Or maybe they were as awed by her ability to talk and kill at the same time. "How about the three of you get your shit together before I text Mitchell and suggest he fire your asses on Monday morning?"

The one who'd pulled Doug back stood up as straight as he could. "Sorry, Tori. We'll leave."

"Thank you, Skip."

Doug wasn't done, yet, though. "I'll leave when I'm—"

Skip was drunk but smart. "Hey. Asshole. You'll leave *now*. With us. Cuz if Mitchell fires your ass, he'll make sure everyone in the industry knows why. See who hires you after they learn you were sexually harassing a manager in public. If you want to be an unemployable dick, you'll do it alone. Sorry, Tori." He and Levon turned and shuffled away.

Doug quickly figured out that he was standing alone in the crowd and his future was balanced on a very thin alcoholic thread. "Shit. Sorry, Tori." He looked at me. "Sorry, Mr. Tori. No harm, no foul."

I shook my head. "Harm *and* foul, big guy. Good luck."

Doug drifted off in search of the other two. Tori waited until he was out of sight, then leaned over and kissed me on the cheek, without missing a shot. Probably trying to contain Rage Grrl, she was radiating heat like a furnace. "Thank you, Max."

"For what? I didn't do a damned thing." I had no idea what I should have done.

"For not jumping in to defend my honour, for trusting me to handle it myself, and for standing there, quiet and firm, as backup."

"You hardly needed me to back you up. I never doubted you for a minute."

"That's sweet, but *I* doubted me. It was a toss-up between being professional, and hitting him with this gun." She dropped the game gun into its holder and held her hands out. They shook like mad. "Adrenalin is a bitch."

"Let's get out of here." I could see her three coworkers wander into the men's room. "The 'dudes' are in the bathroom. We can slip out now while they're trying to find their zippers."

She laughed. "I would almost pay to see that. The three of them standing at urinals fumbling, swearing, and wetting themselves."

"I'll wait here if you want to go watch."

"Yeah, *no*. Then who would be the one up on sexual harassment charges? 'Hey Tori, what exactly were you doing in the men's room videotaping the boys at the urinals?'" She took my elbow and turned me to face the door. "Let's go home. It's late, we both have to get up early, and it's been a weird evening."

"You sure know how to show a fella a fun time, though."

"Maybe next time we'll try axe throwing. I don't know too many drunks stupid enough to step up while I'm holding an axe."

"Or too many sober guys, either, I expect."

"Good point."

"Do the axes bounce, though? I don't need an axe scar in my head, to match the one in my leg." I touched a spot on my inner right thigh about five inches from my groin. Tori lifted her eyebrows, shook her head, and chuckled.

A cool breeze blew in off the lake so we opted to make the ten-minute walk outside.

"So that's the kind of crap you have to worry about." I pointed behind us at the gaming lounge.

"Just about every convention or meeting where alcohol is served. Not every guy is like that, but there are enough of them."

"Will you tell your boss about this?"

"I probably should. I'll downplay it a bit, tell him they were a little too drunk to be representing the company."

"But you won't tell him about the sexual comments?"

"It was minor stuff. I handled it."

"True. But if you don't tell him, then he can't make an educated decision. He can't have your back if you don't tell him the truth."

"You want me to ruin Doug's career based on a couple of inappropriate drunken comments? That's a little harsh, Max."

"That's not what I said. Do you trust your boss?"

"Mitchell? Yes. Of course."

"Has he ever behaved like that toward you?"

"No. He never drinks to excess and has never even given a hint of that kind of douchery. He's happily married with three kids."

"Is he known for knee-jerk reactions, or is he more known for reason, logic, and fairness?"

"The latter."

"Then tell him the truth, without emotion, and let him decide. If he's as reasonable as you say, then he'll probably call Doug in and give him shit, then maybe send him for some sensitivity training."

"He *is* reasonable, but Doug has already had that training. I taught the class."

"And that's information Mitch has. A good boss would weigh the evidence and make their decision based on what is best for both the company and the employee. If he thinks Doug can be redeemed, then hopefully he'll try. But what if yours isn't the first such complaint against Doug? What if there's a long list of similar complaints? Or what if there are no complaints because no women have thought that the offences were serious enough to get him fired? You could be either the first to get the ball rolling or the last straw for the camel's back."

She stopped there on the sidewalk beside Front Street and gave me that look of hers. "I'd accuse you of mansplaining, Mister Maxwell Walden, except that you're right, and I wasn't seeing the big picture."

"You can still accuse me of mansplaining, but sometimes it just takes a step to the side to get a clearer view. And sometimes I'm just full of shit, but I'm pretty sure you'll call me on it when I am."

"Definitely."

We continued east along busy Front Street. "So what's this training you're doing in London over the weekend?"

"It's a three-parter. The first part is sort of a Code of Conduct Train-the-Trainer. I'll be teaching managers how to deliver the lecture materials the company has developed."

"Code of Conduct? Like how not to talk to female coworkers when representing the company?"

She blushed. "Sort of exactly like that. Hey, we can only deliver the materials, we can't force them to absorb and live by them. Every now and then we get a lost cause who just won't follow along."

"Like douche-nozzles named Doug."

"Exactly."

"What's Part the Second of the training?"

"The second half of the day is about website maintenance and ensuring that the information available to the public is accurate and up-to-date. Each franchise has their own local menu specialties and themes, so they have to maintain their specific pages themselves."

"Makes sense."

"We have a group dinner on Saturday night, then Part Three on Sunday morning is about how to see the positive in customer criticisms and reviews."

"You said you wouldn't be back until late Sunday night."

"Your memory isn't as bad as you think." She smiled warmly, from her eyes down to her mouth. "I'm taking the really long way home via Collingwood, to celebrate my sister-in-law's birthday. It's about a three-hour drive from London, then after dinner an hour-and-a-half back south to the city."

"A long day."

"Nah. I like to drive. I spend so much time in and around the city that I like to stretch my lungs and get some of that good old Southern Ontario farm air."

"Manure baking in the summer sun! Nothing quite like it."

"You tease, but there isn't. I love the smell of farms."

"Me, too. Especially horses."

"You ride?"

"Not well, but better than motorcycles, yes."

"If you ever want to go for a ride, let me know. There's a public stable just outside Milton that I've been to a couple of times."

"That could be fun." My phone chimed with a text and I took a quick look. A quick, disastrous, should-have-left-it-in-my-pocket look. It was from Michelle. *I miss u. Think I need 2 come back 2 TO.* Really? Let's talk about settling the house, oops, now I want to come home to it? It was just another damned head game. She played more than a few of those when we were together. Things like *I know you love me, but I wonder sometimes if you're IN love with me.* Or *Do you even notice when I stay at work late?* I must have worn my confusion on my face because Tori saw something.

"Are you okay, Max? You look like you've seen my expense account."

Up until thirty seconds ago, I was having a great time, one of the best in a while. Now, I was sliding back into cynicism. "It's from my ex. I'm never sure where I stand with her. First, she goes but says she'll be back, then she's staying there with her old fiancé, maybe, and wants me to buy her out of the house, but now she misses me."

"She sounds like she doesn't know what she wants. Do you know what *you* want?"

"I thought I did. I was just getting used to her not being around and my life being happily settled with kittens, making maps, and the shop."

"Do you still love her?"

Shit. The sixty-four-dollar question. "Maybe, but it doesn't matter. If she comes back she'll only eventually leave again. I care, but she's gone. Life moves on. I've called my lawyer."

"That's a healthy way to look at it, especially if she's all back and forth on you. Having been through this a few years back, I wish you luck."

"Thanks." And right there I felt like our tone had shifted slightly. I'm not sure which direction it went, but there was a definite shift. For the rest of the trip back home it was Small Talk City—the weather, the Blue Jays, the Argonauts football team, the smell of the subway when the summer heat causes humans to be at their most odiferous and crammed into a train. We were both a little distracted. I know what was distracting *me*, but I had no clue what was going through Tori's head. Was she thinking about my situation with Michelle, or her relationship with her absent husband, or maybe just thinking about the weekend of training ahead of her?

When we finally got back to the house I thanked her for covering my tabs and reiterated the promise of beers next week, and she even sounded like she might still take me up on the offer. We said a quick goodnight as I headed up the steps to the front door and she went around the side to the back one. I had a terrific time hanging out with Tori, but Michelle was now stuck in my mind like dysfunctional gum on the bottom of my shoe. Exhausted, I dragged my ass into the house and quickly dealt with the kittens before going up to bed. I only barely noticed how nice and cool the house was. Thank you, Leona, for the AC.

o0o

As the August long weekend approached, the shop got busier. After I dropped the world's ugliest shirt in the donation bin, Saturday went by in just enough of a blur that by the time I got groceries and got home, I was seriously doubting my ability to host the potluck. I fed the little ones, made the house secure from exploratory paws, set the alarm for thirty minutes before everyone arrived, and then all six of us napped on the couch. Or at least I hope the other five napped. Three settled on top of me before I dozed off and all five were there when I woke up, though they spooked and jumped off as I stirred to shut off the alarm.

My phone screen also had reminders to respond to my buddy Ed's query about a map for his novel, and Michelle's text. I sent Ed a quick *send me the details of what you need* note, and I ignored Michelle's text. If I encouraged her to return was I being completely honest with myself or with her? And if I discouraged her, what cascade of events would I set off? If she was serious, then I could hurt her and... *I don't know.* She was never a truly nasty person, but I saw her anger on more than one occasion. She'd already mentioned settling the house and I'm sure that was her friend Mandy outside watching the place that one time. If I pissed Mish off, would she push hard and force me to sell in order to buy her out? Maybe serve me with Separation Papers even though we'd never been legally married? She left. Maybe she wanted to come back, but then, like everyone else, when she got bored or tired or insulted, she'd suddenly leave again.

But was it really sudden? That last year was nice, but more and more issues had popped up. Michelle stopped coming to the club with me, though I didn't blame her, since I never got up on stage. But she also found other things to do on potluck Saturdays and when we were invited out to friends for dinner or karaoke or whatever. I see now that she was slowly disconnecting herself from segments of our life together. Had she already been communicating with the dentist for that year, finding something in what they once had that we no longer did? Of course, I could suggest that she come back to town and we could discuss it all and see where we went off the rails and how could we get back on them, but what would be the point? I had my friends, my work, foster kittens, and no desire to give her another opportunity to abandon me.

It wasn't that I'd met Tori and she'd stolen my heart. She hadn't. She was amazing and fascinating and talented and fun, but aside from the fact that she was married, I think hanging out with her just reminded me that it's a big world, and I don't have to stay cooped up inside, nor do I have to take up the hunt to find a perfect RayRay420 to make me feel whole. That's all the bullshit society feeds us. At thirty-five I was a long way from being old and I was comfortable enough with myself to not need to be half of anything. It drove me nuts hearing of friends who went from one relationship to another because the mere idea of being single was an affront to their sense of place in society, or their identity, or... whatever.

Like Socrates said, *all I know is that I know nothing*, which isn't entirely true because I *did* know that my best friends were all going to be arriving shortly and I needed to do a quick kitty-corralling and vacuuming.

Chapter 8

"SO, WHO WANTS TO give us their horrid worst date story, and who wants coffee?"

Argaw, Lydia and Rose wanted coffee, and Joe raised his hand. "It maybe wasn't the worst date, but it was certainly my most awkward *only* date." The kittens all jumped off their respective laps and followed me into the kitchen. I could still hear the conversation as I fixed coffee and put a little milk in each of the kid's bowls.

"Was it with Rose?" Aba asked.

"Actually, no. Every single date I've had with Rose has been wonderful." He squeezed her hand and she raised it to her lips and kissed his knuckles. "This was back in my last year of high school. I was working as an usher at the Varsity Theatre in the Manulife Centre and had asked out one of the candy counter girls. We worked in a theatre with all the latest films so we decided to walk down to the Eaton Centre and see what they had playing at the repertory cinema. All of the movies were nearly over except for one that had started but wasn't too far along. Since our plan was to go back to the Varsity to join our workmates when they were done their shift and then all go for a drink, we were really just looking to get off our feet and kill time."

I returned with the coffees, and the kittens in tow. They each found laps and went back to their temporarily adopted human. "So, what did you see? Some goofy seventies RomCom?"

"*A Clockwork Orange.*"

"On a fuh—on a *date*?"

Argaw laughed. "That would not have been my first choice, my friend. Or even my last."

Joe grinned. "Not mine, either, now, but since neither of us had seen it and knew almost nothing about it, we thought we'd give it a try. We walked in right in the middle of the—"

Rose cut him off. "Oh no. The rape scene?"

He nodded. "The rape scene. *I'm singing in the rain, kick kick...* We sat down and neither of us said a word. I was horrified, both at the violence of the scene and at the fact I'd brought Wendy to this hot mess. We lasted twenty minutes before I turned to her and said 'Do you want to go?' and she said 'Yes'. We were out of there so damned fast."

Shannon said what I was thinking. "But it's a great film. A classic and such a strong message."

"It is," Joe agreed. "And I eventually saw it from beginning to end in college a couple of years later, but it is *not* a date movie in any way shape or form."

"Agreed." I've only seen it once, but it was enough.

Unlike the absinthe party two weeks before, when this potluck gathering broke up no one had trouble making their feet work in the prescribed manner. Just before midnight Uncle Argaw handed me Ginsberg and placed his long-fingered, dry, warm hand on my arm. "Thank you for opening your home to us, Brother. As always, it was a wonderful evening."

"You're very welcome, Uncle. It's always a pleasure having you here." And it was. He was a kind, soft-spoken man with a heart of gold, a wry sense of humour, and not a mean bone in his body. The world needed more like him.

o0o

Sunday strolled on by peacefully, spent alternating between custom map work, laundry, Netflix, cleaning the kitten room, some cursory catching up on social media, thinking about the fascinating woman living downstairs, and wondering how hard I was going to have to fight Michelle for the house.

Rather than text her back, I did what every reasonable person does at such times and locked my doors, cranked up the A/C, powered off my phone and computer, and turned on the TV... after feeding the beasts and opening a beer.

o0o

Mondays. Can't live with 'em, can't live without 'em. Mine started with ass-dragging at the scream of the alarm, kitten vomit after they bolted past me out of their room, a toe stubbed—but not seriously—trying to embrace the incoming love attack but avoid sitting in Burrough's warm hairball/kibble/puke combo. By the time I deactivated the *Do Not Disturb* on my phone for the day, I was ready to go back to bed.

Two seconds later an incoming text from the Cat Rescue buzzed at me. Tuesday—*tomorrow*—was set for the inspection. 9:00 am. Oh well. I knew it was coming. The text said that it should take about half an hour, which would still leave me plenty of time to get to work—*if* I got up an hour early and shat, showered, shaved, and ate before they arrived. Yippee. I texted back that I'd see them at nine. Just below that text was one from Michelle from two hours ago, and below that was one from Tori last night. I opened Tori's, my heart beating a titch faster than it really should.

Hi Max. Just letting you know I got home safe & sound—it was a loooong day—& 2 thank you again 4 the fun on Friday. I hope we can do it again soon, but without hypnotist & drunk coworkers. ~T.

I couldn't help but smile. I sent a quick text back, keeping it simple. *Thank you for letting me know. I did too! I'm up for more fun!* Maybe at the Black Horse on Bloor, or one of the other pubs for a beer and some pool.

Retrieving the text from Michelle, I was both relieved that it was short and sweet, and concerned that it simply said *I just sent you an email. It's open and honest. Please read it soon, and don't mock me like my mother did.* Shit. She had an emotionally exhausting habit of writing epic, rambling emails. I sure wasn't starting my week with one of those, so I did what always I do and got myself to work. I also crossed my fingers that my lawyer got back from holiday early.

The morning foot traffic into the shop was a steady two or three people an hour, with probably three-quarters of them buying something, so my lunch break rolled up right on time. The home-feed-eat-cuddle went smoothly, but now that the house had AC, it was a bit harder to leave than usual. Once I was back at the store with just the fans to keep me company I envied the kittens and their new cooler quarters, for as long as they're with me. I wasn't too worried about the pending inspection, but I was getting quite fond of this crop of little ones. Glad they had some comfy coolness, I spent the first hour of the afternoon reviewing the shop's newest bills and filling the few online orders. Just before three o'clock I was bored enough to open Michelle's email. I regretted it almost immediately.

It started simply enough with *I miss you and the kittens, Max*, but it soon escalated with *My bounty is as boundless as the sea, My love as deep; the more I give to thee, The more I have, for both are infinite ~ Romeo & Juliet*. That's lovely and all, but she left me for her dentist dude and wanted to settle up the house, so what was the point of that quote? Was she really interested in coming back? I couldn't even say "coming home", because I no longer felt like the house was her home. Sure, I missed her laugh a bit and the house still held her essence in many little ways, but between the one evening with Tori and my regular potlucks with caring friends, I'd seen that life is more fun without guilt trips or insecurity and having to constantly bolster someone else's self-esteem.

The letter rambled on with two paragraphs about how Ottawa doesn't feel like home anymore, then smacked me again for the "inconsiderateness" of my proposal when she was trying to leave, finishing with her usual backhanded snark in a comment about how I didn't even have a ring when I got down on one knee. She followed that with *I've always felt that you are my hiding place; you will protect me from trouble and surround me with songs of deliverance. Psalm 32.*

From Shakespeare to a psalm? Oy vey! There were a couple hundred words about some reading she got from a palmist quack that reflected something she'd seen when meditating after yoga class, then *"You can be too rich and too thin, but you can never be too well-read or too curious about the world" ~ Tim Gunn.*

Project Runway. That curiosity about the world is one thing I love so much about you, Max.

Yes, she actually quoted Project Runway. I admit that it was a pretty poignant quote, but I was done attempting to interpret whatever message she was trying to send. I don't know—maybe I'm completely obtuse. I skimmed the rest of the email to see if there was anything other than emotional outbursts, quotes, quips, and pleas for understanding while repeating that neither of us had anything to apologize for. By the time I reached the end of what had to be a two-thousand-word slog, I was still confused as hell about what she really wanted and I had absolutely no idea how to respond to it all. I was starting to wonder if she'd started drinking again and that's why her missives were all over the place. I closed my email and grabbed the feather duster and Pledge to attack the fast-growing layer of road dust that covered everything no matter how often I cleaned.

"Hey, Siri." Beep. "Shuffle Totally Groovin' playlist."

"Playing Totally Groovin' playlist, shuffled."

Kiss You Inside Out by Hedley bounced out of the speakers and I cleaned, not completely immune to the multiple meanings of the song. I sang along, loudly and not entirely in key, getting lost in the dusting and rearranging as I went.

o0o

I spent the early part of the evening tidying up the house and making sure that everything was good for the inspection the next morning, then fell onto the couch and into Netflix. Being both needlessly nervous about the inspection and necessarily confused about Michelle's bouncing, mixed messages about our relationship and the house, I was too keyed up to get any work done on maps. Maybe tomorrow. Besides, the air conditioning was best enjoyed downstairs, in the living room.

On the coffee table, my phone buzzed with an incoming text. The kittens all hopped down off my lap when I reached for the device. "Sorry guys. If it's more mess from Michelle I'll let you give her crap." It wasn't. It was from Tori, just saying hi and asking how my day went. She was running late with meetings but taking a quick break for "fresh air".

Grinning like a goof, I texted back *Had a good day, thx. The usual. You?* I suspect that she was just making textual small talk while she snuck a smoke and didn't really need to hear about Michelle or the inspection or even the cat puke and stubbed toe that started the day.

A moment later she came back with *Typical Monday. Crazy workload. Still at work. Need to talk to the boss about the hours. Off to Kitchener tomorrow. We should grab beers later this week. I'll know my schedule better tomorrow.*

Her life was go-go-go so I wasn't going to hold my breath that she would have a free evening, but just in case she did, I texted back that beers would be good and for her to have a safe drive to Kitchener. Her reply was simply *Thx. Give the kitties cuddles from me.*

A little rush of emotion bumped into me. I wanted to text her back that her husband was a lucky guy, but that was what I think they call passive-aggressive flirting. Flirting? Yeah. Definitely. I know she started it, but as fun as flirting is, I have to draw a line somewhere, and I hate passive-aggressive anything. I refrained from mentioning her husband and double-thumbed back a relaxed *Will do.* Besides, if she'd leave her husband for me, it's probable that she'd eventually leave me for the next someone. People like to run away.

o0o

Restlessness nudged me repeatedly during the night, keeping me from a single moment of decent sleep. Anyway, that's what my FitBit update and a hot blanket of crankiness told me when the alarm went off at 7:30, an hour earlier than usual. Inspection Day. The place was perfect. Ready for the pickiest of the pickies. Just to be sure, though, I checked the To-do list on my phone, ticking each box beside the task I'd done last night.

Oh shit—*literally.* I didn't remember cleaning the litter boxes! It wasn't a medical emergency, but it was high on the list of health and safety issues. I dragged my ill-tempered ass out of bed, made a pit stop in the bathroom to brush the gack out of my teeth, etc., then down to parole the purr monsters and scoop the litter clumps. I was mauled as soon as their door was open and that furry, mewing, rough-tongued pile-on was exactly what my spirits needed. Flat on the floor, I surrendered to their attack and even managed not to shout in pain when they each separately and together bounced on the still-healing Kerouac wounds on my chest.

Once the kids realized that I didn't actually have food hidden somewhere on my person, most of them abandoned me and scrambled, stumbled, or galloped to the kitchen where there just *had* to be a big two-legger waiting to serve them breakfast on silver platters. Only Calliope remained. She was a food beast as much as the others, but she adored cuddles more, so she curled up right over my heart, a little motorboat of love.

Food failed to magically appear in their dishes so the four-cat rush returned, voicing their squeaky displeasure with each step. I couldn't remember what I'd started downstairs to do so I gently picked Calliope up and led the parade back to the kitchen.

o0o

"I'm a little concerned, Max. The litter boxes were a bit fuller than I'd like and the one food dish high up on the kitchen island is a kitten fall just waiting to happen. I *am* pleased they all passed their physicals and got their shots, and I'm impressed with the temperature in their part of the house during this insane heat wave." Beth-from-the-shelter looked at the front window. "When did you get the air conditioner? Is that a new thing? My records don't show it."

Her records? There was something hinky here. Even with my shit memory, I remember Michelle and Beth being friends, and although I couldn't recall if she'd ever been in this house before, she hadn't appeared to be familiar with it when she'd first arrived. I'm pretty sure she knew Michelle had gone back to Ottawa to donate a kidney, but she hadn't mentioned Michelle and now it was feeling like this was as much an inspection of me as it was of the house. Until Michelle moved the rest of her stuff, she was still technically a resident here and part of the fostering. Unless Beth knew something I didn't.

I'm not stupid, though. I kept my mouth shut and just agreed with whatever changes she said needed to be made. My Furry Five were soon to graduate from foster school and find forever homes, but I really wanted to continue to foster kittens. It gave my life a little more purpose and joy than just running the shop, writing poems, and streaming movies in the evenings.

Beth-the-Inspector-General finished off with a couple of points that were clearly just picky little crap, then departed. The kittens didn't seem to notice her absence and trailed after me. I got them fed again and watered, not changing the location of Kerouac's bowl one damned centimetre. Beth had his health records so she knew exactly why he was separated, which made her point about his dish on the high counter only half valid. Yes, he would get hurt if he jumped down, but I never left him alone up there, and when he wanted down he padded over to me, meowed loudly, and swatted me with a paw. Our communications were highly sophisticated and very effective. He had me so well trained that I even gave him high fives just before I fed him.

While he munched and slurped loudly I put a reminder in my phone to clean the litter boxes before I left for work. I *think* I passed the inspection, but nothing Beth said was definitive on that and deep in my gut I felt a grinding that the inspection had Michelle's DNA all over it. The fact that the two messages—one scheduling the inspection and the other guiding me to the rambling, off-balance, must-read email—arrived at virtually the same time made me wonder if the two were connected. But that sounded stupid and paranoid, so I went to work... after cleaning the litter boxes in response to the reminder alarm that caught me going out the door, of course.

oOo

Rather than mull the inspection/Michelle thing from my usual thousand useless angles, I got out the vacuum cleaner and the sponge mop and bucket and gave the shop's carpet and linoleum both good cleanings. When they were as spotless as they could get without the skilled hands of that cleaning company whose ads I always misread as either Prostate Cleaning or Pornstar

Cleaning—either of which made me gag a little—I filled the bucket with clean, soapy water, found the window squeegee buried in the back of the utility closet and attacked the windows from the street side. The insides needed cleaning, too, but that involved removing all of the recently arranged product displays. I was industrious but not *that* industrious.

oOo

By the time five-o-five rolled around, dark clouds tented the city and a light warm drizzle pretended that it was there to cool off the hot day but in fact, just added to the humidity. I keep a spare umbrella at the shop for such an occasion but the rain was sporadic and the walk home was a short one, so I confidently left it in the stock room.

I shut off the fans, turned on the alarm, locked up, and stepped out into the humidity and sprinkles. With every step the rain increased, until I reached the Baptist church on the corner where the first little hailstones bounced off the sidewalk and melted. They were so innocuous as to be cute. I smiled and walked on.

It was only a hundred-and-fifty-feet from that corner to my front porch, yet in that short, sprintable distance the cute little hail point guards yielded to an orc-hoard onslaught of icy, wet, hammering, thumb-nail-sized hail and rain. It hit so fast and hard that I had no chance to run to stay dry. I was soaked to the skin in the first three seconds. Of course, I *did* run, but only in a desperate attempt to keep my phone and wallet from getting completely ruined.

Thunder cracked as I plopped my wet ass onto the plastic chair on the porch. The hail tried its damnedest to curl its way under the eaves and get at me, but in the absence of a strong easterly wind, I was safe. I retrieved my wallet and phone from my back pockets and set them on the arms of the chair where I would prefer to set a beer.

Head to toe, I was drenched, but there wasn't a thing I could do out on the porch without at least a towel. The light breeze combined with the sopping wet clothes cooled me off, though, drawing the summer heat away from me while the little air conditioner hummed contentedly from the window beside me. The evening was still hot and muggy, but the evaporation effect was a wonderful respite. I leaned back, closed my eyes, and enjoyed a few more moments of wet mellowness before dragging myself inside.

o0o

The kittens weren't happy when I ignored them, stripped naked in the front hall, squeak-stepped off to drop my clothes in the laundry closet, and then had a quick shower before finally letting them out. Kerouac even took a clumsy swipe at me before rolling over on his back in anticipation of a tummy rub. He's such a slut-boy.

o0o

My mad, wild, unbridled, feral lifestyle overwhelmed me around nine, so I abandoned the shipwreck map I was detailing and the six of us retired downstairs to the couch. I lasted ten minutes into an episode of the dark-as-shit, super-bleak Black Mirror before I was asleep under a blanket of kittens.

o0o

Wednesday the shop was quiet for the first hour but a text from Tori sparked a little fire to burn away the boredom. *Hey. How goes your day?*

I smiled to myself in the empty shop as I replied. *Hey T. Stupefying. Yours?*

Same. Getting things booked for a course in Goderich on Labour Day weekend. Nothing exciting. How did the inspection go?

Good, I think. Waiting for the verdict.

Fingers + toes crossed. Beers to celebrate when you pass.

I liked that idea. I sent the little blue thumbs-up emoji, and that's when Leona strolled in, another pair of cold drinks in hand.

"This is beginning to be a habit, boss. Thank you."

She handed me a drink. "I can't have my star manager succumbing to the heat now, can I? Besides, I need to use the toilet, didn't dare show up empty-handed, and will never use a coffee shop bathroom if I can help it."

"I'm the same. Thankfully we boys have the option to stand."

"Braggart!" She placed her drink on the counter and went into the back to the little bathroom. As the lock on the bathroom door click-thumped into place, the bell on the front door rang and I turned to present my best sales smile to... Flat-Earther Robin in his shorts, sandals, and glowing teeth, and a slightly older version of him who could only be his brother, albeit with big so-out-of-style mutton-chop sideburns and thinner hair.

I gave Robin my best stink-eye and he flinched. "Gentlemen. Welcome to *Long & Lat*. How may I help you today?" I *really* didn't want the shop to become a focal point for these wingnuts. Some may argue that a wingnut's money is the same colour as everyone else's, but it didn't take much for a respectable business to get a bad rep by attracting members of a fringe element, and flat-earthers were seriously fringe in the world of cartography.

Robin took a shy half-step forward while his brother took himself on a tour of the display area. Robin flashed his creepy veneer smile. "Hi. Remember me? I'm sorry, but I was hoping you had another copy of that 'azimuthal projection' I bought. Even a small one." He did air quotes for 'azimuthal projection' and I almost smacked his hands.

"I'm sorry, but that was my last one." I actually had a dozen of them in the back, but I would rather lose the sale than encourage these two.

Big Brother piped up, far louder than necessary in the small space with only the soft whirring of the fans to speak over. "Why do you carry all these fakes? It's not a globe, not a globe, *not a globe*."

He sounded like a broken, socially-delayed, fact-stunted record. Then he picked up the softball-sized model of the moon and tossed it to Robin who caught it, but barely.

"And we've *never* been there. No man has *ever* set foot on the moon. Not even close. I met a documentarian in Vegas last year who took a Bible and camera and visited every living astronaut that NASA claimed had stepped foot on the moon. He asked them all to swear on the Bible on camera that it was all true, that they'd gone to the moon, and no one would do it. Not *one*. Proof that it was all faked."

At that point I really wanted to meet the knuckle-dragging parents who'd produced these conspiracy-spouting trolls, but since I couldn't do that I decided to compound the problem with my own bullshit. "Of *course* the moon landings weren't real, unlike the Christie Pits tunnel."

"The what? I know about the riot, but not about any tunnel."

"Of course not. They don't want you to, either. It's soaked in the blood of American soldiers."

"*Christie Pits Park?*"

"The very one, just down the street. It was the northern terminus for the Underground Railroad."

"What?"

He sure was thick. I gently took the $199.99 moon model out of Robin's hand and walked it back to its display stand. "Oh yeah. The tunnel ran all the way to the lakeshore, then under Lake Ontario, coming up three-and-a-half miles south-southeast of Olcott, New York. That was the irony because the slaves weren't 'all caught', they were 'all freed'."

Brother-of-Robin stopped his fidgeting and stared at me. "*The* Underground Railroad, in Christie Pits? Are you shitting me?"

"Not at all. They still use the last fifty metres of the tunnel as part of the Bloor subway line." They did no such thing, of course, but if it kept muttonchops from tossing the globes around, the tale would be spun.

"So, can we get into the tunnels? Can we walk under the lake to the U.S.?"

"I wish! On their last run on... Christmas Day, 1860, former slave Jefferson Washington led a parade of two hundred through the tunnel lit only by hand-held torches, just minutes ahead of a battalion of Confederate soldiers intent on recapturing or killing them."

Robin whispered, concern in every word. "They didn't catch them, did they?"

"Well, when little elderly Octavia Parks shuffled up and out of the filthy, damp, fish-smelling tunnel after three days of trailing behind the group, Jefferson pushed down the plunger on the dynamite and blew the whole thing up, drowning or crushing every last Confederate soldier down there."

The Brothers Numbnut stared at me like I'd just made a ferret appear out of my ass. Robin was the first to find his words. "A-may-zing. I remember hearing rumours, but that connection to Christie Pits makes it all fit. Is there any proof, though?"

"Proof?" Oh crap. "Um, have you ever seen Niagara Falls and Niagara Gorge?"

"Uh, yeah."

"There's your proof. When the tunnel collapsed, the...uh... lake bed shifted and the gorge and falls were formed." I'm going to go to Hell for this whopper!

The sound of the bathroom door closing startled us all. "Oh shit! The Feds! They've come in the back!" I leaped to the front door and pulled it open. "Go guys go! Before they see your faces! Watch the sky for drones! I'll hold them off as long as I can! This place is blown. It's not safe to come back! *Ever.*"

They were deer in the headlights until a loud cough from Leona lit a fire under them and they were out the door and gone, one going west along Bloor and one east. A moment later Robin bolted from the east and followed his brother west, head down, hand shading his eyes.

I let the door close and Leona joined me, retrieving her drink. "Did you just recycle the story of Moses parting the Red Sea as a local anti-slavery tale?"

I picked up my own drink and took a careful sip. "May-be."

"That was brilliant. I could barely keep from busting a gut laughing. Chasing off customers is bad for business, but I think we'll do fine without the likes of those two."

"I'm sure we will, Boss."

Her phone chimed. She checked it then tucked it away. "Reality calls. I have a client wanting to see a retail space near, of all places, Christie Pits."

"Good luck with that. Watch out for a couple of kooks trying to find the Underground Railroad."

"Thanks. You *do* know that it wasn't exactly underground nor a railroad."

"*I* do, but anyone who believes the earth is flat and that the moon landings were hoaxes might not be privy to those small details."

While I carefully sipped my ice-cold piece of chocolaty paradise, I texted Tori. *I hope your day is more sane than mine.* I stashed the phone in my pocket, found my spare notebook behind the counter, and jotted down the first line of a new poem that just started bouncing around in my head. An hour later I had a rough draft of something that might be worth trying out at the club tomorrow.

Chapter 9

A S I EDITED THE poem, tightened it up, and second-guessed myself on word choices and rhythm, my phone chimed with a text. *Nope. Crazy here, too. What's insane at the shop?*

Poem forgotten for the nonce, I thumbed back. *Flat-Earther-moon-landing-denying brothers.*

WTH?! I want to hear all about it! Going into a meeting, then another this evening. Drinks tomorrow?

Drinks? Of course! *Sure! Someplace with AC.* Or a patio.

Cool. Of course AC. Or a patio. Will pick you up @ the house when I get home around 7.

The bell rang as a small dog led an older dressed-for-the-heat-in-loose-white-linen lady into the shop. I recognized the senior from the area but couldn't remember her name. The hairless crested Chinese dog on the other end of the leash was Oolong, I think.

o0o

After Oolong and his mistress left with a copy of my West End dog parks map, the muggy day slogged along without incident. I made five Cottage Country map sales, filled three online orders, and then spent an hour sketching out an idea for a map of the top twenty dessert places in this part of the city, based on an article in Toronto Life magazine. A simple map with the locations was easy but *boring*. I wanted something fun. I doodled landmark-shaped desserts in places of the buildings and blocked in where I'd add snippets of classic recipes along the borders: Black Forest cake, tiramisu, and Canada's own Nanaimo bars.

By the time I'd looked up each shop online and gleaned what their specialty was, I was freaking starved for dessert. Conveniently enough, number eight on the list was half a block away, so I set a five-o'clock reminder to stop in on my way home. I then spent fifteen minutes scouring their menu in order to select the perfect two or three desserts that would give my taste buds a rush without turning me into a diabetic. I settled on a strawberry shortcake tart and a slice of key lime pie. Not too heavy, not too sweet. I also wondered what Tori would have picked. I was doing that more and more lately, probably because Michelle confused the hell out of me and Tori was straightforward and clear as a bell. Except where her marriage is concerned. I suppose I could step up and actually ask her about it if it was such a big deal to me. The big question would be *why* was it such a big deal? As attractive and funny and fascinating as Tori is, I'm not wrecking a home. I'm not an Ottawa dentist. I'm also not rushing into something that will inevitably end.

Ten minutes later a text from Tori made me doubt everything I'd just decided; it was only a happy face emoji followed by the two-clinking-beer-steins emoji, but it made me grin like a twelve-year-old with a crush. Or a thirty-five-year-old with a crush.

We texted back and forth for an hour while she waited for a late-to-arrive appointment and I tidied up or served the few customers who wandered in. Our texts weren't anything deep or profound or even "Hey Baby, what are you wearing?" Just stuff about the kittens, the weather, the shop, and the last training session she ran. It was fun, light, goofy, and didn't in any way drift into flirting territory.

Her late appointment arrived at five o'clock, just as my phone reminded me to get dessert. Five minutes later *Long & Lat* was closed and I was on my way to pick up a tart and piece of pie.

o0o

The kittens mauled me, we all ate, and eventually, I alternated between messing with the new poem, doodling on the new map, and nibbling on the delightful desserts, but even when I gave up and settled for streaming a movie, I kept picking up my phone and checking for messages from Tori. Finally, I just lay on the couch in the coolness and let the Furry Five smother me with little nips, rasp-tongued kisses, adoring purrs, and trusting snores.

o0o

Thursday morning a customer waiting for me to open the shop, but as I started to greet her, my phone blasted at me that I had a text. A quick glance showed Michelle's number so I muted the phone, put it in Airplane Mode, and stuffed it into my back pocket.

"My apologies. Give me a quick second to open up and we'll find what you need."

"Thank you." Her big smile said she was in no hurry, but her rocking back and forth and hands in and out of her pockets told another story. I hurried.

As I turned on the lights and fans, she told me she and her family were leaving for the West Coast in a rented motorhome in eight hours and her husband hadn't bought any maps for their ten-thousand-kilometer round trip. He was a tech nut who intended to rely on digital navigation apps and his GPS the whole way. She on the other hand was a practical, experienced traveller who needed a good old-fashioned hard copy in her hand. I started quizzing her about their route and $160 in hard copies later she was much more relaxed and ready to have fun exploring.

I finally checked my phone. Michelle's text was a simple *We never talk anymore. Why?* I was so dumbfounded that I stuck the phone on the charger in the office and distracted myself by designing a tiered, spiral display for the smaller globes. I measured and sketched and did my best to refrain from sending a snarky *We don't talk because you're playing fill-my-cavity with your pet dentist while stressing me about the house, my home* reply to the text. At lunch, the kittens were all the distraction I needed, and the afternoon was spent building the new display and polishing the poem about bottle pickers.

oOo

I actually got *Bottle Picker's Dreams* ready in time for reading at the club but at almost four hundred words it was too damned long, so I sat back and enjoyed the show. A few new faces took to the stage and they stammered and sweated, but we all showed them love for trying, snapping our fingers enthusiastically. Seeing the flush of success on the one young guy's face made me wonder if maybe it was my time. He shook, he nearly cried in fear, and then he read a mediocre poem about Starbucks baristas always getting his order wrong. When he was all done and didn't get booed and was instead given cheers and finger snaps of support, he *did* cry and laugh. If he could do it, maybe I could, too.

I took my phone out to send a quick *I've had an epiphany* text to Tori, and when I took it out of Airplane Mode I was greeted with two texts from her.

I'm @ the house. Where are you? That was sent at 7:15. Oh shit. Did we have plans for tonight? The second text was a simple *Is everything ok?* It was sent half an hour ago. I frantically scrolled up in my messages from her and there it was. Drinks. *Will pick you up @ the house when I get home around 7.*

FML. I had failed to put it in my calendar and Tori was paying the price. I texted back. *So sorry. No excuse. Epic memory fail. On my way. There in ten.* It was only a five-minute walk but I had to settle my bill and then go to the bathroom.

Shit shit shit shit shit shit. Maybe it was just a 'meet for drinks' thing, but I hate being unreliable. Michelle had done it to me more than once when she'd gotten distracted by her friends or family and I'd been more than a little hurt. To do that to Tori went against my grain.

I was paid up, peed out, and striding down the street when my pocket vibrated. *I'm out back @ the fire pit. Saved you a couple of beers.*

Hmm. No sarcasm, no anger. If it were Mish, the text would have been loaded with both. Or she would have called and turned a thirty-second call into a one-hour harangue.

I skipped the kittens and went through the side gate, straight to the fire pit. Despite the heat of the evening, Tori had a small, cozy fire going. Her body language spoke volumes. Her eyes were closed, but she was facing the house, not sitting with her back to it in dismissal. She was also leaning back, her tanned legs stretched out straight and crossed at her ankles. She looked relaxed. It's not quite the reaction I expected. I mean, it wasn't like I'd stood her up for an actual date, but she still had a right to be angry, or at the very least disappointed. Then she opened her eyes, smiled, and raised a can of beer in salute. That's when I knew she wasn't like the handful of women I had experience with. Michelle would have been hiding in the spare room binge-watching eleven seasons of something, ignoring both me and the kittens.

"I'm *so* sorry."

"No worries, Max. You *did* warn me you have a shit memory, now I know to send a reminder text when we have anything planned." She lit a cigarette and took a long drag.

"You're seriously okay?" I had to ask. 'No worries' doesn't always mean there are no actual worries. Surely every man over thirty knows that.

Tori retrieved a can of beer from the cooler by her side and offered it up. "Sit. Relax. Stop worrying. If this had been dinner with my family or some work function I'd invited you to, I'd be seriously *not* okay. But it was just a beer after a long day."

I accepted the cold, perspiring can and sat in the other chair. "Thank you." I opened the beer and sipped. It was wonderful.

"Just don't make a habit of it. Please."

"I wouldn't dream of it."

"Thank you." We drank in silence for a moment, enjoying the cold brew and the cedar smoke, which nearly overpowered the pungent stench of summer dumpsters in the alley behind the house.

"Kakis and a collared shirt... I'm guessing you weren't at work or home cleaning litter boxes. A date?"

Her tone was casual, but there was a hint of hurt in her eyes. I got the feeling my answer was going to be a big deal for her. "Poetry slam open mic. Every

Thursday at the comedy club around the corner."

Wide-eyed, but still skeptical, she leaned in. "You write and slam poetry?"

"I write it, but I haven't slammed it, yet."

"Stage fright?" My sin of forgetting forgotten, for the moment.

"Crippling. Or it *was*. Tonight I think something changed. Maybe I'll slam next week."

She took a drag and considerately blew the smoke away from me. "Fear is a harsh mistress. For me, it's heights."

"So you haven't been up the CN Tower with its glass elevators?"

"Oh, I've been up. But I nearly puked and had to get really drunk at dinner just so I could make the trip down. You're okay with heights?"

"Yes and no. I'm not afraid. I can look down just fine and have even jumped out of a plane at three thousand feet, but I get mild vertigo. My toes go numb and my bowels threatened to loosen."

"Isn't that the actual definition of fear?"

"Not for me. I'm afraid of certain insects like centipedes and earwigs, and the feeling is completely different than vertigo. Racing pulse, sweaty palms, desire to burn the world down to kill one earwig—you know, the usual."

"Yup. Earwigs and fire... a good combination. The day camp I worked at when I was a teen was overrun by them."

"And it doesn't help when adults tell kids about how earwigs climb in your ears, can't turn around to get out, and have to use those big pinchers to claw their way through your brain and out the other ear."

"It definitely doesn't help. Plenty of nightmares came from *those* stories."

"So, how was your day?"

"Long, even though I finished on time. Three meetings, a mini training session, and a subway ride home in a cloud of hot, sweaty humanity. The usual."

"And stood up by your landlord."

"Like I said, the usual." She winked at me and I sipped my beer to hide the flush of my embarrassment.

"How was your day?"

"Steady, uneventful, hot."

"I hear you. Didn't you say something about flat-earther brothers yesterday?"

"Oh God. I don't think I've ever met such a willfully stupid pair of siblings in my life."

"That bad?"

"Flat-earthers *and* moon-landing-deniers. The earth isn't round but the moon is, though man has never even stepped on it, or so the Brothers Numbnut claim."

"Did you ask them whether they thought the moon was a disk or a globe?"

"Hell no, I spun them a story about the Underground Railroad tunnel beneath Lake Ontario."

"*No.* I bet they ate it up."

"Like it was a Mars bar covered in whipped cream."

"That's a bit sweet for my taste, but I get what you're saying. I guess it takes all kinds to make the world go 'round."

"Not if it's flat." I tipped my beer at her.

"Touché." She tipped back. "Back to the poetry thing. You've piqued my interest. What was the poem you were thinking of reading tonight when you should have been here answering my every whim and listening to me drone on about my day?" There was only a faint hint of hurt in her tone.

"Bottle-Picker's Dream? It's about misperceptions and assumptions."

"*Really?*" Was she doubting me? "Can I hear some?"

"Of course." I mean, it wasn't up on a stage with a mic and lights, so I should be okay.

"I'm not usually a fan of poetry, but I've had five beers and can't get out of the chair, so consider me a captive audience until I fall asleep."

"Since you put it that way..." I pulled out my phone, found the file, and started reading. Maybe it was this beer on top of the two highballs I'd had at the club, but I didn't even stumble or gag.

"The daily life of one is the nightly dream of the other.

A dumpster-diving bottle-picker dreams dreams of tightened spokes, spinning pedals, and knobbed tires between clinking pickings, and his thoughts are full of having his own bicycle shop...

A bicycle shop owner dreams of lift and drag and someday soaring eagle-like through the clouds above his world.

I dream, you dream, even a king can dream a dream.

The thirty-ish lawyer dreams the dream of being a parent...

The scattered, harried, young single mother dreams of court and of one day representing terrified, troubled teens.

They put one foot in front of the other..."

I looked up to see if she was still awake, and she was staring at me, her eyes moist.

"Wow. That's it?"

"Not hardly. It's almost four hundred words long."

"Can I hear the rest of it, please?" She reached over and gently squeezed my arm.

How could I resist?

When I was done, she levered herself awkwardly out of the low chair and stood up, unsteadily stretching the kinks out of her back. "I have to pee. But first..." She leaned down and kissed me smack on the lips. Confused, I kissed back, but when she started to tip over she broke off the buss and stood back straight again with a bit of a wobble. "That was beautiful. The poem that is. The kiss was nice, too." She took a step toward the house. "But I still have to pee." She wasn't falling down drunk, but I could see that her long day combined with the five beers she said she'd had was fuzzing her edges. Halfway to the house, she checked her watch, the Fitbit's glow abruptly illuminating her face in a creepy campfire ghost stories kind of way. "Shit. It's late and I have a meeting at ten."

I worked my way up out of my chair. "And I should get in and take of the kittens. I'll clean up here, first." I was afraid if I started walking to the house while she stood in the way I'd want to go for a second kiss and then a third, but like I said before, I'm no Ottawa dentist. The one kiss was nice, but it would be the last one. I took the last two beer cans out of the cooler, then picked the whole thing up and dumped the ice and water over the fire pit, getting a face full of smoke and steam. I coughed and spit and, temporarily blinded, stumbled back into my chair, caught my foot on it, and went over backwards, landing hard on my ass, but still clenching the handles of the cooler. I expected a cheer or at least snickers and giggles from my audience, but my clumsiness was greeted with only crickets and the traffic sounds of Bloorcourt on a summer evening. I squinted over at Tori, but she was gone. She really must have had to pee.

I picked up my pride, poked around the fire pit to make sure it was well drowned, then cleaned up and dawdled over and into the house, more than half hoping Tori would come back out after she'd drained her bladder. No such luck. Depositing the cooler and beers in the kitchen, I released the furkids, fed and cuddled them, and eventually put them back in their room and made my way to the shower. The last of the little bandaids from Kerouac's wounds separated easily from my chest hair as I sluiced away the day's sweat. Between the residual cleansing heat, the epiphany that I might actually have the nerve to get up on stage, and the unexpected but wholly enjoyable kiss from Tori, I'm sure I was still smiling when I fell asleep.

o0o

Friday morning at the store was so crazy busy with last-minute road-trippers having the nerve to interrupt my back-and-forth casual texting with Tori, that lunchtime arrived before I was hungry. But, hungry or not, I slogged home in the repressive heat just to make sure the wee ones were behaving and fed. I was going to just slap together a sandwich to take back to the shop with me, but if the morning was any indication of how the afternoon was going to go, I wouldn't get a chance to eat, so I ate as much as I could and stuck the rest back in the refrigerator. Either the heat and the humidity were starting to mess with my appetite, or I was just spending too much time thinking about that damned kiss last night.

That kiss. That beery, cigarettey, soft, enthusiastic kiss. That kiss that I would never forget, no matter how shit my memory got. It was our first and last kiss, but it was a stellar kiss. Back at the shop, between map enthusiasts, I texted Tori a quick *Beer by the fire pit tonight* note. We hadn't actually discussed each other's weekend plans, so I had no clue if she was even in town that evening.

I kept plugging away at the day, joking with customers, chatting about their upcoming trips, and showing kitten photos to the locals who knew about my Foster Five. I also kept a close eye on my phone for a reply from Tori, but as of five o'clock, there was nothing. I checked at least once every ten minutes to make sure my phone was turned on, not muted, and not in Airplane Mode, again. It wasn't. What there were, though, were a half-dozen customers who rushed in just before I started to close up, each on their own personal map-buying missions. By five-fifteen the number was down to two, but three more slipped in.

It was six o'clock before I managed to close up. The day was still rotten hot, my shirt was soaked through before I got to the corner, and there, in one of the chairs on my little front porch was Tori, cold cans in hand.

"You didn't reply to my text about beers. I wasn't sure you got it." I accepted the beer. "Thanks."

"It wasn't a question so I didn't think it needed a reply. It seemed more like a statement."

I pulled out my phone and checked the text. Sure enough, there was no question mark at the end of it. "Oops. How long have you been waiting this time?"

She patted the chair next to her. I sat. "Just a couple minutes. I was done early and knocked on your door but you weren't in, obviously. Since I didn't know your store hours off by heart, I wandered over to say hi. I peeked in but you were a little busy. I left you to it, picked up more beer, came home, and got changed. I sat my ass down about five minutes ago, so this is just my first beer."

"But it's a Friday beer, and they're the best."

"Amen to that." She tapped my beer can with her own.

"Unless you work on Saturday." I sipped. The beer was deliciously, teeth-numbingly cold.

"I only have a short meeting in the afternoon, so not too bad. You open the shop at ten?"

"I do."

"Then how about we take care of your kitties, barbeque some steaks, and maybe go to the pub for a game or two of pool. Your treat."

"My...? Of course. I'll even remember to bring my wallet."

"And I will remind you to, just in case."

"But I haven't got any steaks thawed and nothing to go with them."

She hoisted up a cloth grocery bag she'd hidden from sight on the far side of her chair. "Steaks, coleslaw, baked potatoes. Do we need anything else?"

The lady was way ahead of me! But I needed to be careful. The memory of that kiss was fresh enough to make me pliable and receptive to another. "Not that I can think of." Except maybe a long chat about your marriage.

"Excellent. Now, since you have AC, I propose we let the kittens out of prison and get some food in our bellies before we have too much beer. And yes, I am inviting myself into your home." She stood up and I followed.

"Um..." I had no objections, but couldn't remember how clean the place was.

She saw my hesitation. "Unless you'd rather I not."

Her own hesitation decided for me. Whoever had hurt her in the past had done a helluva job. She was strong and powerful and radiant and pure alpha, but at least some of that was a mask hiding a hurt. "You are more than welcome to come in. I paused only because I couldn't remember if the place was presentable. Plus, I need a shower." I unlocked the door and held it for her to precede me into the coolness.

She stepped far enough inside for me to close the door behind us. "Oh my God that feels *so* good. She twirled around in the cool air while I let the kittens out. They went straight for the stranger and Tori stopped spinning immediately to sit amongst her new worshippers. "Go have a shower. I'll keep these cuties company and out of trouble."

"Don't let them sell you any homemade catnip. It's really just parsley. I'll be back." I slipped my sandals off and went upstairs. Calliope made to follow me, but Tori made a kissing sound at her and my little Torby scooted right back down to the fray.

oOo

Either our kiss had been forgotten or Tori had decided to take a step back from whatever direction she'd been going, because we cooked, ate, and cleaned up side-by-side like we were old friends. There were gentle hip bumps, high-fives, beer can toasts to Fridays and steak and kittens, shaking our stuff to my cooking soundtrack of The Lumineers, Lord Huron, and Mumford and Sons. But there was no second kiss in that intimate shuffling around each other and the kittens, right there in my sanctuary.

We laughed, goofed around, and not quite flirted. No looks of longing, brazen innuendos, or gentle touches as we passed each other. I don't know if I was more relieved or disappointed. Either way, I knew not to get used to the idea because she would be moving back to her condo soon, and with the issues of the house and Michelle far from settled, I didn't even know if I was going to get to stay in the neighbourhood. Also, I hardly needed to fall for another woman who had another man.

Plunked down on the couch, digesting the rib-eye feast and being smothered in kitty love, I wasn't sure how I was going to find my way to a pub, let alone play pool for a few hours. I was about to suggest we postpone the ass-kicking I invariably got at pool and opt for streaming a movie, but her phone rang in her back pocket and stalled that idea.

Chapter 10

"HI, MITCH... OH NO! Is he okay?... Are they keeping him overnight?... Good. How can I help?" She looked truly concerned for whomever they were talking about, leaning forward, chewing her bottom lip, bouncing her heels. She nodded while Mitchell spoke at length.

"Of course. I have it all on my laptop and will be fine. Nine o'clock start... Stratford store... see the chef, Cheryl. Got it. Please text me her number and I'll coordinate with her... Of course... of course... Thanks."

She disconnected the call, sighed, and turned to fully face me on the couch. "Don't hate me. I have to call it a night."

"Hate you? Not even close. It sounds like something pretty serious happened at work."

"Thank you. Bashir—the manager of our new Stratford location—wiped out while cycling with his son and broke his collarbone. He'll be okay, but he can't work for a few days. Unfortunately, he was due to give the orientation training for a dozen staff all day tomorrow and we have a soft opening on Wednesday."

"And your boss needs *you* to do it. That makes sense. It's what you do."

"You're okay with me leaving? I have to be up at six to get there and set up for a nine o'clock start, and although I could play a few hours of pool and still function tomorrow, I'd rather not be dozy for the drive."

I wasn't even sure why it was an issue with her. Her company needed her and she had to get some sleep. "It's all good, Tori. We had a wonderful dinner and will just get a rain check for pool and beers. Will you be back tomorrow?" Saturday evening would be better for me anyway because I wouldn't have to open the store the next morning.

"I won't be back until eight at the earliest, but instead of making plans that may get screwed up by changes to my schedule during the day, how about I text you when I'm on my way and I'll drop by for a nightcap when I get back? If it's not too late."

"Sounds good. I tend to be up late on Saturdays anyway." I had plenty of map projects to keep me busy after work.

"Thank you!" She scooped Ginsberg and Kerouac off her lap and transferred them to mine, then leaned over and gave me the second kiss I was both dreading and hoping for. Before I could say a word or dare to deepen the kiss, she pulled back and smiled. "Stay. Don't disturb the kittens. I'll see myself out. Thanks, Max."

"No, thank *you*, for dinner and the beers. I still owe you." Three kittens got up and followed her, butting her ankles for attention. I couldn't blame them at all.

Slipping on her sandals, she tickled the kittens and laughed warmly. "Yes, you do. And I will definitely collect that debt, soon."

"I'm counting on it. Have a safe trip tomorrow and I'll see you whenever you get back." And think about her every second until she does. Damn that second kiss.

"Yes, you will." Then she was gone, and it was once again the kittens and me. Her life moved at a speed mine didn't even recognize. It was both invigorating and exhausting, mostly because of the summer heat, I suppose. I picked up the remote and found a movie I'd been wanting to watch, but the beers and steak convinced me that lying down with the kittens was a better idea. I checked my phone for messages and reminders, was relieved there was nothing from Michelle to harsh my happy, and stretched out on the couch in my best imitation of a cat bed.

o0o

While preparing breakfast for us all I got a text from Tori. *Three coffees later have arrived safe and ready to go. Sorry I bailed last night. Looking forward to picking up where we left off. Have a good day, Max. Text ya later, Map Man.*

'Map Man'. I liked it. I'm not a fan of labels—Michelle often used them to make digs like 'Retail Hero' or 'Pot Luck Prince'—but coming from Tori, it made me smile.

Just after three, I was finishing up with my fifth customer of the busy hour when a flash of lightning lit up the street and seconds later a cracking, primordial explosion of thunder scared the shit out of me and shook the 'hood. The storm rolled in hard and fast. In seconds it was as dark outside as ten o'clock at night. I propped open the shop's front door to get some of the cooler, ozone-heavy air. At four-forty-five it stopped as abruptly as it had started and moments later the sun came back out. The deluge had washed away the worst of the summer stink, and yet it had mixed with the various botanicals from plant oils to now revitalized loam and turf to give the neighbourhood that fresh-washed scent of life.

My phone chimed at five with a reminder to pick up a few things at the corner store. At the bottom of the note was a reminder that tomorrow would have to be a full grocery shopping day because the fridge and freezer were nearly empty. I confirmed that a reminder and shopping list were entered into my phone and put it away.

My mango pork on rice was just starting to make itself at home in my belly when a text from Tori startled the kittens and me. *Just grabbing a quick bite. Will be on the road in fifteen. See you in a couple hours. Long day. Need beer.*

The pork did a little hop of joy and settled in for the duration. Keeping it simple, I replied *Have a safe drive. Fresh beer and kittens will be waiting. :)* That promise made, I returned the wiggly, non-compliant kittens to their room and made a quick trip to the aptly named The Beer Store two blocks east on Bloor, where I picked up a 12-pack of bottles of the same Canuck Pale Ale she'd been drinking last night.

Back home the Ferocious Five acted like I'd abandoned them for a week instead of just half an hour and once the beers were in the refrigerator I let the kittens herd me back to the couch.

The sharp rap of brass on steel kicked me out of sleep so violently that I jumped up and nearly stepped on Zwerling and Ginsberg, while the other three ran for cover. Kerouac didn't go far and swatted my foot to pick him up, which I did.

I opened the door just a crack, blocking kitty egress with a foot. Tori leaned on the doorframe like it was the only thing keeping her from face-planting on the porch. "Beer me. Pleeeease." Her voice was an exaggerated I'm-dying-out-here rasp.

"Of course. Sit. I'll bring libations."

"*Please...*" She smiled up at me and slumped her way to the porch chairs. I made sure the door was clear of kittens and closed it. Once I was in, I scooped them all up, placed them in their room, and got two beers from the fridge.

Back out on the porch Tori was once again leaning back with her legs stretched out and her eyes closed. Without moving even one eyelid, she held up her hand and made grabbing motions. I opened the bottle and put it into her grasping claw and she held it tight. She drank, longer and deeper than I probably could. When she finally pulled the bottle from her lips and opened her eyes, half the beer was gone. "Thank you. Just what the barkeep ordered."

"I'm guessing it was a long day." I drank and listened.

"Painfully so. Two of the staff for this new location were rude and disrespectful not just to me, but to the other women on their team. I did my best to redirect their energy and give them the lowdown on Montgomery's workplace Code of Conduct, but they were oblivious.

"So you had to fire them?"

"I don't have that kind of authority, especially at a franchise location, but I sent Bashir a very pointed text and told him to."

"That's good."

"Not so much. They're his youngest son and the son's best friend."

"Ouch. No, not so much."

"But he promised to do it, tonight. I left my business card with each of the women and quietly asked them to keep in touch and to let me know if Benny and Paul aren't let go."

"Good idea."

"Bashir has invested a *shitload* of money into the franchise license and reno-vations but there's a clause in the agreement that allows Mitch to pull the plug if Montgomery standards aren't met. He's done it once before."

"I'm impressed." And I was. Too many companies didn't back up their em-ployee-protecting policies.

"Oh, I forgot to tell you. Mitch *did* have a file on drunk Doug and terminated him immediately. His buddies, Levon and Skip were put on notice, too, but I think they'll stay out of trouble now that Doug isn't their ringleader. When I told Mitch that I almost didn't tell him because it was so minor, he said pretty much what you did about trusting him. Then he told me about what his wife went through as an administrative assistant before she became his business partner, and he promised me that Montgomery's will *never* be a place where women feel unsafe. He even wants me to put together some ideas to keep female patrons safe and comfortable, too."

"Wow."

"He's a good man. Will you help me?"

What? "Come up with ideas?"

"Sure. I'd like a man's point of view and you've already proven yourself to be intuitive and sensitive to women."

"I'll help however I can."

"Thank you. But not tonight. Tonight I need another beer and to talk about anything but work." She held up her now empty bottle.

I laughed. Mine was nearly done, too. A mosquito landed on my arm and I shooed it off. "More beer it is, but how about inside where it's cool and mosquito-free."

She swatted her leg. "Let's." As thirsty as she was, when we got inside she went straight for the kittens instead of the beer. "Can I let them out?" She peered over the half-door.

"Of course. I'm pretty sure they don't care who grants their parole."

She opened the door and stepped back. The first to bolt to freedom was Kerouac, of course. His black-and-white blur bounced off Tori's ankle before racing into the kitchen where I'd just opened the fridge. "Hello, you little shit." I picked him up and put him on my shoulder. While I retrieved two more beers he head-butted my cheek then licked my earlobe. I returned to the living room and found Tori on the couch with her feet tucked up under her and four kittens exploring her lap, accepting scritches and tickles. I handed her a beer and sat at the other end of the couch, friendly but not intimate.

"Thanks. I was going to suggest we try the pub again, but it's so nice and cool here and I'm so comfy with the kittens. Would that be okay? Just chill here?"

I don't mind going out to the bar every once in a while, but I was much more of a homebody than a social butterfly. Michelle always had trouble sitting still, and getting bored easily, so she often toodled off to visit her bestie in Mississauga. "I am *very* much okay with relaxing here."

"Cool." She sipped her beer and rubbed Zwerling's tummy.

"Hey, Siri." There was a telltale beep. "Please shuffle the Acoustic Mellowness playlist."

Siri's Aussie sweetness replied from the speakers on either end of the couch. "Playing Acoustic Mellowness playlist, shuffled." There was a beat of silence, and then Tori Amos' live acoustic version of *Total Eclipse of the Heart* filled the room.

"Is that my namesake, Tori?"

"It is. Good ear."

"This album got me through middle school."

"Now I feel seriously old."

"Not as old as Tori. She's been around since the eighties. My *Mom* was a fan."

"I've only been a fan for a couple of years, since I heard one of her songs at a wedding."

"Cool."

We sat and sipped and spoiled the kittens through *Total Eclipse*, and then through Mumford & Sons, but when Barenaked Ladies and the Persuasions' delightful version of *Maybe Katie* started up, Tori stood slowly enough for the kittens to relocate safely. "May I have this dance, monsieur?"

"Dance?" Oh shit. That was dangerous turf. The problem wasn't that I couldn't dance, it was that I *love* to dance. Michelle's sense of rhythm was criminally awkward, so we'd never done much more than rock back and forth at family weddings. Tori swayed invitingly without being overwhelmingly erotic. Erotic would have been better. It would have been easier to turn down; but her smile, her reaching, beckoning come-here-you finger wiggles, the gentle side-to-side swing of her hips in a one-two-one-two-three-four rhythm... I moved the kittens to safety and stood, taking her hands in mine, feeling stupid for making assumptions. I mean, really, we'd only kissed twice.

She led me away from the big coffee table, but we couldn't avoid the fur-balls that rushed to play on our feet. We shuffled and swayed, taking turns leading each other through the mewing kitten obstacle course. The song ended and I could sense the next kiss coming when Tori smiled slyly at me, but Port Cities *Half Way* infectious beat kept us moving just fast enough to forestall trouble.

This whole scene was ridiculous! Here I was with a sexy, funny, intelligent, amazing woman, wanting to forget Michelle ever even set foot in this house, and that amazing woman was *married*. Everything about her said I was an idiot for ignoring the obvious attraction. From the dry warm strength of her hands to her subtle soap and tobacco smoke scent, her thick, dark-gold-blonde braid, the sparkle in her too-blue-to-be-true eyes when she looked right at me, and the way her curves moved beneath her loose cotton, spaghetti-strap dress, she was beguiling and bewitching. Then the light bounced off the diamond in her ring and reality hit me like the ice bucket challenge. I let go of her hands and stepped back.

"I'm sorry, Tori. We have to stop. I can't." I don't think I could have hurt her more if I'd physically slapped her. Her whole body seemed to curve in on itself. The transformation was heartbreaking, and I was responsible.

"I thought we had a connection, Max."

"We *do*. That's the problem."

"I don't understand. Why is that a problem?"

"Because you're married, Tori. Even if I hadn't just been abandoned for the dentist, I can't get between you and your husband." And, like I said, if she'd leave him for me, eventually she'd leave me for someone else.

I expected her to agree, cry, or tell me he was an abusive bastard and she wanted me to save her, but I didn't expect her to laugh. Not a snicker, but an honest-to-God roar. She held up her left hand, reached over with her right, tugged her rings off, and tucked them in the pocket of her dress.

"Tori, are you saying that your marriage doesn't matter?"

"No, Max, I'm saying that it doesn't *exist*. Read my lips... I. Am. Not. Married. Never have been."

"But the rings?" I was confused as shit.

"Are armour. They give me gravitas, respect, and a bit of protection in an industry where a twenty-eight-year-old woman is still often seen as little more than booze-serving eye candy. Sure, the rings attract a few creeps who think the married chick is up for fun, but for the most part, the illusion of marriage gives me a bit of a mother image which comes in handy as a trainer. Mitch and a few other people know, but generally speaking, my marital status is no one's damned business at work."

"So..."

"So shut up and kiss me."

"Yes ma'am!" So I did. And boy, did she kiss me back! We kissed like we'd never see each other again while at the same time like we'd just found each other after searching for centuries. Every cell of my body sang with the current she sent through me, the feel of her dress under my hands, the moist fullness of her lips, the heat of her breath on my neck when we broke briefly for air, her little moans as I traced my nails gently across the skin of her back. I'm sure I was making sounds too, but I heard, felt, saw, smelled, and tasted nothing but her.

Then she pulled back just far enough to say, "Couch. Quick."

We shuffled back to the couch and nearly fell full length on it, oblivious to anything but our passion, but a soft *mew* stopped us. We nearly fell on three of the kittens. I released Tori. "Bedtime for the kittens. Can't have them getting crushed." I scooped up the three and deposited them in their room.

"Definitely not!" She grabbed her own armload and as we passed each other we leaned in and traded a kiss.

I dimmed the lights, turned up the music a notch, and waited by the couch.

Tori slipped into my open arms and gave my neck a nip. "I need to use your bathroom, please. The beer..."

"Me, too. Door on the left, just before the kitchen. I'll use the one upstairs."

"Hurry." She tore herself away from me.

"Race you!" I scooted up the stairs pretty sure I wasn't going to win this race. I really had to drain my bladder, but the 'physiological response' of my body to the intimacy was going to slow me down considerably.

By the time I was finished and washed up, Tori was sitting on the top step, leaning back against the wall. I held out my hands and she took them, letting me help her to her feet and into another long, deep kiss. When we finally broke out of it she leaned back and I could clearly see that she wanted to say something but wasn't sure about it. "Say it. Whatever is on your mind. Quick, before I kiss you again."

"That's what I was going to say. I *want* you to kiss me again. But I don't know whether I want you to make love to me or to shag me until I pass out from sheer exhaustion."

"*Shag* you?" I couldn't help but smile and raise my eyebrows. We were both on the same page, but we obviously weren't done 'dancing' yet.

"*Screw* me, *hump* me, *boink* me."

"But what about shtupping? Or jumping your bones?"

"God, yes! Those too. Take me and dance with me between the sheets!"

"That too! And maybe we can even take the bald-headed gnome for a stroll in the misty forest..." I couldn't resist and regretted the words immediately.

Tori froze. "Take the bald-headed gnome...?"

I pulled her in and whispered in her ear, "I'd rather explore your body all night long until we *both* pass out from exhaustion."

"Promise?"

In answer to that I scooped her up in my arms and carried her to my bedroom. At the last second, I swerved to keep her head from banging on the doorframe and instead smacked her feet against it on the other side. "Sorry."

"Shut up and take me."

"Or what?"

"Or *I'll* take *you*."

"Promise?" We reached the bed and the conversation ended. But nudity didn't happen immediately. Once we were horizontal and where we needed to be, we took our time. fastenings were undone carefully and with great teasing and anticipation. As my fingers fumbled with the buttons of the front of her dress, my lips found hers, then her neck, and finally her breasts. Her hand found its way under my golf shirt just as she sunk her toenails into my calf. *Toenails*?

"Ouch! What the...?" I pulled back, looked down, and in the dim light saw a black-and-white shape spring away from me and land on the comforter. *Mew.* "*Kerouac*!"

"Kerouac? You naughty little boy!"

I disentangled my legs from Tori's and scooped up the furry little *kittius interruptus.* "Save my place?"

"You betcha. Hurry back."

"Just call me The Flash." I got Kerouac downstairs with his siblings, and was back upstairs in record time, for *me* at least.

Tori patted the bed beside her. "Saved it."

"Yes, you did." I joined her on the bed. "I have just one request." It was going to sound really stupid, but I was so ready for 'liftoff' that I had to say it.

"Um, okay?"

"It's been a while for me. I just ask that we commit to, you know, at least twice, so I have a chance to redeem myself if I'm a bit *quick* the first time."

"Map Man, that is the most practical, unromantic thing I've ever heard, yet at the same time, the thought of more than once is so sexy... Yes. I agree. Twice. At least."

"At *least*."

Without going into details, before we dragged ourselves out of bed for breakfast and to release the kittens, we did indeed do it twice, twice. And we managed to stretch that first time out for a full hour, most of which I spent fulfilling my promise to explore her body *very* thoroughly. And what a body it was. Tori wasn't ticklish, but every nerve ending of her skin was on high alert and I fed off the current running through her.

Down in the kitchen just after nine the next morning, the kittens ate while we waited for the water to boil for coffee. Tori snuggled up behind me. It was the simplest, most wonderful feeling in the world right then.

"Do you have plans today, Max?"

"I'm all yours. Just don't ask me to run a marathon."

"The marathon was last night. No, I was thinking of Centre Island. I don't think either of us could manage to run to the end of the block, but maybe a stroll on the island. I haven't been there in a few years and one of my friends was posting pics from there on Instagram yesterday."

"A stroll I can do. Just so long as we take frequent breaks. Take lunch with us or buy it there?"

"How about a compromise? We'll buy sandwiches from a little place I know near the ferry terminal and we can find a nice bench on the island with a view."

oOo

And that's how we found ourselves sitting on the tabletop of a blue plastic and steel picnic table next to a willow tree on a beach packed with sleepy sunbathers, squealing and giggling children, and daring water-lovers who didn't care that Ontario was a Great Lake and not a tropical ocean. The view was primarily beach umbrellas, towels, and half-naked bodies of every size, shape, and colour, but we weren't far from the water's edge, and that's what counted. Grey gulls waddled around us, waiting for one of us to drop crumbs from our corned beef on rye, but neither of us was so inclined.

We sat side by side, occasionally leaning toward each other for a kiss between bites or drinks, or shoulder bumping simply to confirm physical contact. For me, it was to reassure myself that Tori was real and we'd somehow jumped into this with both feet. The warmth I was feeling there on the picnic table had nothing to do with the summer sun and everything to do with Tori.

I was halfway through my thick, meaty sandwich when a gull with nerves of steel dropped out of the sky like the Red Baron on Snoopy and snatched it in his beak. To add insult to injury, he smacked me in the back of my head with a wing tip during his escape, and abruptly lost half the sandwich into the sand. His five siblings then started World War III over the scattered meat while I stared at my lost repast. Tori laughed loud and long and then handed me half of her own sandwich.

"Here. Eat. We'll find something else at the café later."

I leaned in and kissed her. "Thank you."

The Battle of the Gulls quickly chased us off. We ate as we strolled. I say 'strolled', but I hobbled along sore and stiff and pissed off at my body for not being able to handle a simple night of vigorous, limb-bending, torso-twisting sex. Okay, maybe it was the best sex I'd ever had, but I'm thirty-five, not sixty and should have been in better shape. I hoped Tori didn't expect such sexual callisthenics from me *every* night. I'd be dead in a week. I'd have a huge-ass grin on my face, but I'd still be dead.

She squeezed my hand, and, like she could read my mind, smiled with a hint of a wince and said "Thank you for last night... and this morning. I hope we didn't set the bar too high for ourselves."

"Thank *you*, and unless that bar comes with a hoist, a harness, and an assistant to operate it all, it's going to take me a while to even be able to *see* that high, again."

She sighed. "You, too? Thank God! What was I thinking, suggesting we walk around the island after a night with that much fun?"

I pulled her in for a quick kiss, but there were people all around us, on the grass or the pathway, and the kiss was brief. "Too public?"

"Much. My ex was all about showing the world how hot he was because he had a girl, so our public life was all about *him* kissing, *him* grabbing my ass or my tits in public. We never just walked hand-in-hand. He always had to have his arm around my waist pulling me in, or around my shoulder like he could put me in a headlock in an instant. His narcissism made what could have been romantic gestures all about his ego and my second-place finish to it. But I really like what we're doing today, so ignore my knee-jerk reactions."

"They're valid reactions, so I'm not going to ignore them. But I have an idea. I pointed to a dark copse of trees and bushes next to a barbwire-topped chain link fence surrounding a long, man-made mound. "How about we find some privacy in there? I promise not to put you in a headlock, although I might grab your ass."

"You'd better!"

"Shall we see where that trail leads?"

"Sounds yummy, but let's try to look a little casual about it and not just run for the woods like horny teens in a horror movie."

I squeezed her hand. "I couldn't run if I tried to, so I'll just follow your lead."

"Oh, so now *I'm* leading *you* astray. Nice turnaround, dude." She gave me a quick peck on the cheek and tugged me along in a circuitous stroll that tried hard not to look as urgent as it felt.

Chapter 11

THE THICKET WAS ONLY about twenty feet wide, but it looked to be over a hundred yards long and the growth was so dense that once we were past the first bend of the snaking path, we couldn't be seen by the outside world. I spun Tori around in place like we were on a dance floor, and then reeled her in for a kiss as deep as any last night. When we finally came up for air she slid her hand up under my loose shirt and ran her fingers through my chest hair.

"I've been wanting to do that all morning!"

In retaliation, I ran my hand up inside the back of her blouse, my nails lightly trailing along her spine until my fingers reached her bra. With a quick pinch and a twist, I undid the clasp. "And I've been wanting to do *that* all morning."

She kissed me, hard, pressing her body into me. I slid that hand around to the front and lifted her bra away from her breasts.

A young girl's voice tore the moment right down the middle. "We can hide in here, Sophia!"

I whipped my hand out of Tori's shirt and then stepped between her and the approaching voice so she could rearrange the clothes I was trying to remove only a moment before. A split second before whoever and Sophia came around the bend in the path I realized that I was about to be betrayed by a too-eager bulge in the front of my cargo shorts. I spun around to face Tori, lifted her chin up so I could look into her shocked eyes, and said probably too loudly, "I can't see anything in your eye, Honey. Blink a couple of times and see if that feels better." She fumbled with her bra and quickly got herself rearranged while I blocked her.

"You're right, Sweetie. I think that got it. Whatever it was, it's gone now."

The girls saw us. "Who are you? Are you parents?"

My shorts were not yet presentable, so I stepped behind Tori and stood with my hands on her shoulders while I answered our interrupters. "No, we're not."

"Oh. Cuz this is school property and you're not supposed to be here unless your children are students here."

Tori straightened her glasses but kept me covered. "School? Cool! I didn't know there was a school on the island."

"It's the Natural Science School. I'm Sophia and I'm in grade three. I'm specializing in deciduous trees."

"I'm Lily and I'm an entomologist, in grade four. Entomologists study bugs."

I glanced down and saw that I was now presentable, so I stepped up beside Tori. The girls stood about ten feet away. "That's very cool. I'm Max, and I'm a cartologist."

"I *love* maps! I've mapped the whole island!"

"You did? That's what I'm trying to do!"

Tori took my hand. "Since we didn't know this was school property, we'd better scoot before we all get caught. We wouldn't want you to get into trouble for harbouring trespassers. Which way should we sneak out while you hide?"

Lily pointed down the trail behind them. "That's the only way out. The other way comes out by the teachers' patio, and you'll def get caught there."

"Then it's back where we came in. It was nice meeting you ladies. Have a good day!"

"Bye! Nice meeting you too."

Tori led me past the two and out into the sunshine. As soon as we were clear of the trees we could see the long log-cabin-style, sloped-roof one-story school a hundred yards to the east. A small group of children were gathered around what we now knew to be a teacher, not a parent or nanny. We walked in the opposite direction, not daring to look back once we were back on the main road amongst the baby strollers, joggers, and occasional cyclists.

The noise started as a squeaky giggle from Tori, but it was contagious and quickly evolved into howling laughter. We stopped and hugged, laughing until we cried. People flowed around us.

"Holy shit that was close. I think my bra is twisted."

"*Too* close! I *know* my pants are twisted."

"We need to find the bathrooms and get ourselves straightened out."

"You *had* me straightened out, which is why my pants are twisted."

She slapped my arm. "Who started it, Mister?"

"Guilty as charged." I raised my hands in surrender. "But can I help it if that's how my body reacts when it gets close to you?"

"I guess we'll have to duct tape Little Max to your thigh."

"Ouch! I'd rather walk into the cold lake thank you very much."

"That would work, too, at least for a while. In the meantime, I still need to find the washroom."

Another minute of walking took us to a sign with arrows pointing exactly where we wanted to be. Five minutes later we were back on the road, hand-in-hand, the affectionate goofballs we were.

"Where to now? The hedge maze?"

"Do we dare? What if we find ourselves in another dark corner?"

"Mmm... good point. Let's save the dark corners for when we get home."

"Deal. How about Centreville, the little amusement park with farm animals, rides, and food?"

"Centreville it is. What time do you need to be home for the kittens?"

"We left late, so they're good for quite a few more hours. They won't be happy, but they'll survive."

"How much longer are they in your care?"

That was something I was trying not to think about. "A few weeks at the most. If the verdict on my inspection is positive, then I'll be offered another batch shortly after that."

"You really love fostering, don't you?"

"I do. I didn't think I would when Michelle proposed the idea, but I've grown attached to having baby furry company."

"Do you miss Michelle?"

"Yes." I felt her hand tense in mine. "But only in terms of her veterinary experience." Her hand relaxed a bit.

"How long were you together?"

"Six years. Three in the house."

"You didn't marry?"

I laughed. I couldn't help it. She stopped walking and looked at me with an odd intensity, but she kept her grip on my hand, her fingers laced in mine. "No, we didn't. I proposed but in a hotel room surrounded by her friends as a last-ditch effort to show her how much I loved her and to give her a reason to come back." She laughed.

"Where did she go?"

"Home to Ottawa. Her mother was sick."

"And she stayed? Told you it was permanent?"

"She got back with her dentist ex-fiancé, at least according to her emails, texts, and Facebook relationship status."

"Facebook? Well then, it *must* be true." She winked at me. "You don't want her back, not thinking of fighting for her?"

Was Tori suggesting I should? "No. I think I've come to realize that I didn't propose earlier than I did because I wasn't completely sold on the idea of 'us'."

"Could it have been a fear of commitment?"

"Probably, but there's more to it than that. A fear of committing to someone who will likely leave eventually anyway."

"That's a little fatalistic."

"Maybe it is. My parents divorced when I was ten, then Dad died. And so did Mom, a few years later. Is it fatalistic when it comes true? Michelle *did* leave."

"Maybe more like a self-fulfilling prophecy."

Maybe. "I suppose always having a thread of thought that *she* would leave me too could have worked its way into our relationship and undermined our confidence in it."

"Or she was a fickle bitch and you knew it all along."

"Or that."

"Have you seen her since she left?"

"In person, just once. She flew back two weeks after she left and picked up her Rav4 and a load of clothes. The surgery was scheduled for the following week so it made sense to have the car and more clothes."

"What if she came back? Dumped the dentist and returned to Toronto?"

"She's actually hinted at that a couple of times. Her long, tortuous emails have covered the entire spectrum of emotions and desires, but no, I don't want her back."

"Have you told her that?"

"I don't dare. Her moods swing so fast and her name is still on both the mortgage and the title of the house. She even suggested I sell and buy her out, but two sentences later she says she misses me and wonders what she's doing in Ottawa. I've even seen her realtor BFF scoping the place out."

"That's more than a little screwed up."

"You think?"

"Her behaviour sounds like one of my friends who's bipolar."

"It's possible. If Michelle's ever been diagnosed, she never told *me* about it." We arrived at Centreville. I referred to it earlier as a 'little amusement park' but it's only small if you compare it to the huge annual Canadian National Exhibition, or Canada's Wonderland north of the city. It has a couple dozen rides and a dozen or so food outlets. It's a late-nineteenth-century-themed amusement park with a log flume, bumper cars, and a century-old carousel, for starters. It was low-key and fun.

Having lost the sandwich to the gulls, I was still hungry. "Do you mind if I grab a burger or something? We can split it, since you shared your sandwich. Or we can each get our own."

"Food good. Hunger bad. Let's split one." She pointed to a red-brick-white-trimmed-cedar-shake-roofed building with a sign labelling it as a smokehouse. Yum.

We spent nearly two hours taking it as easy as possible. We split a bacon cheeseburger, went on a few rides—though not the Ferris wheel because of the height—fell in love a dozen times with everything from goats to chicks at the petting farm, took selfies like insane tourists, and ate even more because beavertail pastries are *not* to be passed by. I was having the best weekend of my life and so as to not jinx it I silenced my phone, put it in airplane mode, shoved it back in my pocket, and took Tori's hand in mine again, kissing the back of it as we walked.

"What was that all about?"

"I don't mind talking with you about Michelle, but she has this sixth sense and would probably call or text if I didn't turn my phone off."

"Really? That's almost creepy."

"Almost?"

"Okay, it *is* creepy. Like she senses when you're thinking about her? Or do her ears burn and she just assumes it's you?"

"Honestly, I stopped trying to explain it years ago. It's just a knack she has. Most women do, in my experience."

"I suppose we do. I know I've had strong hunches and made a call to someone just when they needed to hear from me... or really *didn't* want to hear from me at that moment. Caught them in the act, so to speak."

"It sounds like you've been hurt." Would her past pain drive her away eventually?

"A couple of times, which would mostly explain my trust issues."

I tugged her to me for a quick kiss. "Aren't we the pair? You expect men to lie and I expect women to leave."

She leaned back and gave me a serious look. "Are you saying we should stop this before we both get hurt?"

"Should we? Do *you* want to?"

"Not a chance. I feel... *comfortable*... with you. That may sound wishy-washy, but I don't remember ever feeling this kind of comfort in a relationship, even though it's less than 24 hours old. It's like, I don't know."

"Like we've known each other for ages?"

"Yes! I'm having fun, I'm relaxed and not worrying about work, and I want to see where this leads. Wanna come along with me?"

I answered her with another kiss. How does one say no to a relationship with a beautiful, funny, smart woman? Yeah, maybe she could leave like everyone else has, but in the meantime, she makes my heart feel good.

"Is that a yes, or were you just kissing me to shut me up?"

"Yes." I smiled and she let me tug her down the path toward the little bridge over the water fowl-filled pond. We stood and watched geese, mallard ducks, children, seniors, and enthralled tourists who seemed amazed by the simple beauty of it all. Two teenaged girls in hijabs laughed, blushed, and pointed at a mallard drake as he climbed on his mate's back, ducking her under the water while he had his way with her.

Tori kissed me on the cheek and whispered, "I want you to duck me."

"Me, too."

oOo

The view of the skyline from the ferry is always magical and the deep blue late afternoon sky behind the eighteen-hundred-foot-tall CN Tower and all of the skyscrapers just made the sight pop. We both got a few great photos of it, then we did the requisite selfies before finding a bench and plopping ourselves down. I was exhausted and was sure I'd need a long nap before I was capable of hopping back into bed.

Tori hugged my arm tightly and leaned her head on my shoulder. "Thank you for today."

"Thank *you*." I kissed the top of her head and struggled to keep my eyes open.

oOo

The kittens forgave us for abandoning them, but only after we fed them treats and stretched out on the couch with them on top of us. It didn't take long before we were both asleep, wrapped around each other in what was physically-not-so-comfortable, but was emotionally heavenly.

oOo

Tori started to get a hint of a migraine so while she went downstairs to take a prescription pain reliever, I started making spaghetti for the two of us. By the time we were done with dinner, her head was much clearer and her headache was a faint, fading throb, so we relaxed and forced the kittens to watch *Spider-Man: No Way Home*.

She had to lead a training class downtown at nine in the morning, which meant it needed to be an early night. After the movie, we put the furkids back in their room, chased each other briefly around the house, and finally dragged ourselves to bed in order to further explore naked gymnastics.

oOo

Apparently, Tori tried to wake me at six when she got up and returned to the basement suite to shower and change for work, but I was out cold and responded with only a grunt. By the time my alarm went off at eight, I'd come far enough up out of the deep sleep of shagged exhaustion to hear it. I levered myself up to hit snooze and was greeted by a silly text asking if I'd be more comfortable sleeping in a coffin, like other dead-to-the-world creatures. She even attached a vampire GIF. There was also a waving hand text from Michelle. Two guesses which text I sent a Nosferatu GIF to and which one I ignored.

Around three in the afternoon, Tori texted me she had a pre-scheduled squash game after work and could she stop by afterward if it wasn't too late. Haha! Why would I *not* want her to stop by? Did she think I'd be tired of her already after only a day and a half? But it was sweet of her to ask. I would have done the same, although I wouldn't have been playing squash. My game, all the way back to high school where I was on the school team, was badminton.

I texted back: *Well since you asked so nicely... sure. Even if it is late, just use your key. The whole house works on just one key. I forgot to change it back before you moved in.*

Her reply came quickly. *Oh really! Well, no hurry to do it now. Any time you want to sneak into my suite and have your way with me is just fine.*

That sounded like fun. *Ditto.*

Then I'll see you after squash tonight. You won't even have to work too hard because I'll already be hot and sweaty.

But getting you hot and sweaty is half the fun!

Naughty man! c u later! xo

xo. Uh oh. In thirty-six hours we've already graduated to exes and ohs. At least we didn't jump straight into the L-word. We weren't twelve after all. We were at least thirteen.

oOo

She was indeed hot and sweaty when she tiptoed into my bedroom just after ten, but she quickly did a little dance as she peeled off her workout clothes and slipped into the bed. She tasted wonderfully salty and sexy and we didn't get to sleep until eleven.

oOo

Tuesday was hot and humid and slow at the store, especially since Tori couldn't text too often because she was in and out of meetings all day as they prepped for a new advertising campaign launch. She finished late and after the requisite celebratory beers with Mitch and their management team, she dropped by to find me asleep on the couch downstairs where it was much cooler than my bedroom. I moved over to make room for her, but she kissed me with a blend of beer and smoke that I found oddly sexy, and whispered, "Hey Handsome. Why not come to *my* place? It's a lot cooler than your bedroom and more comfortable than this couch." The kittens mewed softly for attention. We ignored them.

I gave a gentle tug on the front of her pale blue blouse and she tumbled willingly on top of me. We kissed enthusiastically for a minute or two before I gave her an answer. "I've never slept down there, even once. Let me grab my phone and charger and I'll be ready."

She reached her hand down to my shorts. "Oh, you're ready *now*." She was a little drunk but it was fun to be the focus of her attention.

"Yes, but if we shag up here, I won't have the energy to go down there." I kissed her. "Your choice."

"I don't want to wait to take you... but I will." She climbed off of me, slowly and not without considerable rubbing of her thigh against my shorts. "Get your phone and whatever and I'll wait here. I'm not taking any chances that you'll fall back on the couch and go to sleep without pleasuring me."

"You make me sound like some sort of sex slave." The phone was on the charger on the kitchen counter next to my keys so I didn't have to go far to get either.

"I would like to think that you're a willing participant and it's a complete team effort, Map Man."

Extremely self-conscious of the bulge in my shorts as we left the house, I followed her out the kitchen door and down to her suite. I kept my voice low. "Ready, willing, and able. Go Team Shag, go!"

"Go Team!"

She was right. The suite was quite cool compared to the sweaty heat outside even at midnight. Tori closed and latched the door behind us and spun to face me. I reached for her blouse buttons and she reached for my shorts and the cool basement suite heated up damned fast. My last thought as I responded to her tipsy, horny enthusiasm with my own was that her bed was a lot more comfortable than I expected. And a lot bouncier.

o0o

Tori's first class wasn't until noon at the Scarborough location, so we started the day the way we ended the night a handful of hours before, then we stepped into the shower together and I had that stupid thought we all have at some point in every relationship: *What did I do to deserve this amazing woman?* Then she soaped us both up, slid up against me, and I stopped intellectualizing.

Upstairs we eventually freed the cats, fed them, and made a simple French toast breakfast because I forgot to buy groceries after ignoring the reminder when it flashed on my phone while we were on the island on Sunday.

"Can I walk you to work, Max?"

Uh oh. Michelle used to do that in the beginning, but it tapered off pretty quickly when she got bored of the little store. I really didn't want to repeat Michelle's patterns with Tori, but then, walking to work with Tori sounded like the best thing in the world. "Only if you want to spoil me."

"You betcha."

One day at a time. "Then I'll go shave and get changed."

"Me, too. See you in fifteen? Twenty?"

"I'll be ready in ten, but I don't have to leave for twenty."

"I'll come up as soon as I'm ready." And she was gone, careful not to let any of the little ones follow her.

Since it was almost time to leave for work, I rounded up the kittens, made sure they had fresh water and litter in their room, gave them each a little headbutt as I deposited them over their door, and finished getting ready for work.

My phone chimed while I was looking for a clean work shirt, but instead of the half-expected message from Tori saying she'd been called in early to work and would have to walk me to work another day, it was from Michelle. *Hey Max! How has the weather been? How did the cat inspection go? Maybe we should Skype sometime and catch up! xo*

What the hell? Part of me wanted to grab her by the shoulders, look her in the eyes and demand she decide whether she was going to fight over the house or come back and convince me she wasn't going to leave again. But part of me just wanted her to leave me alone, stop rubbing salt in the wound, and let me get my lawyer to deal with it all. Maybe Tori and I would only last another week before she realized that my tortoise-pace lifestyle was no match for her hare-speed one, but I'd rather have only that week than any more time at all with Michelle. Maybe I'm just an asshole.

So I ignored the text until I could think about it for a bit and obsess over it a lot. Tori arrived just as I was having a final glass of orange juice. I offered her a glass but she just smiled and kissed me with gusto.

"*That* is all the orange I need to get me through the day, Mister."

I had no answer to that, so I just finished the juice and repeated the pulpy kiss, pushing Michelle further and further from my mind. My phone chimed that I had five minutes to get to the store, so we quit making out, Tori said goodbye to the kittens, and we left.

The day was already hot, but I forgot about the heat when Tori took my hand as we walked. This wasn't just a Public Display of Affection, it was a PDA in *our own* neighbourhood. What a delicious feeling it was, too.

No one waited at the store, so once we were inside, I got the lights on and the fans going while she explored the space, humming as she sauntered around, gently spinning globes as she passed them or picking up atlases or maps that caught her eye.

"Martha's Vineyard. I've never been there, but always wanted to."

"Me, too. My family used to 'own' it, sort of."

"Are you shitting me? Your family used to *own* Martha's Vineyard?"

"Plus Nantucket and the Queen Elizabeth Islands. Maybe 'own' isn't the right word. My tenth-great-grandfather bought the rights to governance for forty pounds sterling and some beaver skins, back in the 1600s."

"That is *so* cool. But you've never visited?"

"No. I only just found out about the family connection last year. Michelle and I actually booked flights to Boston for a week in October, but then she got the news about her Mom and eventually left."

"Why can't you go without her?"

"Alone? That would hardly be much fun."

"Then I suppose you'll have to find someone else who really digs you and thinks it would be a blast exploring your family history with you. I wonder where on Earth you might find such a person?" She glared at me sideways, like she was pissed that I didn't think about it first.

"Gee, I don't know? I'd need someone who has a passport." She raised her hand. "And someone who loves to travel." She raised her other hand. "And someone who could bunk in with me because getting two rooms would just be too expensive." She waved her arms like she was landing a 747 and stared at me with one squinty, accusing eye. "It could take me months to find someone like that." I picked up a stack of maps and walked them over to the cash counter. "Unless *you'd* like to come with me."

"Who? Me?" She folded her arms across her wonderful breasts in her loose red Montgomery's golf shirt and I nearly forgot what we were talking about. "I suppose I could free up some time."

"Cool." It wasn't just cool, it was freaking amazing! I'd forgotten all about the trip until this conversation but now that we'd discussed it, I was excited to go, especially with the sexiest woman on the planet.

"Then kiss me and seal the deal." She walked over to me and leaned in for a contract-sealing kiss with comically puckered lips.

I kissed her. "Deal." Although it was two months away and our romance was only days old, I wasn't stupid enough to bring that up. Let hope have its time.

"Thank you." She looked around the store. "Quick change of subject before I get out of here and go to work. How are your online sales?"

"Online sales? Tepid, at best. Some weeks are better than others."

"Online marketing is where my main strength is. Do you mind if I look at the website and maybe put some ideas together?" She picked up one each of the dog park and gay wedding maps and examined them. "*You* designed these?"

"I did."

"These are great. Now I *really* want to see the website. Do you have any more ideas? Two is nice, but I think your own line of custom-to-Toronto maps could do really well." She looked at her watch. "Shit. Gotta go. Think about it and we'll talk when I get home tonight."

"Sure. Of course." My brain blanked on map ideas as soon as she said 'when I get home tonight'. That had such a soul-dipped-in-the-sun sound to it. Oh, shit. I was falling hard.

She kissed my dazed lips and fled.

o0o

How I got any work done at all amazed me. By the end of the day, we had exchanged eighty-nine texts, though admittedly probably a quarter of them were goofy emojis and taunting GIFs. We were quickly creating our own communication shorthand. One final text just before five warned me that she was bringing home dinner in the form of leftovers from their new menu-tasting day. I guess they shuffled the menu at least twice a year and management gathered to test the new dishes before sending them out to the restaurants and officially putting them on the menu.

After dealing with a mini sales rush of three people at 5:05, I sauntered home, wondering when the endless heat was going to give way to cool autumn temps. It was only coming up on mid-August so we were likely stuck with sweat and exhaustion for a while yet, but a guy can dream, can't he?

The kittens had more energy than they had a right to, but I suspect it was due to the magic sub-arctic world created by the air conditioner. When I opened their door they all charged past me as if there were someone else they'd rather see. "She's not here yet, you ungrateful little shits. It's okay, though. I miss her, too."

I shuffled my way to the kitchen and got them all fed. While I enjoyed a tall glass of ice water, Kerouac threw himself down on the counter and exposed his little black and white belly.

"A tummy rub? You think you deserve a tummy rub?"

Mew.

"Did you puke today?" I wiggled my fingers over his stomach, just out of his reach. He squirmed.

Mew.

"Good boy. Did you only pee in the litter box?"

Mew.

"Alrighty then. A tummy rub it is." I vigorously tickled and rubbed his belly, trying in vain to avoid the affectionate nips from his needle-sharp teeth and swats from his extended claws. It didn't take long before the other four twigged to the fact that love was being doled out and they weren't getting any. They didn't try to climb my bare legs, thank God, but they assaulted my feet until I made my way to the couch.

When Tori knocked on the front door, the love fest abandoned me as if they knew exactly who was pounding brass on brass. I rushed to scoop them up. "I'm gathering cats! Come on in, slowly!" I grabbed Kerouac just as the door cracked open. Tori was becoming a pro at Feline Exodus Prevention and even managed to plant a kiss on me between sneaking through the narrow space, slipping off her sandals, and transporting bags of delicious temptation taunting me with tendrils of curry, mango, bacon, and something deep fried. I followed her to the kitchen, letting the kittens run free again.

Chapter 12

ONCE TORI HAD THE various-sized compostable food boxes set out on the island counter, she turned, threw her arms around me, and kissed me like we'd been apart for weeks.

"I missed you. Sorry."

"Ditto." Our second kiss was shortened when Tori pulled back and nodded toward the food.

"We should either eat while it's all lukewarm or put it on low heat in the oven before we run upstairs to 'renew our acquaintance'."

"Hmm... that's a tough one. We'd better eat now. Once we start 'renewing' we could be up there all night. I'd hate to waste great food and die of starvation."

"But if we die in each other's arms..."

"Then the kittens will feast on our rotting corpses."

"Oh no." She smiled.

"And Kerouac would overdo it as always and end up puking us up, all over ourselves."

"But we won't care because we'll be dead."

"Yeah, but... I wouldn't wish finding us rotted, chewed, and puked on, on anyone."

"Good point. Eat now, 'renew' later."

oUo

And that's exactly what did, though, between the two activities, we had a beer or two and streamed the live Lion King remake for the kittens. I joke about playing movies for the kittens, but this time Calliope, Zwerling, and Ginsberg actually sat and stared at the screen, jumping when scary things happened and periodically mewing or hissing at the screen when a big cat filled it.

Tori and I sat, curled up in each other, fingers laced and occasionally tracing shapes on each other's fingertips or nearby kitten bellies. It was peaceful and so relaxing that I could feel my heartbeat slow right down to a 'life-doesn't-get-any-better' rhythm. The lizard part of my brain nibbled away, though, whispering that it was too good to last, that she'll leave, too, and that I was shagging another woman under the roof Michelle still had partial ownership in. I told the voice to go screw itself then leaned down and kissed the top of Tori's head. She purred, wiggled closer, and squeezed my hand.

o0o

Morning came much too early. "I have a bit more time to myself today, so I'll finally take a look at the map shop website and put together some ideas for you if that's okay." She passed me a fresh cup of coffee as I doled out food into kitten-sized dishes and the kittens begged like they were holding cardboard *Hungry and Homeless* signs.

I turned and kissed her. "Of course it's okay. Why would I not want to improve our sales?"

"But you and Leona didn't *ask* for my help. It's really none of my business. If Leona is only keeping the place going as a tax write-off, maybe she's happy the way things are."

"She is and she isn't. She's always been open to new ideas. She has some personal reasons for keeping the place open that I'm not privy to, but if you can help me move us off the profit-loss line and steadily into the black, I'm all for it and will gladly pitch your ideas, or let *you* pitch them."

"Cool. Let me see what I come up with.

Rolled up empty cloth grocery bags in hand, I walked Tori two blocks over to the subway station at 8 a.m. then made my way to the Sobey's grocery store at Dumont, a short fifteen-minute stroll. We'd made a grocery list based on things we wanted to cook together plus the essentials I always tried to have on hand like canned soups and a couple of frozen pizzas.

I was in and out of the store in half an hour and rather than try and carry what had to be thirty pounds of groceries all the way home, I grabbed a waiting cab. Better to fork over a few more dollars than stretch my arms two inches.

o0o

With the long weekend behind us, the store was quiet even for a Thursday, so I was able to do the one thing I *never* did—I had a nap at work. I brought my desk chair out of the office and into the storage area, pulled the map-pattern curtain closed, set my alarm for thirty minutes, and closed my eyes. I won't deny that I was fast falling in love with Tori—and probably had been since I shared my fries with her on the street—but my sloth-slow, totally chill lifestyle wasn't used to hours-long conversations, dinner-making marathons standing in the kitchen, and enthusiastic sex. I can't even say that the sex was the best part of it all. It was incredible, but so was the flirting, tasting, and touching in the kitchen. The house felt like a home in a way it hadn't for ages.

Tori's condo repairs were almost done, though, so we both knew she would be leaving the basement soon and then when she said "home" she would mean the condo, not the house. Too, this weekend was Potluck Saturday and I knew that as soon as I introduced Tori to the crew they'd be dropping hints both narrow and broad that she was *the one*. Hell, maybe she is, but after only six days together I wasn't betting on anything relationship-related, especially until I got the house mess with Michelle sorted out. First, though, I needed a nap.

The bell over the door snapped me out of a bizarre chasing-Canada-geese-with-a-Supersoaker-squirt-gun dream.

"I'll be right out." A muffled 'okay' answered from the shop front. I ducked into the bathroom, splashed water on my face, dried it quickly, grabbed a box of maps I didn't need out front, and took my best customer service smile out to do what I do.

"You're not a music store." She looked pissed off.

"Sorry, no. In the next block. Similar name, different product."

"That's dumb. Naming yourself after a music store."

Dumb? Most people just shake their heads and leave, but she insults us? "Well, theirs is probably named after their founders, while 'Long' and 'Lat' are actually map terms, short for Longitude and Latitude."

"So? It's still dumb, and a waste of people's time when they come to the wrong store. It's inconsiderate is what it is."

"I suppose from some points of view it must look that way." For someone so against wasting time she was hanging around a little longer than she needed to give me shit about a store name I didn't pick but still love.

"It *is* that way, no matter how you look at it." Hands on her bony hips, she glared a 360 around the shop. "What kind of maps do you sell?"

Got her! "All kinds. Road maps, Bruce Trail hiking maps, maps of shipwrecks, dog park locations in the west end of the city, world m—"

"Dog parks?"

Ah ha! "What kind of dog do you have?" I really only wanted her angry ass out of the shop, but if I could make a sale, too, it would be a win-win.

"A Shih-Tzu-Pomeranian."

A shits-in-your-palm? "Do you ever have trouble finding a dog park when you're out in the West End with little..."

"Choo Choo. Like the Queen's pup."

I thought the Queen had corgis. "...when you're out with Choo Choo? Then this map might help." I handed her a copy of the map because it's harder for them to say 'no' when they have it in hand.

She opened it, looked for a location that interested her, found it, and one eyebrow edged up. I'm not a master at reading people but I've seen the 'map experience' enough to recognize it. It's like Googling an old flame and finding them, but instead, it's looking for something on a map and seeing it right there, between the folds.

"I'll take it."

I took her money and directed her to the music store, silently wishing them luck with her. Some folks just seem to have a grumpy default setting.

Even though it was Thursday, I really didn't feel like going to the club. Whether Tori was done work in time or not, I just wanted to get some work done on a few maps. The shipwreck one for Kevin had a bit of a deadline, plus the Best Desserts one was starting to gel in my mind. Of course, now that Tori had put the idea of a series of a half-dozen local maps by my hand, I was itching to start sketching. I did some restocking at the store, gave the floors a sweep, then filled the online orders and was done with an hour left in the shift. I texted Tori to ask when she'd be home.

While I waited for her reply, I texted Michelle back. I didn't want to, and I know I said I wished she'd leave me alone, but the house wasn't going to settle itself. If nothing else, I wanted to avoid pissing her off until I could find out what she wanted me to do about the title and the mortgage. We really needed to sit down in the same room and sort it out with the lawyers in tow, but in the meantime, a quick text would keep the line of communication open and friendly. It was when she stopped talking to me that I usually worried.

Hey Mish. Damned hot here. Leona gifted me an old AC unit, so the kittens are spoiled. How is the weather there? How is your Mom doing? Yes, we should Skype sometime. I don't know why I said that. I really didn't want to Skype her. She would read all sorts of things into my expressions and probably hang up on me. I'm lousy on Skype. My mind wanders and I look like I'm bored when I just really prefer conversations without screens and distance. I was fine with voice-only, but Michelle used to call and talk on and on and get angry if I cut the call short because she had interrupted my dinner or I was working on a sketch. Oh well. Deep breath.

Tori texted back just before I closed the shop. *Should be home by 7. Are you slamming at the club tonight?*

Not this week. Maybe next week. Got all that food to cook, a commissioned map to work on, and a sweetie to cuddle with.

Her reply was quick. *Cooking is good. Need help? Or will your sweetie be assisting you?*

And that's the problem with electronic communications. I couldn't tell if she was being a smart ass, knowing that *she* was the sweetie, or whether she was still unsure how much she was wrapped around my heart. *Help would be good, Sweetie.* :)

:) Then I'll see you when I'm done. If you can wait until I get home to eat, shall we BBQ burgers? Simple and quick?

Simple and quick? That sounds like my motto in bed.

Hardly. Or at least not always. Only when that's what we both want. ;) Sometimes a quickie is perfect. God, I wish I was there right now. Just texting about it makes me want to hop on top for an afternoon ride.

That would be amazing! *Me, too. Tonight.*

That a promise, Lover?

I suppose so.

Good! Gotta go. Short but late meeting. C U soon. xoxoxoxoxo xoxoxo

Yeah, we were as bad as kids. But she was so much fun to play with on so many levels. I locked up the shop and walked home via the wine store where I picked up a bottle of prosecco Spumante, a sparkling Italian white she said she wanted to try. I've had the stuff once or twice and it's okay. If I have to drink sparkling, I have to admit that my tastes are peasant simple and I reach for Mateus Rosé. While in the wine store, I had a flash of thought about the potluck and texted Rose to ask if Joe would like to do another absinthe night. I added that I already had the absinthe but needed his expertise. I finished with a teaser, *And I may just be bringing a date*. Once we were confirmed to be doing absinthe, I'd text the group and also let them know that we'd be one more for dinner, just to make sure we each brought enough food.

At home, the cool house pulled me in and took me straight to the floor with my mewing monsters after I let them out.

o0o

The floor is as far as I got. I fell asleep sprawled out on the carpet, covered in kittens. As hungry as I'm sure they were, they let me sleep. Only when my phone alerted me to a text with the Goldfinger James Bond theme in my ears and vibration in my back pocket did I stir. I sat up and the little ones scattered. By the time I got to my feet, five sets of pleading eyes stared at me from the kitchen archway.

The text was from Rose, saying that Joe would be happy to bring the absinthe set-up again. I texted back a quick thank you, then sent out a second text to the potluck group warning them that Joe and one other guest would be joining us, and to be prepared for another round of absinthe, for those who partook in such silliness. Kalani was the only one who replied immediately.

A guest? Does our Max have a DATE?! OMG! Also, I'll be bringing two new tricks to show everyone, before you all get drunk.

I replied with a simple thumbs-up emoji and a grinning happy face and set about feeding the kittens.

Tori's text at seven announced she was home and going to change before coming up. To punctuate her message, I heard the basement door open and close.

See you soon.

Then, like the freaking Twilight Zone my life can be, a text from Michelle flashed on my phone and the vibration startled me so that I almost dropped it.

See you soon!!!!

What the ever-living hell?!

Maybe we should watch the airshow, then go to the Ex. We always have fun on the midway.

Shit. Shit. Shit. We *did* always have a blast on the midway but that's not the point. Since when is she coming to Toronto? And more importantly, *why?*

My thumbs itched to reply with *What are you talking about?* Or more politely, *When will you be here and for how long?* But if I replied now she might call while Tori was here and that would not be good. Don't for a second think I was waffling on Michelle and thinking of taking her back. Like I said before, pissing her off while the house stuff hung in the air was risky. I ignored the text, turned off my phone, stuck it on the charger upstairs, and shook off the thoughts of the clinging, confusing past in favour of the vividly vivacious and fabulously funny present.

A moment later that present tapped on the back door and slipped in before any of the claws-and-fur set could slip out. I really didn't have anything to worry about because the second they saw Tori they were all over her. So was I.

o0o

We stood on the deck near the barbeque, sipping our beers, anticipating the lean mushroom Swiss-cheese-stuffed patties sizzling away, almost ready. I considered telling her about Michelle's message but decided to wait until I actually knew what Mish was up to. Unfortunately, Tori didn't give me a chance to wait.

"Something's up. I've only known you for a short time, but something is going on in your head. Are you still hung up on thinking I was married? Or worse, do you think I'm lying about it?" She leaned her forearms on the deck railing, beer bottle in both hands, gazing out into the yard, not at me.

"Definitely not. I no longer think you are or ever were married." I took a sip and composed the words I had only a moment ago hoped I could postpone. "I got a text from Michelle just before you arrived. She's coming to Toronto."

She sucked in her breath and held it a moment. "To stay?"

"God, I hope not, but I have no idea. She didn't say."

"And you didn't ask?"

"No. I didn't want to start a conversation with her when I was looking forward to spending the evening with you."

"Just the evening?" She turned and smiled.

"Okay, maybe breakfast, too." I took a sip. "And the hours in between, if you want."

"'If'? Yes, I want. I also want you to figure out what's going on with your ex and your house, for *your* sake. If you need a lawyer, I know a few."

"Thanks. To all of that. She said something about watching the airshow, and that's not until Labor Day Weekend, so we have a few weeks." I put my beer on the wide deck rail and tugged on her elbow, urging her into my arms for a perfect-fit embrace and a long kiss.

The kiss could have gone on much longer but Tori broke out of it and pushed me away. "The burgers!"

o0o

The burgers were a little well done, but still delicious, as much by the stuffing and honey Dijon mustard as by the company of the woman beside me running away with my heart. When the plates were rinsed and in the dishwasher, we snuggled on the couch and discussed the shop's online presence. I brought out a notepad and pen to sketch ideas and make notes, of which there were plenty once we opened the website on my iPad. We went over everything from the layout to the colours to the ordering system and catalogue. After two hours we had a helluva plan laid out and she'd even convinced me to start writing a weekly blog about the history of maps and why we still need them even in the age of Google Maps and GPS.

At midnight the timer on the living room lights clicked and plunged us into darkness. I was torn between turning the lights back on and starting to make the website changes she suggested, or dragging her upstairs to thank her profusely. Fortunately, the lover in me beat the artist and I left my notes on the kitchen table after we retired the little ones.

o0o

Friday started early when Tori slipped out of bed at seven to shower. I tried to follow her but she waved me off. "Sleep, Lover Boy. I have a class in Scarborough, but *you* went above and beyond the call of duty last night, so relax."

"Okay." I blew her a kiss and tumbled right back down into sleep.

oOo

The shop was glacial slow for a Friday so I had plenty of time to work on the website. I emailed Leona with Tori's ideas and what I was doing with them. She called me five minutes later.

"Max! That all sounds fabulous! This Tori knows her stuff. While I was reading it over I got an idea for a map I could use here."

"For real estate?" That makes sense.

"Yes. I've been doing more and more sales of heritage homes and think it would be great if we had a map of historic sites and areas of Toronto overlaid with current neighbourhoods and the subway line. I would pay for all the costs through *this* office and give them away to clients, but you could add them to the online catalogue."

It was a smart idea. "I love it. Things like the St. Lawrence and Kensington Markets, but also Casa Loma, Fort York, the Distillery District."

"Yes, but some of the less well-known, too. The Black Bull Tavern, Spadina House, Mackenzie House. I'll send you a list to start with and we can pare it down to find something throughout all areas of the city and all cultures, not just old Scottish homes and pubs."

"What style do you want the map in?"

"Good question. I'll do a little digging and send you samples of ones I like."

"It also sounds like a plan, Boss."

"Sounds like you have a brilliant woman in your life, Max. I mean, other than me."

I think Tori and Leona would get along famously. They both had what I call a "strength of personality" which draws people to them. It's more than charisma, it includes the sound of their laugh, their willingness to engage the person they're talking to, eye contact, and a lack of patience with ignorance and stupidity. I might just have to introduce the two of them, just to see if the universe implodes.

"I'll watch for your email and get started ASAP."

"I know you will. How are the kitties? Is that old air conditioner still working?"

"It is. Thank you. I've even spent a night or two down there on the couch." When I wasn't doing the horizontal mambo either upstairs or down in the basement with Tori.

"Excellent. Must run. Have a good weekend, Max."

"Thanks, Leona. You, too."

Half an hour later I checked my email for her list and map samples and right there at the top of my inbox was an email from Hogtown Cat Rescue. If it hadn't said "Congratulations!" in the subject field I wouldn't have opened it immediately, but it did, so I did.

Congratulations, Max. You not only passed your recent inspection but you've also been approved for more fostering. We here at Hogtown Cat Rescue clearly see how you've done a wonderful job and would love to have you continue.

It's also time for your current fosters to find forever homes. Due to scheduled staff vacations and an upgrade to our grooming room, we've set the date for a week from this coming Monday.

You know, with all the shit going on with Michelle leaving, nothing about that hit me in the gut like the thought of my Furriest Five leaving. It's the hardest part of fostering. The little ones grew as attached to us as we did to them. The agency was on top of it, though. To help us deal with it when we first started the job we were allowed to watch each bonding and adoption, to see the kittens each find the home they would become an intrinsic part of. It helps but doesn't ameliorate all the pain.

o0o

Tori got hung up at work with a trade show function she couldn't avoid, so I went straight home to give the five all the love I had. Ten days left. Damn.

I fed us all and retired to the upstairs office, but it was so damned hot I just took the sketchpad back down to the air conditioning, kittens following along like I was the pied piper, or had cat nip between my toes. Kerouac and

Calliope joined me on the couch, Zwerling climbed to her usual perch atop the big cat tree in the kitten room, while Ginsberg and Burroughs climbed into one cardboard box together and proceeded to wrestle over whatever cat toy was in the particular container.

Just after eight Tori texted. *Home. Finally. Changing. Up soon. xo*

I texted back a Snoopy-dancing-for-joy GIF, then finished roughing in an outline of Casa Loma, the Gothic-looking mansion built in the early twentieth century. It started out as a private residence but is now a popular tourist destination and has been featured in film and television for decades. It's only three blocks from my Mom's old condo as well as near the ravine my great-great-grandfather used to walk through with a pistol in his pocket to get to work back in the 1930s.

o0o

After dinner, Tori went for a run and I worked on the shipwreck map. I was astounded at her dedication. Even in the evening the heat and humidity were overwhelming. She was back in fifteen minutes, sweaty and smoky.

"No, nope, no way. Too damned hot." She was soaked, like she'd run in a salty rain. She kissed the top of my head. "I'm going to go shower and change. If you're busy, I can stay in the basement and not distract you."

It was a considerate offer, but seeing her dressed in skin-tight running gear, hot, wet, and flushed from the effort was distraction enough. I wanted to climb in the shower with her but compromised. "I've got about a half-hour's worth of work to do before I change gears on this, so why don't you go shower and relax and I'll put the kittens away and join you downstairs? If it's not too hot."

She smiled. "It's never too hot for *that*."

"Then I'll see you in a bit."

o0o

The basement was cooler than my top floor by far, but it was still warmer than the air-conditioned main floor, so we curled comfortably around each other in post-coital spooning on top of the sheets. I pulled her hair to the side, kissed the sweat-salty back of her neck, and she purred like a panther. That sparked a memory.

"I forgot to tell you. Good news, sad news."

She wiggled in tighter. "Give me the good news first."

"I passed the inspection and have been approved to continue fostering."

"That's wonderful! So what's the sad news? You have to move to Hamilton or Peterborough to do it?"

I laughed and held her closer. "Not a chance. No, the kittens are ready to find forever homes. They leave a week from Monday."

Tori wiggled around until she was facing me, with her legs entwined in mine. "Oh, no. I mean they'll find wonderful homes, I'm sure, but they're all such characters that you'll miss them terribly."

"That's an understatement. Especially Kerouac and Calliope. He's such an affectionate asshole and she's just the cutest cuddle monster of them all. Five families are going to be *very* happy."

"But what about you?"

"I have a week to clean the place up after they leave and then we get a new batch. They could be orphaned siblings or even newborns with their mom."

"Max..."

"Mmhm?"

"You said 'we'."

"Yeah, I guess I did. You and me."

"Cool." She kissed me slowly, then not so slowly.

Chapter 13

TORI HAD THE DAY off, so she took my short grocery list for the potluck and headed off to Sobey's after walking me to the shop. I knew my friends were all going to love her, but my gut was a little twisted up in nervous anticipation. Fortunately, the shop was busy for the first three hours, so I was sufficiently distracted.

Just before I locked up for lunch an idea for a brilliant custom map walked into the shop. A young father and his two boys ducked in to quickly pick up a Southern Ontario map for a day trip tomorrow, Sunday, when one of the boys asked Dad when the splash park closed and if were they going to make it in time. I realized that I had no idea what splash park they were talking about, which meant it would be a good map. I could even add outdoor rinks, to make it a year-round map. As soon as they were out the door I frantically made notes so I wouldn't forget, then I was off home for lunch.

Just inside the front door, Tori sat on the floor, smiling in a lotus position with the wee ones on or around her lap. It was the most wonderful sight in the world. I guess seeing that father with his sons made me think about the future, though the kittens leaving soon probably contributed a lot to my emotional overload, too. Having Tori in my life was amazing, the unicorn sparkle sparkle shine still burning bright on the whole thing. But how long until the lustre was gone and we drifted apart or she moved on? Shit. Why did my mind have to stumble down that dark alley?

I shook off the dark thought and concentrated on the simple fact that I was ass-over-teakettle in love and was determined to enjoy it for as long as it lasted.

I flopped down on the floor beside them and submitted to the best lunch hour molesting *ever*.

Tori strolled along beside me, her cool, soft hand in mine, our paces perfectly matched, stride for stride. Her walking me to the shop was spoiling me and I wish there was a way I could spoil her back. I couldn't exactly walk her to work, or make her lunch when she worked for a restaurant that fed them as a perk. I wondered if she likes flowers. After Tori left I called Kalani at their shop and asked her to pick up a dozen red roses for me and bring them to the potluck.

"Roses? Oh, I *so* can't wait to meet your new sweetie. I don't remember you *ever* buying Michelle roses."

"Because she preferred live plants. She wasn't keen on gifts that would wilt and fade."

"And new chick likes roses?"

"I have no idea, but there's only one way to find out."

"A dozen reds will def make an impression."

"Fingers crossed. I'll call and place the order now."

"And I'll bring them with me."

She was the best! "Thanks, K. Love ya!"

"Back atcha, dude."

Why didn't I pick up the roses myself? I had a hunch Tori was going to drop by the shop to escort me home. Maybe she would, maybe she wouldn't, but the bases were covered. Or they would be, once I actually ordered the flowers.

I made the call, gave them my card to charge, and let them know Kalani would be picking them up.

oOo

"Well, Tori so far you've made an impression on all of us, but there's one last test you have to pass before you can be an official member of the Potluck Crew." Aba leaned in, a goofy semi-drunk-on-absinthe grin shining in his dark brown face.

"Another test? I thought my reaction to those amazing roses was the test." Wedged between Lydia and Shannon on the loveseat, she laughed and stuck her tongue out at me.

"That was a *Max* test. This is a *group* test."

"Fire away."

"Tell us about either your worst date or your best one."

"That's it?" She twisted her face in an adorably thoughtful way. She was at least as drunk as I was, which was a bit more than Aba. "And everyone in the group has done this?"

"Yup."

"I'm going to guess that none of you ladies told your own date-rape story, so I'll go with my *best* date."

The room got deathly quiet except for soft kitten purrs. Shannon took a loud breath. "We didn't, but maybe one of these dinners we should; to let the men know it happens and to assure the sisters here that we're not alone. But not tonight."

Rose nodded. "Not tonight." Joe took her hand in his.

Tori picked up her glass of absinthe. "Best date story it is." She took a sip. "This stuff is both horrid and wonderful."

A chorus of agreement sounded. I looked around at this gathering of my most intimate and trusted friends and wondered where I'd gone right. What did I do to deserve this incredible woman and amazing friends in my life? Then Calliope started heaving, probably to upchuck a hairball. I scrambled and stumbled and scooped her off of Uncle Argaw's lap. I almost fell once and bounced off the wall, but I got her into the kitten room without dropping her and closed her in where she could puke to her heart's content, or her stomach's.

"Sorry about that, folks. Crisis averted." Forcing my wobbly legs to take me back to the ottoman, I gave my attention to Tori and her best date ever.

"So, my best date ever... it involved a long romantic walk, finding someplace private, and then... getting caught tearing each other's clothes off by a couple of school kids."

Oh shit. She was telling *our* date story.

Rose gasped. "You were having sex at a *school*?"

"Not *at* a school, sort of beside one; and we weren't having sex, we were just, um, making out enthusiastically."

"And you got caught? Did they call the police?" Ever since Aba and I nearly got caught moving an administrator's car as a prank in college, he loved to hear about other people getting unwanted police attention.

"No police were called, and the girls didn't figure out what we were doing."

"Lucky you. Why was that your best date, though? You got stopped."

"It was a day full of silly fun, sun, seagulls stealing sandwiches, and more laughs than I've had in years."

"Very cool. Where was this magical place?"

"Centre Island."

Kalani turned to look directly at me. "*Max!* You dog, you!"

Joe looked confused. "Max?"

"Yes, it was Max. They went to Centre Island last weekend."

I blushed. I didn't know what else to do. Not only wasn't I used to having my sex life discussed by my friends, but I was royally touched that our simple day together was Tori's best date story. I raised my hand part way up. "Guilty."

Tori tried to lever herself up off the loveseat, but her limbs wouldn't cooperate. Instead, she laughed at her own clumsiness and blew me a sloppy kiss. "Best. Date. Ever. My Map Man."

o0o

It was the most memorable potluck in the three years we'd been doing them, with Tori jumping right in, feet first, and treating everyone like the family of mine they were. She turned out to be better read than I'd imagined, especially of science fiction both old and new, and when music was discussed, her love of pounding rock and heavy metal won Kalani and Shannon over completely. My tastes run more to the mellow, but I knew a few of the bands they went on about so I wasn't totally lost.

After dessert Kalani sat us facing a TV table I brought out for her. Her first trick was what she called a 'zombie ball' that consisted of a gold metal ball floating up off the table under a big silk cloth, and drifting around in a creepy cool way. Mad applause showered her when she floated the ball back into her magic case but stopped abruptly when she brought out a foot-tall miniature guillotine.

"During the French Revolution, the real king was the guillotine," she began her patter. "It was usually at the whim of... Joe? Are you okay?"

It took a moment for all of us to understand that her question wasn't part of the trick. She dropped the prop into the case and leaped across to the couch where Joe sat with Rose and Uncle Argaw. Joe was perspiring heavily and looked a little wobbly.

"I'm okay. It's not a heart attack, just indigestion." Kalani placed two fingers on his wrist and took his pulse while Rose felt his forehead with the back of her hand.

Not convinced, Kalani repeated what Rose did, then looked closely at Joe's eyes. "You don't feel pain in either arm or numbness anywhere? Shortness of breath?"

"No, no, and no."

"Please stick your tongue straight out."

Joe did that and Kalani seemed to relax. "It doesn't look like a stroke."

He smiled. "No. Nor a heart attack. Only the Tabasco sauce in the jambalaya. Just the same, I think I'd better call it a night. Sweetie?" He looked at Rose whose look of concern said it all.

She nodded and squeezed his hand. "He does have a problem with Tabasco sauce, but if his symptoms get worse or change, I'm dragging his ass to the hospital."

Kalani kissed the top of Joe's bald head. "Listen to her. Be well. Don't be brave."

"Yes, ma'am. Thank you all. I had a terrific evening. Max, do you mind if I leave the fountain and come pick it up tomorrow?"

"Of course. I'll put it up out of the reach of the kittens. Give me a call tomorrow and I'll bring it over."

"There's no need—"

Rose cut him off. "There *is* a need, Mister. You're going to take it easy. Doctor's orders."

Joe stood as Rose helped him to his feet. "But you're not that kind of a doctor. You're a PhD, not an MD."

"I'm the kind of doctor who will sleep on the couch if you don't stop being obstinate."

"Yes, Doc. Whatever you say, Doc."

"Perfect. You're learning. It only took you forty years."

Tori squeezed my arm and whispered in my ear. "They're so cute, but I hope it doesn't take you forty years to learn."

I was drunk and pleasantly stunned by what she was implying, so all I managed was a snort and a tossed-out "No way. Thirty. *Tops.*"

o0o

Since it was nearly 11:30, the party dissolved and my wonderful guests all agreed to walk Joe and Rose six doors down to Rose's apartment. Between stolen kisses, Tori and I shuffled the dishes to the dishwasher, the rest of the kittens to their room, and ourselves down to the welcoming coolness of Tori's suite. I just hoped the memory foam mattress didn't tell anyone some of the things it might remember.

I have no idea what time we finally fell asleep, but it didn't seem long before the rising sun peeked through the cracks in the blinds to see if we were decent. We weren't. We were sprawled naked on top of the satin sheets, entwined in each other. Interlimbed as we were, we stirred at the same time. I was still a little groggy, so I lost the race to the bathroom simply because I didn't even try. Tori was in and done and back on the bed before I even managed to sit up. She slowly and lightly dragged her nails down my arm, and as much as they caused the desired physiological response, I still needed to go.

Reluctantly I pulled away from her touch, blew her a kiss, immediately tripped over my sandals, fell sideways onto the edge of the bed, bounced off, and thudded to the floor. Not only did Tori not jump up naked to my rescue, but she laughed so hard she cried. With as much dignity as I could scrape off the carpet, I crawled naked to the bathroom.

It took me a little longer than it took Tori, but I eventually climbed slowly back onto the bed without falling off. Once we stopped laughing, sleep was the last thing on our minds.

o0o

It was the need to feed the wee beasties and clean their kitten room that finally coerced us to get showered, dressed, and back upstairs. We had no specific plans for the day so we played with the kittens and eventually started unloading the clean dishes.

After a quick smoke break, Tori commented, "I can't believe they'll be gone in ten days."

"Eight now. A week from tomorrow."

She hugged me from behind, her arms tight around me, and her breasts pressed hard against my back. "Too soon."

"Definitely. They've kept me grounded for the past five weeks. But now I have *you*."

"You do, but it's not the same. I don't purr quite like they do."

"True, but they don't snore quite like you do."

"I do *not* snore."

"Not loudly."

"Not like *you*."

"Sorry about that."

"I hardly notice. For some strange reason, when we're in bed together I end up so exhausted I'd sleep through an earthquake."

"'Some strange reason'?"

"Maybe not so strange, but definitely a *great* reason."

"The best."

"Yup."

"God, we're starting to sound like a greeting card."

We moved to the couch, kittens in hand. "Yuck. Anything but a greeting card."

"Do people even send cards anymore? There used to be a card shop east on Bloor, but it closed a couple of years ago."

"E-cards, texts, SnapChats, Tweets, Facebook birthday reminders—who needs paper when social media has it all covered?"

"Covered, but lacking the human touch." I took hold of her hand and lifted it from scratching Zwerling's head up to my lips. I kissed her cool, soft palm. "I'm kinda fond of the personal touch."

Tori closed her eyes and hummed with pleasure. "Mmhmm." I kissed her fingertips one at a time and she groaned, low and deliciously feral.

Her phone rang on the coffee table just as I started on the back of her hand. She glanced at the device but didn't pull her hand away. I stopped the kisses but she purred "Don't stop now, it's just a text." I kept exploring, fully intending to make my way up her arm to her neck, but when she flipped her phone over to read the screen, she twitched, so I paused.

"My condo's finished!"

It's odd how a simple statement can make a dude both happy and sad. I was happy for her because I know how stressed she was with the whole flood thing and all her floors being replaced and walls repainted, but it meant she was moving out of the suite.

Like she could read my mind, she turned to face me and looked me in the eyes. "I'm not leaving you, Max. It's just a few blocks away, and no one says we can't have sleepovers anymore." She kissed her fingertip and touched it to the end of my nose.

"I know, but I'd better stick to making the hot cocoa because I suck at making s'mores."

"How could *anyone* suck at making s'mores? That's just sad." She kissed me, I kissed her, and the kittens leaped away for fear of getting crushed as we shifted position.

oOo

We dropped Joe's absinthe fountain off at Rose's and confirmed that he was feeling much better. I know Rose well enough to be sure she *would* drag his ass to the hospital immediately if things had worsened. As it was, she promised us she would call Joe's doctor the next morning and book an appointment. He had a family history of heart disease and had dealt with arrhythmia a couple of years back, so she was taking it all *very* seriously. Joe on the other hand wasn't worried at all.

We gave them both hugs and continued on east to Christie Pits and Tori's condo.

"It's not very big, but it's not bad, considering the real estate prices in Toronto. I've only owned it a year and it's gone up 50k in value. I imagine the same is true with your house."

It was. "In three years it's gone up enough that I couldn't hope to buy it today with the same investment. We were lucky to get it for what we did."

"And Michelle is still on the title *and* the mortgage?"

"Yup. She helped with the mortgage payments for a couple of months but went back to school to upgrade her degree. Then she bought her car and since then the mortgage has been all on me."

"The shop makes enough money to give you that solid a credit rating?"

"The shop's revenues, no. But Leona pays me a good salary, just enough to satisfy the bank. And I made a huge down payment on the place and have some investments as backup, so the bank is chill so far. I'm not sure how they'll react if Michelle wants out."

"She might not?"

"I have no freaking idea. She says she wants to talk about it and I spotted her realtor friend out front scoping the place out, but I guess I'll find out when she shows up at the end of the month."

"The Waiting Game—I hate it. I've never had much patience myself, so I don't know how you do it."

"I've learned over the years that a soft, quiet approach is best with her. She doesn't respond well to a raised voice, threats, or even firm words. Her family tells the story of how she and her brother were driving somewhere and they disagreed on the route to take. Frustrated, her brother snapped, "Just shut up and let me drive!" At the next red light, he stopped and she jumped out of the car and ran away. She turned her phone off and didn't show up at home until twelve hours later. To paraphrase Boromir in Lord of the Rings, one simply does not get angry with Michelle."

"Wow. That's some seriously passive-aggressive behaviour. If someone in my family pulled a stunt like that we'd change the locks while they were gone."

"*My* family would have rented out her room after the eighth hour."

"Yet you managed to last six years. You must really love her."

"You'd think so, but now I wonder how much of it was just letting myself be pushed around by guilt and fear of her fragility. Asking her to marry me as a grand gesture is the dumbest reason *ever* to propose."

"Even dumber than being drunk?"

"They'd be tied for first place, I think, but drunk would win if it led to eloping."

"You wouldn't elope?"

Hmm. It suddenly felt like I was being tested. "There's nothing wrong with eloping. Joe told us last potluck that he was a wedding photographer for a while and that at least half of the couples whispered to him afterward that they wished they'd eloped and used the wedding money instead for a down payment on a home. Even my own sister has said that. I guess the rush of the dream wedding wears off damned fast after the event when the bills roll in."

"I wouldn't know. I've never had to plan my wedding. I've never even been a maid-of-honour, fortunately."

"Fortunately?"

"I have a cousin who has been in at least seven wedding parties in the last five years and she has a closet full of expensive, ugly-ass dresses she can't ever wear again without spending hundreds on alterations. Based on that alone, eloping while on vacation sounds like a viable alternative."

"My wedding experience is limited, but I was Aba's best man and it was a simple affair with suits and dresses and nothing too elaborate. You're right about eloping on vacation, though—definitely a viable alternative." We arrived at Tori's condo building and the thoroughly awkward topic of conversation evaporated like sweat dripped on the griddle-hot sidewalk. Weddings? Eloping? WTF?

The building was only four stories and simple pale yellow brick with balconies just big enough for a café table and two chairs.

"That's mine, up there." She pointed up and left, to a third-floor balcony.

"Nice. Not too high, but not right at street level."

"Exactly. I can actually stand at the rail and watch sunsets without wanting to puke or pass out."

"Not puking or passing out... always a bonus in condo ownership."

"Pretty much." She squeezed and released my hand so she could open the building's front door and hold it for me to enter. I did, and after she unlocked the inner door I held it for her.

She kissed me on her way past. "You're so cute."

"Back atcha, Honeybuns."

It was a simple lobby typical of buildings that had once been rental units and were now condo-ized. The tiled area was probably fifteen by thirty and divided in two. The first part was the foyer with mailboxes, a monster mirror that looked like a seventies leftover with a fake wood frame with gold trim, and two nice, clean, utilitarian, comfy-looking beige couches near the big front window, for residents to wait for their rides in comfort. The second section was simply the area around the elevator, with marked doors leading to the stairs and the parking garage, and corridors on either side probably off to the first-floor units. Unlike my mother's building, there was no concierge, which I suspect lowered Tori's condo fees.

She led us to the stairwell and up. "I've missed a few runs, so it's the stairs for me. You can take the elevator if you want, Map Man."

"Ha. I think I'm good. As long as I have that cute butt to follow, I could climb the CN Tower."

Without warning she took off up the stairs, taking them two at a time. I did my best to keep up, despite the lack of AC in the stairwell. As much as I wanted to stare at her taut backside the whole way up, though, I needed to watch the steps more. At the third-floor landing, she waited with the fire door open and a kiss. "Look at you, all sweaty but not naked and horizontal. It's a good look."

"It's summer in Toronto. It's hard to avoid sweaty in any position. Does your condo have AC, or will we have to strip down to keep from passing out?"

"It does, but we can still strip down."

"Then lead on, Trainer Lady."

She gave me another quick kiss and I followed her into the nicely carpeted, well-lit, art-adorned corridor, and along to her door. Sheet plastic like a painter's drop cloth peeked out from under the door. Tori sighed. "Shit. This isn't a good sign. The message said it was all done and I could come home. Only one way to find out, I guess." She unlocked the deadbolt but the doorknob was still locked. "At least they secured the place." She unlocked the knob, too, and slowly, hesitantly pushed the door open like she was expecting an attacker. I stayed silent, mostly because I didn't think anything I said would help. I was just there for support.

Since the carpet, hardwood and tile had all been replaced, as well as some of the walls painted, according to Tori, I was surprised when my nose was greeted by a lingering hint of some floral incense rather than chemicals. There was a hint of paint taint in the cool air but someone went above and beyond in the cleanup.

"Oh my God!" Tori stepped in, onto the square of plastic, and removed her sandals. I followed and did the same. "It looks perfect! The furniture's all in the wrong places and the pictures need to be hung back up, but it looks amazing!"

In fact, it looked like there'd never been a flood at all. I needed to get the name of the firm that did the work. Just in case. "I'm guessing you're happy with repairs."

Her answer was to take me by the hand and drag me into the small living room where we danced around the small coffee table. There was no music, but that didn't matter. Her laughter was the only song we needed as I followed her lead. We spun and wiggled and jived until she noticed something through a barely open door and she broke off to examine it. She pushed the door open to what I could now see was a modest-sized bedroom and dropped to her knees to examine the dark green carpet.

"Ooh! This is *gorgeous*. My adjuster said that the carpet was nice, but this is so *plush*." She stood and jumped into the room, hopping up and down like a rabbit on a soft lawn. "Come in here and try this, Max!" Her outstretched hand was all the invitation I needed, though my heart wasn't in it quite like hers was. Yes, intellectually I knew this was her home and it was more than reasonable for her to be happy with the work done to put it back together after someone else's overflowing bathtub ruined so much of it, but her cute little space was already drawing her away from the space she occupied in *my* house, and maybe the space she occupied in my heart. Or was I just being an idiot? What was it Michelle's friend Stephanie had said? 'True love doesn't run away'? Maybe it just slipped away quietly, back to its own condo.

Tori was right, though. The carpet was like bouncing on a sponge, or forest moss. It was impossible to succumb to my threatening blue mood when her own joy was so infectious. I pulled her in for a bouncy kiss but instead, she tackled me onto the bed and then pulled me down to the floor.

Chapter 14

T HE RUG BURNS ON our knees, elbows, and backs weren't too serious, but we definitely proved that the carpet and underlay were more than sufficient padding for our favourite vigorous team sport. Back on the bed where we'd retired to recover, I had time now to look around and notice that all of her bedroom furniture was beautiful antiques. A cardboard banker's box on top of the tall-boy dresser had a couple of picture frames poking out and probably contained whatever usually resided on top of the dresser and the dressing table with a bevelled oval mirror. "You've got gorgeous furniture in here. Family heirlooms?"

"Yes, but not *my* family. I bought them a couple of years ago at an estate sale in St. Marys, just outside Stratford. I was driving to London and saw a sign by the highway. I followed it to a lovely Confederation-era farmhouse on a former dairy farm. The weather was crap and they'd sold very little, so they gave me a helluva deal. I only had the car but paid for it all upfront and returned the next day with a truck. I've got a few more pieces in storage that I don't have room for, yet."

"Amazing. And they're all this quality?"

"Most of them. The husband spent his retirement refinishing furniture he and his wife found around southern Ontario and into Michigan. When the wife died of cancer, the husband—Carl—decided to just sell it all and move to Florida to be near his brother and sister-in-law." I ran my hand along the edge of the nightstand on my side of the bed. The room was cool, but the dark wood was warm. "That piece is walnut, as is the matching one on this side. The dresser is ash, pine, and poplar. The bureau is rosewood and mahogany."

"The workmanship is stunning. The grains are all so different but pieced together beautifully." I suddenly wanted a house full of this furniture but didn't express that out loud. On the heels of the elopement conversation and while lying in her bed, the timing was disconcerting. Instead, I gave Tori a quick kiss and got up to use the bathroom. I grabbed my cargo shorts and boxer briefs off the floor on my way.

"Are you leaving, Max?"

"Not a chance. I just want to check out your newish bathroom."

"Before *I* do? I don't *think* so!" She leapt off the bed and bolted buck-naked into the bathroom while I was still putting on my pants. The door latched shut behind her.

"How is it, Track Star?"

"I don't know. I can't reach the light switch from the toilet. It's tile, that much I can tell. Cold as hell under my feet. The old bath mat was ruined by the flood so I need to go shopping." The toilet flushed and a crack of light appeared at the bottom of the door. "It's really nice. Cold to the touch but warm to the eyes. Come on in." The door opened and Tori stepped out, still naked and unashamed. Right at the moment I didn't give a damn about her bathroom floor and instead opened my arms and welcomed her into my embrace.

o0o

Although I did get to the bathroom, somehow we ended up back in bed, which I didn't protest in the least. Eventually, though, Tori got fidgety and hopped up to get dressed and start putting her home back together. The first thing she did was retrieve the coffee maker from under the sink and get a pot started. "I hope you like it black. The fridge is empty and has been unplugged all this time, so no cream or milk. I have sugar, though."

"Black is good, thanks." I looked around at the little place. "How can I help?"

"Just relax. I'm going to have a smoke, then we can kick back with our coffees before heading out. I'm sure the kittens are missing you." She picked a cigarette and her lighter out of the pack in her back pocket.

"Us. They're as fond of you as I am."

"Aw. They're such cuties. I'm going to miss them."

I followed her out onto the balcony and closed the sliding door behind us. "Me, too, but there'll be a new batch in the house in no time. There's never a shortage of kittens to foster."

Once she determined which way the slight breeze was blowing, Tori shuffled us so that her smoke was carried away from me. "This is my final pack, I hope. I'm going to try and make it last the week, to wean myself off. I promise. Cold turkey doesn't work for me. I've tried."

"What about vaping?"

"Hell no. Douche flutes can be more toxic than cigarettes."

"Douche flutes?"

"Sorry. One of the girls at work calls them that and I sort of picked it up from her. The vapes are the flutes and the guys who stand right next to the entrance to our corporate offices blowing that god-awful fruity vapour at us are the douches."

"Ah. Walking the gauntlet of strawberry and vanilla farts. There ought to be a law."

"Agreed. So, no vaping, or gum. The gum burns a hole in your stomach and can lead to more nicotine consumption than the smoking did. I heard of one woman who chewed eleven packs of gum a day."

"Holy shit! Did she live?"

"That I didn't hear. I tried the patch once and got really sick. I blame the beer."

"The beer?"

"The beer I drank too much of that made me forget I already had a patch on my left arm and told me I needed one on the right arm. Never drink and patch."

"I'll remember that. I once drank and *ate* a cigarette, but that's hardly the same."

"You did *what?* You *ate* a cigarette? You're hardcore, Walden!"

"I didn't eat the filter. Just the tobacco and the paper. I'm not crazy."

"I want to throw up just thinking about it."

"I did. Throw up that is."

"Just how drunk were you? Was it a dare? I've done some stupid crap on a dare."

"We were sitting in the campus bar and I took a cigarette out of my classmate Susan's pack, but she wouldn't let me have her lighter. I wasn't a smoker and she knew it and was just trying to save me from my drunken self."

"Good for her."

"But I told her that if she wouldn't let me light it, then I was going to eat it. She said I wouldn't dare, so I did. Washed it down with an entire rum and Coke and still couldn't get the disgusting taste out of my mouth."

"Silly boy." She blew smoke away from me and leaned in for a quick kiss I was more than happy to bestow.

"That's pretty much what she said, with a few more f-bombs thrown in."

"Don't *even* think of pulling that crap with me. I'll light your beard on fire. Your smoking will *not* help me quit. The fact that you're even out here with me warms my heart, though." She picked up a little soup can I hadn't noticed in the corner, butted out her cigarette, dropped it in the can, and returned the can to its spot.

"Any time with you is time well spent. And to be honest, although I don't smoke and can't stand hanging out with smokers, you manage to make it sexy. I actually enjoy kissing you after you smoke."

"You're very strange, Map Man."

I shrugged. "I know."

"Don't ever change. I love it."

Uh oh. The 'L'-word. It wasn't used directly at me, but close enough. Honestly, I wasn't sure how I felt about it. Being in love is amazing, but with great love comes great risk, to badly misquote Spider-Man's Uncle Ben. Not change? Nope. Too old for that. "I won't. Strange I am and strange I'll stay."

She slid open the door and we returned to the coolness of the condo. "Good. Now kiss me before we have our coffees, then we get home to the kittens."

I did as I was commanded, with extra enthusiasm born from hearing her call the house 'home'. When we finished, she snuggled in, arms tight around me, and her head nestled sideways against my cheek. "How's that coffee looking, T?"

"Ready." She went and poured us two cups and we retired to the couch. It felt strange to sit without being pounced on by kittens, but it was a nice, peaceful few moments.

"Don't you need to hang your pictures and get everything back to normal?"

"There's no rush. Today is *our* day. There'll be plenty of time to sort this place out. I still have two weeks left in the basement suite, don't I?" She looked at me. Her eyes glistened with emotion, and maybe a little fear.

"Of course you do." I leaned in and licked the end of her nose to break the serious mood rolling in like a fog.

"Ew! Yuck!" She wiped the lickiness off her nose, then licked mine.

o0o

The cats were as happy to see us as we were to eventually see them, and once they were fed, Tori and I took our sandwiches to the couch where we spent as much time fending off the little moochers as we did eating.

Halfway through watching *Ad Astra* starring Brad Pitt, Tori's phone rang. She glanced at it sitting on the coffee table, then reached over and tapped the screen. "Hi, Mitch. You're on speakerphone with Max next to me."

"Hey, Tori. Hi Max. I hate to bug you on Sunday evening, but Tori would you be up to doing me a well-paid favour?"

"Um..."

"Sorry. Let me explain it first. As you know, my little brother in Ottawa is about to open his dream neighborhood pub next weekend; but his assistant manager just eloped and quit."

Tori looked wide-eyed at me and had to clap one hand over her mouth to keep Mitch from hearing her laugh. I mouthed "Eloped?" at her, then followed her example by putting a hand over my own mouth to keep from squeaking.

Mitch continued. "She was also his primary trainer. As soon as I confirm that you're on board, he'll book you a flight out first thing tomorrow morning and you'll be there until Wednesday evening at the latest. He'll pay you a thousand dollars plus expenses for two-and-a-half days of intensive training of our own Modules One through Four. And I will also count them as workdays for Montgomery's, not using vacation days or days off. What do you say? You worked with Zach and his wife for a month last year, so you know who you're dealing with and how serious they are about quality service and superior work environment."

The line went silent while Mitch waited for Tori's answer. She looked at me and I nodded. Work was work and it was an extra $1000 in her pocket. "Call Zach and tell him I'm in, Mitch. I'll be glad to help them out however I can. Are you sure they only need me for two-and-a-half days?"

"Yes. Two-and-a-half at the most. His staff have already been through a week of basic training, so you might even be done in two. They'll be long days, though. At least one and maybe two twelve-hour stretches."

"No problem. It'll be like that messed-up opening in Barrie last fall."

"Exactly, but this time you'll have good local leadership to lean on. Shall I give him your usual list of audio-visual needs?"

"Please." She thought for a moment and held her hand out toward the phone as if Mitch could see her. "Actually, please have Zach get me *four* easels with whiteboards. I've been working on a way to speed up and intensify Module Three."

"Four easels it is. I really appreciate this, Tori. I'll be up until midnight waiting for Lynda to get home from her date, so if you have questions or more equipment needs, give me a call. Max, again, I'm sorry to interrupt. I know I keep stealing her away to work out of town, and we're both grateful for your patience."

We'd only been dating a couple of weeks, but Mitch made it sound like we were married. "It's the nature of the business, Mitch. It just makes it all the sweeter when Tori gets back."

"That's what my family says when I go away. I'm glad we're on the same page. I look forward to buying you a beer at our downtown flagship pub whenever you have time. I can tell you everything you didn't know you wanted to know about Tori."

Tori jumped up. "Like hell you will! I'm not letting you two in the same room together without me there to monitor and censor every word you exchange."

I reached up and took her hand. "But you'll be in Ottawa, T."

Mitch laughed. "Like Max said."

Tori sighed theatrically and sat back down, careful not to land on Zwerling. "I'm outnumbered. Great."

"Goodnight you two. Tori, I'll have Zach email you all the flight info and copy me on it. He said he'll meet you at the airport in Ottawa and get you checked into the Chateau Laurier, which is only three blocks from the pub."

"I'll watch for the email and call you if I don't get it by midnight."

"Perfect. Goodnight guys."

"Goodnight, Boss."

"Goodnight, Mitch."

The call disconnected and Tori leaned back into my arms. "Now, where were we?"

"Dozing off while Brad Pitt tried to keep himself from dying of boredom on the way to Saturn or Neptune. I don't remember which."

"Me neither. How about we pick something a little livelier? Have you seen *Train to Busan?*"

"The zombie flick? No, but I've heard great things."

"Cool. Since I'm now flying out early, I'm going to stop with the beer. Do you mind if I make myself a tea? I noticed you have a nice herbal decaf."

"I do? Sure. Go ahead and help yourself. It must be one of Michelle's. Speaking of whom, with my luck, you'll ruin into her in Ottawa."

We got up and led a kitten parade to the kitchen. "Oh shit. That's right. She's in Ottawa. What does she look like? I'll keep an eye out for her." She smiled wickedly.

"Well, she's about my height, shoulder-length brown hair, although she likes to play with the colour so I have no idea what colour it is now. She's got green—"

"Max, you must have at least one picture left of her on your phone. That would be so much easier than trying to describe her."

Duh! "Yup." My phone was on the charger on the hall table, so I went to get it.

"Do you want a tea?"

"Sure. Please." I returned with my phone and scrolled through the photos while Tori started the electric kettle and fetched down a couple of mugs. I hadn't actually cleared any of the Mish pictures from my phone, yet, so it wasn't hard to find one. I picked my favourite, one of her looking off into the distance, not knowing I was taking her picture. When Tori was done, I held it up for her to see. "Last summer in Peterborough."

"Wow. She's pretty."

"She is. But don't tell her that if you see her on Parliament Hill or wherever she hangs out. She'll wonder what your 'hidden agenda' is. She doesn't trust compliments."

"She's smart, too. I'm the same way, at least with strangers."

"Well, some days she's stranger than most." I fixed the kittens each a little bowl of food. Up on the island, Kerouac purred like a motorboat while he buried his face in his dish.

"She couldn't be all that bad."

"She's not."

"Then, if I run into her, I'll be as sweet as pie and not yell at her to get her shit together and stop messing with your head."

"Thanks. At least until I talk to my lawyer and figure out what's up with the house. After that, you can yell at her, take her out for drinks, or forget she exists."

"Which one of those will you do?"

"Michelle who?"

She grabbed the front of my shirt and pulled me in for a lips-on-lips collision.

When the teas were ready I hoisted Kerouac onto my shoulder and we led the purr parade back to the couch to watch Korean zombies take over a high-speed train. Twenty minutes later Tori's phone buzzed with an incoming text. She read it out. "Check your email. Again, thanks T." She checked her emails. "All booked. Air Canada flight 444 at 9:10. I'll book a taxi for 7:00, just to be safe. Better to be early than late, and Monday morning traffic can be as crazy as Friday afternoon's." She opened an app on her phone. "Sorry. This will just take a second." And it did. She was done like a pro, which I suppose she was. "Okay. Booked. Now, about those zombies..."

oOo

The movie was great, and I was still awake enough to watch another one, but Tori passed.

"I have to go pack, Sweetie. Rain check?"

"Of course. Whenever you like."

"Thanks. Do you mind if I come back up when I'm done?"

"Are you sure? With that early start don't you need a good night's sleep?"

"Trust me, Mister. I never sleep better than with you. You wear me out."

"*Me* wear *you* out? I'm going to need a gym membership just to get in shape to keep up with you."

"Or you could come running with me."

"Run? Me?"

"Or rollerblade alongside."

"Maybe. You go get packed and come back up whenever you're ready."

"Good idea. Why didn't *I* think of that?" She kissed me quickly and was gone. I sat back down and sipped my tea. It was too early to go to bed, but it was too late to start a movie. Maybe an episode of *The Good Place*. Short, sweet, hilarious.

oOo

For someone who had to get up with the sun to get to the airport, Tori was in absolutely no hurry to get to sleep once we got into bed. In fact, there was no hurry for anything we did and it was after one when we conked out, sweaty, sated, and smiling.

oOo

Ten minutes after I opened the shop the next morning I got a text from Tori saying that she'd arrived safe and sound in Ottawa and for me to have a wonderful day. She signed off with *xoxo*, which I tagged onto my reply telling her to have fun and that I missed her already. Oy. I was smitten.

The shop was busy enough to keep me from falling asleep or checking my phone every twelve seconds for a text I wasn't going to get while she was cramming as much training into the day as she could. Lunch with the kittens was quick. The house smelled of Tori's perfume with a hint of tobacco and it made me miss her even more, so I cut lunch short and returned to the shop a few minutes early.

Just before four she texted me a photo of taken in front of the pub, captioned "Zach & Ashley". It looked like every Canadian version of an Irish pub I'd ever seen, but the smiling, exhausted-looking couple standing in front of the heavy double, dark wood doors made me want to wander in and order a pint. The sign above their heads simply read *TUPPER'S*. I replied *Looks great! They look so happy! I hope you're having fun, too.*

A moment later her reply came up. *I am, but I wish you were here, too. It's a pub like any other, but the menu is amazing and their microbrew is to die for. Break's over. Back at it. Give my love to the kittens. xoxo*

Will do. Maybe a road trip to Ottawa is in our future. xoxo. Maybe, but as inviting as Zach and Ashley may be, Ottawa wasn't my first choice for a road trip with Tori. I'd rather go to Buffalo. I didn't *want* to go to Buffalo, but the odds of running into Michelle and her dentist in Buffalo were slim to none. God, I hope Mish wasn't bringing him with her at the end of the month. It didn't sound like she was, but with her, who knows?

The day cooled off a bit, or maybe I was becoming numb to the heat and humidity, but either way, I was up for a plate of The Nigerian Prince's daily special. I closed up the shop right on time and started off east toward the restaurant. Dark clouds on the west horizon hinted at the storm the weather app predicted and I welcomed the scrubbing the 'hood would get from a day or two of rain.

A familiar face weaved in and out of the foot traffic on the sidewalk. Flat Earth Robin was coming right at me. "Shit!" I ducked into McDonald's and waited for him to pass by, but he turned and came into the restaurant. Keeping my head down and my back to him, I pivoted slowly in time with his shuffle to the self-order kiosk. I worried that he'd recognize my green Long & Lat golf shirt, but he appeared to be oblivious to anything but placing his order. While he squinted at the big screen and earnestly tapped in his selection, I left and continued my mission to The Nigerian Prince.

Because it was Monday it was free salad night and the restaurant was packed. This shouldn't have been a surprise to me, but my brain was so occupied with happy thoughts about Tori that even facts that were welded to my memory were missed. I placed a take-out order with young David, exchanging hugs with Lydia and Aba when they each darted out from the back while I was waiting.

Aba needlessly wiped his hands on his immaculate apron and pulled me aside. "I will close your dating profile immediately, brother."

"That's okay, Ab. There's no rush."

"No *rush*? She is funny, beautiful, wise, and smarter than the two of us together. If you don't marry her immediately I will—"

"You'll what? Marry her yourself? Lydia might object. And if she divorces *you*, I'll marry *her*."

"Don't even joke about divorce! I was going to say... hell, I don't know what I was going to say."

"Everything you just said about her is true. Tori is all of that and more."

"But?"

"But I still haven't settled things with Michelle."

"Michelle is gone. Move on, with Tori. The house will sort itself out eventually, but your heart needs settling now. Even when you and Michelle were good I *never* saw you look at her the way you look at Tori. You've been more relaxed than ever since Michelle deserted you, but on Saturday you were relaxed *and* alive. So was Tori. Even when you couldn't see her she had eyes for no one but you."

I didn't have a clue what to say. I wanted Aba to be right, but... "Her condo is ready. She's moving out."

"So? Where is her condo?"

"Two blocks from here."

"Oh my God! Two whole blocks? That settles it. Dump her cute ass now. There's no way your feelings for each other could survive that kind of distance."

"You're such a sarcastic asshole."

"And you're an idiot in love, my Brother. Don't lose her because you're afraid to lose her."

He was right, of course. "Fine. I'll have hope, only to keep you from over-spicing my beef just to see me cry."

"I would *never* do that."

"Raptors celebratory party, 2019."

"Okay. *Once*. You just weren't showing the emotion such a momentous occasion deserved."

"Point made. I'll be all emotion now. Do you need me to Skype you when I'm ready to propose?"

"Maybe. Just don't propose at the airport in a hotel room surrounded by her friends."

"Yeah...*no*."

Lydia arrived with my order. "Abdalla, leave poor Max's love life alone."

Aba looked offended. "I *wasn't*."

"Yes, you were. I didn't have to hear a word you said because Max's expressions said it all. Victoria is lovely, and if she's the right one, then you have to trust Max to figure that out for himself."

I nodded and smiled idiotically. "Thank you, Lydia."

"You're welcome. Now, if you don't marry her I'll divorce Aba and marry her myself." She kissed me on the cheek, turned, and left the two of us gaping.

David, whose position at the reception desk forced him to hear every word, laughed. "Burned by the Boss. Mom – one. Dad – *zee-ro*."

Aba huffed, but we both knew his son was right.

"I'd better let you get back to the kitchen before you get too backed up."

"Agreed. Bring her by for dinner when she gets back. I promise to behave."

"I know you too well to hold you to that promise, Brother, but I also know you won't say anything I'm not already thinking."

"Truth."

"Truth. You go cook, I'll go eat. I'll ask her what night is good and will make a reservation."

"Of course. Check with her. Now get home before the rain starts. It's supposed to be a wet week."

o0o

The Kenyan *kachumbari* salad and *karanga* beef stew with rice blew my mind and my taste buds. I knew exactly what I was going to order when we went back for our formal dining experience.

When I got home and went to let the kittens out I could see a puddle of urine in the middle of the newspaper on their floor. "All right you brats. Who's ignoring the litter boxes? There's three of them—count 'em, *three*—so what's up?" They all clamoured at the still-closed door as if nothing was amiss. The reason for the mess could be any number of things. I opened the door to let them burst out, then I ducked back in and closed it again.

I knelt next to the little puddle and examined it for crystals and blood. I wouldn't necessarily see the blood as separate from the urine, but it would affect the colour, turning yellow to orange. But the urine was a pale yellow and crystal-free. Another possibility is that one of my little charges was just angry that I cut lunch short and was late getting home. To find out who that was I'd have to view the video footage of the room.

The camera still hung on the nail on the far wall, facing the door. Ignoring the wails of despair in the other room, I opened the camera's app on my phone. A red alert banner popped up immediately *CHARGE CAMERA BATTERY*. Damn. I laid the camera on the shelf top of the bottom half of the door, looked in the litter boxes to make sure I hadn't forgotten to change them, then left the room, closing the door. Dinner would have to wait a few minutes.

I fetched the camera's wall plug charger from the Drawer of Miscellany in the kitchen, snatched the roll of paper towel off its upright holder, and returned to the kitten room. I plugged the camera into the charger and plugged the charger into the wall plug next to the door. I aimed the camera at the mess, checked that its red charging light was flashing, then gathered up the wet newspaper and wiped the plastic beneath it. While I was in there I checked each of their beds for bodily fluids or solids. They were all clean.

The room all settled, it was dinnertime.

The rain didn't start with the flash of lightning and crack of thunder I expected but rather with a few drops here and there while I was at the sink cleaning up. By the time I was wiping off the counter and stowing the scrub-brush, the rain was a steady, unassuming wetness. I opened the inner door to see if a cool breeze would come in through the screen door but the air was still thick and muggy.

Six full bellies retired to the couch, from where I sent Tori a quick *Miss you. xo* text. The rain continued outside, but none of us gave a whit. The kittens were content playing or cuddling, and I doodled little border details for the dessert map while an episode of Toronto-filmed *Suits* played in the background.

The conversation with Aba and Lydia was 'sticking in my craw', as my grandfather used to say. Tori was terrific and I was happier than I'd been in a helluva long time, but—there's always a 'but'—were our lives actually compatible? How long until the cuteness of evenings home with kittens wore off for her? She's amazing at her job, so when does Mitch start hiring her out coast-to-coast? Will Map Dude and the House of Kittens be a home to return to, or an anchor to shake? Is there a dentist in *her* past, lurking, waiting to pounce? Or a lawyer, or a pub owner?

The thoughts spun like that until I'd had enough and put in The Last Jedi disk. It never failed to draw me in and keep me riveted and I was able to let the goofy ideas float off... at least until her text snapped me out of it.

Done. OMG. What a long effing day. We start again @ 8 AM, so I'm bed-bound, but if you want to call I can chat for a bit.

Poor kid. I checked the time—11 PM. I missed her, but hardly needed to rob her of sleep. *You need sleep. Get it. Talk tomorrow. Miss you much. Xo.* That sent,

I retired the kittens and went to bed, alone for the first time in nearly two weeks. Sleep didn't come quickly so I opened the Kindle app on my iPad and read Philip Pullman's *The Book of Dust: The Secret Commonwealth*, the second book in the sequel to his trilogy that included *The Golden Compass*. It was a wonderful story but, as expected, I started to doze off after about twenty minutes. The light was out and I was asleep five minutes later.

Chapter 15

I SCREWED UP. I woke to a text from Tori. *I'm sorry we didn't get to chat last night. Turns out I was up for a while. Can I call you at lunch?*

Oops. I'm guessing I missed a cue. I sucked at catching cues. Michelle was always throwing subtle hints around like fairy dust at Disneyland, but to me, they were just sparkles, and so I had no end of trouble. I didn't think Tori was like that. I thought she was more straightforward. I went back and read her text from last night. Yup. That was pretty straightforward. I screwed up. I didn't want to apologize by text because it was a lousy medium with very few shades of grey. I would have preferred to talk to her, on the phone at least, but preferably by video chat of one sort or another. Unfortunately, I was going to have to reach out by text in order to set up the live conversation. As I fixed breakfast for the six of us I ran text ideas through my head and even scribbled a couple of notes on the pad magneted to the fridge door. After much consultation with the kittens, Calliope and I came up with a note that we hoped would do the trick.

I'm sorry I didn't call. I'm an idiot. I didn't want to look like I took your long hard day for granted, just to satisfy my need to hear your voice. I miss you so much that I didn't think that maybe you needed to hear mine, too. Yes, please call this idiot at lunch. Or whenever you can. All texts, calls, or messages by passenger pigeons are welcome and much needed. The house was too quiet and lonely without you. I look forward to you coming home. xo

Not very short, not excessively sweet, and just shy of falling on my knees and telling her how much I loved her without actually using the 'L' word. Then again, maybe she was waiting to hear me tell her I loved her before she said it to me, kind of like I was waiting for her to say it first. Aba had said to be careful not to lose her because I was too worried about losing her, and I was. Afraid, that is. But I also had to protect myself, protect my heart. I'd fallen deeply for her and so close on the heels of Michelle's betrayal that I was afraid to invest so much into a person I'd really just met. Like I said in my text, I'm an idiot.

My phone vibrated with a return text. *I'll call when I get a chance. You're sweet. I miss you with all 2000 body parts.* A second message buzzed in while I read that one and a duck-faced, kiss-blowing selfie popped up. On her, it looked cute, but I knew I couldn't pull off the same look so I picked up Kerouac and took a selfie of the two of us, him looking everywhere but at the camera, and me trying to blow her a kiss without looking like a duck. I hope the kitten added the necessary cuteness that my contorted beard-surrounded lips lacked. I looked like the idiot I was in the photo, but sent it anyway, crossing my fingers that she saw the humour in my attempt.

Her reply was simple but to the point. *LOL. xoxoxoxo*

oOo

The rain was a dull, relentless, warm wet thud. If Tori were here it might have been romantic to go for a walk in it, but the walk to work by myself was totally unromantic. The morning shift was slow, with only two separate customers bursting in from the downpour, each shaking their umbrellas outside the door before entering. Each knew exactly what they wanted—one an atlas for a ten-year-old and the other a map of the Kawarthas Lake District—and were gone as quickly as they came.

But lunch was a complete pick-up. Tori called just as I was lifting Kerouac up onto the island, so I tried to juggle chatting and feeding. "Hey, Sexy."

"Hey, Lover Boy."

It was a short chat between mouthfuls of lunch by both of us. She was working hard, couldn't wait to get back to Toronto, and loved having Zach and Ashley in her training sessions because even though there was a young waiter and an older second cook who rolled their eyes a lot and hinted early on they would rather be anywhere but there, with their bosses present, Tori didn't have to even say a word to keep them in line. It was a good thing, too, because as an outside contractor, she had absolutely no authority, unlike being a member of the management team when she was training Montgomery's staff.

Someone in the background of her call shouted her name.

She sighed. "Break's over, Map Man. I'll give you a call when I'm done tonight. I miss you."

"Sounds great. I miss you, too. Have a good rest of the day."

"Will do. Bye." She made a kissing sound so I did, too, and hoped I wasn't just hearing interference on the call. God, we sounded like lovesick morons.

I was five minutes late getting back to the shop and actually had a customer waiting, standing in the rain under a big golf umbrella. Dirk was a regular. A fifty-ish former Army Master Corporal, he was six-one, at least two-hundred-and-fifty pounds, and dwarfed me when we stood side-by-side.

"Max, you're smiling." I opened the shop and ushered him in. "What the hell are you smiling about in this shit weather? You're in love, aren't you?"

"I was just wondering what tale you were going to regale me with today."

"So you're *not* in love?"

"No. I *am* in love, but that's not why I'm smiling. Well, it's not the *entire* reason."

"Okay. I'd say love is for suckers, but my wife would kick my ass."

"And so she should. What brings you out in this ugly-ass weather? Not my love life, I hope."

"Germany."

"You're going there?"

"Going *back*. The last time I was there I was in the Service, back when the Berlin Wall still stood. 86, I think."

"I hear things have changed a little since then."

"Just a little. The biggest change is that I sobered up. We spent the whole time in East Berlin completely shit-faced, touring around in our civvies, raising hell. Got fined, got arrested, got the boots taken to us when they found out we were military, and had to cash almost two grand in Traveller's Checks to pay another fine just to get out of jail and tossed back to West Berlin. But Cindy wants to go. Part of a five-country road trip. I have maps of the other four but never thought I'd need one for Germany."

"You've got two choices." I walked over to my international map wall and he followed. "They're both pretty much the same price and have the same features, except that the Borch one is water-repellant and has a write-on, wipe-off surface."

"Perfect! Just like the ones we used in the service."

I handed him the map. "Anything else you need while you're here? Are your other four maps Write-on/Write-off?"

"No. Good point. Let's load up. Italy, France, Austria, and Switzerland." I pulled the other four maps he needed and handed them over. He turned them over and checked the prices. "Shit! These are a great deal. I'd better get two more. One of Southern Ontario and one of the whole province. We're off to the Bruce Peninsula this weekend and driving to Kapuskasing for a wedding in October. I never trust electronics 100%. "

"Done." I picked out those maps and walked them up to the counter. I'd been to Europe a couple of times when I was younger and would love to go back now. "What are you looking forward to the most about Europe? Venice? Paris? The Mozart Museum?"

"Being able to go into East Berlin without getting my ass thrown in jail."

"Haha. I'm sure Cindy will appreciate that. I'm guessing *she* has never been arrested in East Berlin."

"Not East Berlin, but I think she had some trouble near the Finnish-Russian border on a school trip."

Wow! "She sounds badass!"

"It's why I married her." He picked up a copy of the dog park map on the counter. "This is a great idea! I definitely need one of these." He opened it, saw what he liked, I guess, and added it to the pile of maps I was ringing in. "In Germany, Mandy really wants to see Hitler's Eagle's Nest, near Berchtesgaden in Bavaria."

"That's *seriously* badass. I was near there as a teen, but we didn't get to the mountain top."

"It'll be interesting. Part of history."

"True. I just wished the Nazis had stayed in history."

"I hear you, brother. I have to fight the urge to punch anyone wearing a Swastika. At least it's outlawed in Germany, so I should be okay."

"Yeah, I'm pretty sure punching Nazis will get you thrown in jail even in Germany."

Dirk's phone buzzed. He checked his watch. "Speaking of the Missus. It's movie date night and we're seeing the latest *Mission: Impossible* movie."

"Nice. What's this? Number seven? Number ten?"

"Not a clue. I just know that Tom's in his sixties and I hope I'm in that kind of shape when I'm his age."

"Ha! I'd be happy to be in that shape *now*." Then maybe I could go for a run with Tori.

"I hear you, Max, I hear you. Gotta run." He retrieved his umbrella and was off with all seven maps wrapped up in a small *Long & Lat* cloth bag.

I took a picture of the deluge beyond the front window display and texted it to Tori. *Even the weather is miserable that you're away. ;)* I wanted to again say I missed her but didn't want to appear too maudlin or needy. Hell, she was only gone until tomorrow night. It's not like she's away for a week or, God forbid, a month. I was a little crazy when Mish first left, but whether we knew it at the time or not, we were at the end of the relationship, not the beginning of it. What I missed then was simply another human voice in the house, though not specifically *her* voice. It didn't take long to adapt, especially since Calliope insisted on meowing at me like we understood each other completely. The other four were chatty, too, but the little Torby responded to questions, made statements and even sounded like she was asking me questions in return. If I needed actual human conversation I dropped by to see Kalani or her folks in the store or went to have coffee with Aba and Lydia. Thankfully I didn't have to rely on people like Flat Earth Robin to fulfill my need for human discourse.

Speaking of humans, I texted Rose to see how Joe was doing, apologizing for not doing it sooner. She texted back that he was fine, but bored with the plain food she had to feed him for a week. *I promise he'll be back up and 100% before the next potluck. If you want to win his friendship forever, drop by for a chat and bring him a small bottle of ginger ale. The doctor says it's okay for him to have, but I don't stock soft drinks, so he's SOL.*

Ginger Ale? Will do. How about I drop by after work? Tori is away until tomorrow night. I'd swing by the house on the way and feed the kittens, then go see Joe and Rose. I didn't need any more 'anger peeing' from the monsters.

Perfect! See you then.

Is ginger ale all you need?

Yes, thanks.

I texted back a thumbs-up, then turned my attention back to actually doing my job. I filled the half-dozen waiting online orders then took a close look at our online catalogue to see how to best incorporate Tori's ideas. Six orders in two days sucked. I took a picture of the cover of the dog park map, emailed it to my shop address, then logged on to the catalogue administration on the shop's computer, retrieved the email, downloaded the image, and added a brief but concise description of the map. I optimized the listing for search engines and saved the listing. In the next day or so I would restructure the catalogue so I could feature a map of my choice when it opened, and start featuring the local maps. Of the hundred copies I had printed, I had about seventy copies of the dog park map left, and maybe fifty of the *Runaway Grooms* wedding locations map, so I would be set for a while.

The store stayed quiet, which it never does when I'm on the computer, so I repeated the whole process with the second map. It sounded like a quick process, but when I added in the editing of the images and researching the best SEO keywords, uploading and refining the two listings took me right up to 4:45. A flash of lightning startled the crap out of me a split second after I hit 'PUBLISH CATALOGUE'.

"Holy shit!" I looked up from the keyboard at the street outside and the rain was a little heavier, the street a bit darker, but the world hadn't split open from an alien energy weapon attack. The thunder cracked and rolled through a blink or two later, but I was ready for it and enjoyed it for the deep music of nature it was.

Barely protected by my compact umbrella, I picked up a couple of two-litre bottles of ginger ale for Joe and a six-pack of cans of Coke for myself then splashed my way home to the furries. Their room was errant-urine-free so I didn't need to check the recording for misbehavior, though I did check that the camera was fully charged and still pointed at the target area. I half expected it to be on the floor or buried in a litter box, but it was right where it was supposed to be. I poured myself a strong, cold rye and Coke while the kids ate, and gave them all the time they needed. I wasn't going to be gone long, but I still didn't entirely trust them to roam free without getting into mischief while I was out, so they went back into their room when I finished my drink and changed out of my work clothes.

Rose answered the door with a smile and a hug. She was only sixty, but she was like our block mother. "Hi Max. Come on in. So Tori is away, is she? Think you'll survive?"

Joe met me in the hall and I handed him the ginger ales. "For you, sir."

"Thanks, Max. How much do I owe you?"

"My treat. I'm just glad you're feeling better."

"Thanks. Me, too. Let me stick these in the fridge and I'll be right back."

Rose wasn't giving up so easily. "So you're *not* surviving and you refuse to talk about it?"

"It's not so much a refusal to talk as having nothing to say, really."

She motioned me into the living room. Technically they were seniors, but there wasn't a doily in sight. There were incredible quilts on both the couch and the recliner chair, but Rose was a prize-winning quilter and had been since she was in her thirties, she said.

I continued. "She's back tomorrow night. I suppose I miss her more than I expected because we're in the first two weeks of the relationship and the shine hasn't worn off. Her condo repairs are all done and she'll be moving back there soon, but both she and Abdalla have assured me, separately, that it's no big deal and our relationship will be just fine." I heard the pfft-hiss of Joe opening one of the bottles.

"Either of you two want a ginger ale?"

"Sure, Joe," I replied back over my shoulder.

Rose leaned forward and twisted her torso a bit to aim her voice at the kitchen better. "Yes please, Honey." She turned back to me. "But you don't believe them?"

"Intellectually, I believe them. But Tori and I have such strong chemistry when we're in the same room together that when we aren't, her absence is a chasm. And I *know* I sound like a freaking lovesick puppy, but I've never felt love like this before. It's like a steel spring supporting my whole system, flexing and supporting, and humming in my heart like it just got plucked."

Joe returned with three glasses balanced like a professional waiter and handed two of them off to Rose and me. We thanked him and he sat on the couch, beside Rose. "There's nothing worse than a heart that's totally plucked, Max. That's what happened with Rose and me back in college. I swooned when she was near me and pined when she wasn't. I had serious separation anxiety."

Rose squeezed his hand. "Yes, but that didn't stop you from going to Banff for the summer."

"True, but that was my last summer in Banff. When I took that three-day train ride back from Alberta it was to come back to you."

"And to graduate."

"Well, yes. That, too. But I stayed, instead of going back to Banff like my boss wanted me to. Then my grandfather died. Two months later, Dad died. I was messed up and I took it out on you by breaking up with you."

"You did."

"And I will apologize for that cruelty for the rest of my life, Rose. I never stopped loving you, but I wasn't too fond of myself for a while."

"Me, neither. But that was forty years ago, and we've moved past that. We're supposed to be encouraging young Max, not telling him what got screwed up in *our* relationship. Besides, I think Max knows our story only too well from potlucks. What he probably wants to know is how they can avoid those same mistakes and get to sixty and beyond still head-over-heels in love with each other.

Max?"

"Not really. I'm not thinking that far ahead. One day at a time, at least until we've been together for a month or two. I have no idea if it's love or lust after less than two weeks."

"Bullshit." Joe and I both stared at Rose. "Yes, I said 'bullshit'. I watched you and Tori. When she wasn't looking you weren't staring at her ass or her breasts, you were watching for a glimpse of her smile, or a flash of affection from her eyes. That's not lust. Or rather, not *just* lust."

"She's right, kid. Your heart is in the game whether you know it or not. Maybe it'll last, maybe it won't, but you two are clicking on more levels than the naked ones."

"Yeah, but there are a *lot* of naked ones."

Rose held her hand up to silence me. "TMI, Max. TMI. And none of our business. Or anyone else's but the two of you."

"Sorry."

"So what's bugging you?"

"Besides the fear that she'll get bored and leave me, like Mish did? Just after college, I was in a relationship that got hot and heavy really fast, like on the first date. So fast that her enthusiasm scared the hell out of me. We didn't have much in common outside the bedroom, on *any* level, so I suggested that we back off of the sex for a bit and see how we do. We had coffee one more time and that was it. It turns out that sex was all she wanted."

"Wow. *You* stopped the sex?" Joe was shocked. "You must have had serious doubts about the relationship. But you don't have to worry about that with Tori. I saw the looks she gave you, too. It wasn't just heat, it was genuine affection, which many people take for granted or don't give enough credit to. The two of you strained to hear what the other was saying, completely caught up in the conversation. You are *interested* in each other. Maybe even fascinated."

"That's what Aba said, about looks. She *does* fascinate me. In so many ways."

"There you go. Trust your heart, not your fears."

"Like Joe said, Max. Make sure you show her how you feel. You've already given her a dozen roses, so do a bunch of little things for her. A gift basket for her condo, maybe. A house rewarming gift. It doesn't have to be a big gesture like proposing to her at the airport." She smiled with mock innocence.

"Yeah, yeah. That's almost exactly what Aba said. I'm never going to live that down, am I?"

"Nope." Joe raised his glass to punctuate his promise.

"Not a chance. At least, not until you propose to Tori—*if* you propose to Tori—because it would be uncool teasing you about the last one when you're trying to build a future with the new one."

"Proposing is a long way off. I have to get the house stuff all figured out with Michelle, and I don't think she's going to make it easy. Did I tell you she's coming to visit at the end of the month?"

Rose slowly put her glass on a coaster on the coffee table. "Oh, really? Did she say why? I liked her, Max. She was quiet but funny and sweet if a bit shy sometimes, but after what she did to you, my opinion of her is tainted. I don't trust her motives. You're right to wait to get serious with Tori until you settle the house. Michelle might not react well if she finds out Tori has been sleeping in her bed."

"*Might* not? I think she'll snap, even though she left me for the dentist. I hate all this unnecessary emotional turmoil. It grinds up my gut and is a waste of energy."

"Then get a lawyer. Joe's friend Mark is a family lawyer. He's about to retire, but he's a great source of advice."

"Thanks, but I have a lawyer. I'll meet quietly with him but I'm going to see what Michelle has to say, face-to-face, and take my cue from her. I hardly think she's coming back to me. At least I hope to God she isn't. *That* would make a real mess."

"You wouldn't take her back?"

"I might have, Joe, two or three weeks ago, but not now. It's not so much because of Tori, specifically, but because being with Tori has shown me what my relationship with Michelle was missing and how it had crumbled. No, we're done. Whether Tori and I work out or not, Michelle is in my past, except for the house."

"Good. Speaking of the house, you have five little ones back there that need your love and attention. You've only got a week left with them. I'm really going to miss them at the potlucks. I'm sure the next batch will be just as lovely, but I've grown attached to these ones, especially Ginsburg."

"I know. Me, too, Rose. For me, it's Kerouac and Calliope. I love them all, but those two have climbed right up into my heart."

"Then get home to them. Cuddle them all."

"Will do. Thanks for the encouragement. The situation is whacked, but it will get solved eventually."

"It will. And Joe and I are here if you need to vent."

o0o

I let the kittens out of their room and threw a couple of frozen burgers on the grill in the rain. I put aside the map work for the evening and cuddled and played with the little ones while *The Secret Life of Pets* streamed in the background, again. Just before nine Tori called and I put it on speaker so I could keep wrestling with the kittens and they could hear her voice. At first, they were confused and ran around looking for her, but when she didn't appear they tuned her out and returned to attacking the feathery mouse thing on the end of the string and stick I controlled.

"Another long day?"

"Very. I don't think I've ever crammed so much training into such a short time. I'll be leaving the modules here with Zach so someone can do refreshers and follow-ups, but overall they have a good team with some solid experience."

"That'll make a huge difference in that tough first year. So, another half-day left?" Get back here, hint hint.

"Yeah. Maybe a few hours more. An early start tomorrow to finish it all up by five at the latest. My flight is at 6:30 and I should be home by 8:30, I hope."

"Do you want me to meet you at the airport?"

"*What?* No, I'll be fine, thanks. I'll take a cab on Mitch's dime. But it's sweet of you to offer."

It was sweet, but why was she so shocked when I made the offer? "Of course. Shall I pick up a couple of steaks? I'm sure you'll be starved. Will they even serve food on a flight that short?"

"Snacks only. And maybe one quick pass of the drink cart if we're lucky."

"There's beer here if you don't want to fork over a kidney for one of theirs."

"Sounds lovely. The beer, that is, not the forking over of a kidney."

"I figured that."

"The steaks are a great idea, too."

I put a reminder in my phone to get steaks after work. "How early do you have to go in on Thursday?"

"Mitch hinted that I could sleep in, but he wasn't specific. I'll text him and ask, just so I don't stay up *too* late tomorrow night."

I affected my best Southern gentleman accent. "Why, Miss Victoria, whatever do you mean? What on earth would keep you up to a late hour?"

She replied in kind. "What I meant, Mister Maxwell, sir, is that delighting in a repast of delicious steak might take one through the entire evening and well into the wee hours. One does not rush good meat."

I laughed. "No, Miss Victoria, they most certainly do not." Calliope climbed up on my lap and swiped at the phone. "Calliope says hello. She recognizes your voice and has figured out that you're trapped in the glowing thing on my lap."

"Glowing thing on your lap? That's a euphemism I haven't heard before. Don't let that cute little Torby kitty hurt that glowing thing before I get home." Ah, there it was again. The 'H' word.

"Not a chance."

We chatted for another fifteen minutes about her day, Joe's recovery, and Dirk's past adventures in divided Germany. When we finally hung up it was because she was dozing off. Maybe once the kittens were returned to the adoption centre we could take a weekend off and get away to Niagara-on-the Lake or the Stratford Festival. Just *away*. The two of us.

Knowing that Tori would be back soon and still being warm and fuzzy all over from our conversation and her casual use of the 'H' word, I slept like a rock and was up so early the kittens were still dozy and I was able to put in half-an-hour of detailing on the shipwreck map before work.

o0o

Work at the shop was easy and Tori said she'd be busy training almost until her flight left, so I didn't have to continuously check my phone for messages. She didn't call or text during lunch so I assumed they were busy pushing through and probably eating in the classroom or wherever they were training.

I trudged home in the rain for lunch. The Gang of Five were old enough now that they could go seven hours without food, but they'd be off to forever homes in five days so I wanted to steal what time I could with them.

The wind picked up and the rain went horizontal, so I took a change of clothes back to the shop with me. If the deluge continued, I'd wear my rainsuit tomorrow. Just after three o'clock, I heard sirens and a police cruiser drive past, going east on Bloor. A moment later an ambulance drove by. Neither was going particularly fast and when I looked out the window in the direction they'd gone I could see the reflections of their flashing lights on the reflective surfaces between them and me. They appeared to be at that damned intersection outside Kalani's store.

Even in the rain people were curious and a few walked past, craning their necks and holding up their phones under the cover of their umbrellas. Since I had zero medical experience and wasn't about to photograph someone else's misery, I stayed inside and dry, doing the weekly dusting and checking the online catalogue for the two new map listings, making sure they came up properly and were linked to the shopping cart. I wasn't happy with the image I'd posted of the dog park map so I took a copy closer to the front window where the light was better and snapped a fresh shot. On closer inspection, it had a hint of red and blue from the emergency vehicle lights, but it was clear and crisp and you could only see the colours if you knew to look for them.

I was posting the new image when a siren started up again and moved away.

At least the siren was on and they weren't calling the coroner for whoever was hit. I could still see the reflections of alternating red and blue lights so the police were likely still investigating and taking witness statements. Eastbound traffic backed up, moving at a crawl when it moved at all.

Twenty minutes later the flashing lights were gone and traffic sped up enough to be considered normal. Now that the 'excitement' was over, a couple of customers came in, hung out for a few minutes, then went, maps in hand. I sent Leona a text asking her opinion on the two new listings, then spent the final hour sorting bills, restocking displays, and up on the stepladder moving the extra globes around so they went from smallest to biggest. Sometimes they were arranged by color or manufacturer, but this week it would be size. The reminder to pick up steaks popped up on my phone just as I was grabbing my umbrella.

The rain went on and on, so the walk to Sobey's was a damp one, despite the umbrella. I picked up two nice rib eyes, pre-made mashed sweet potatoes, a California mix of frozen veggies, and ducked in and out of the liquor store for a nice Chilean Shiraz.

The kittens were unusually subdued when I finally wandered in, wet from the chest down, and no one had made a mess outside of their litter boxes.

A text vibrated my pocket as I was setting the raptors-in-training loose. It was from Leona: *Looks great!*

Thanks! I hate the "thx" reply. It's just damned lazy. What's so hard about another three letters? Anyway, I changed into dry clothes and fed my charges.

7:30 came and went with no message from Tori. I texted her. *All good? Did you make your flight? How was your day?*

I whipped up a pair of grilled cheese sandwiches to get me through to the steaks after 8:30. The rain had cooled the upper half of the house enough that I led the bouncy little parade of love upstairs and started the inking of the shipwreck map. Ten minutes in I was twitching to hear from Tori. I Googled flight times from Ottawa to Toronto and found no delays. There was no way to check to see if she was actually on any of the flights, though. I went back to work, using the intense concentration required for the finely detailed ink work to distract me.

I finally took a break and had to check both my watch and my phone to confirm that it really was 9:45. I looked at the kittens curled up on the loveseat. "Where is she? Do you guys know why she's late?" My gut flip-flopped with the unwanted thought that maybe she'd met someone in Ottawa and changed her mind about us. I also knew that phone batteries die, so not only couldn't she call me, but she couldn't look up my number on her phone until it was charged at least a little. Or maybe Ottawa was as rainy as Toronto and she'd dropped her phone into a puddle. No, that was something *I* would do.

I wanted to give her the benefit of the doubt but...

Chapter 16

I PUT THE KITTENS to bed, changed into old jeans, a t-shirt, and sports sandals, fetched the umbrella, and went for a walk. No, it wasn't some random, I'm-in-a-mood-and-need-to-clear-my-head walk like Michelle used to do. I had a purpose. I was a lot worried about Tori and a little concerned about our relationship, and that naturally took me out into the rain and dark for a four-block stroll to her condo. I couldn't remember what her unit number was, but I knew which balcony was hers. If I saw the light on then I'd know she was home but not talking to me. That was okay because we could always sit down and discuss whatever she was angry about. But if she wasn't home, then something else was wrong. Or she was staying somewhere else. If she was mad about something I doubt she'd have returned to the basement suite.

From across the street, I could see by lights behind the closed vertical blinds at the balcony door that someone was home. A tall figure walked between a lamp and the blinds. Tori was 'home' and she wasn't alone. I wanted to puke.

I slumped home, knocked back a shot of bourbon, had a long hot shower, turned my phone off and went to bed. My mind spun, but the bourbon and shower did their jobs and I tripped face-first into a restless sleep.

o0o

The alarm went off exactly when it was supposed to. I jerked awake, thinking it was the phone ringing, but it wasn't. There were no messages, either. Nothing. I checked the phone settings to make sure it wasn't on Airplane Mode, and that it had a couple of bars to prove it would receive a call if such a thing happened. I had a lot of wet clothes, which I grabbed from the shower curtain rod where they were hanging, added them to the armful of dirty socks and underwear I scooped up from the closet floor, and took it all down to the stacked washer/dryer in the tiny room off the kitchen. I was numb. Ghosted in less than ten days. Just tossed aside. I really hadn't thought she was the type.

The rain poured down like it was waiting to drown me, not realizing that I was already drowning in self-pity. I shuffled to the kitten room and let my babies out. I cleaned their litter boxes while they climbed all over me and mewed expressively. It was as if they could sense my malaise and were trying to crush it with love. Oddly enough, by the time I was done with the third litter box, their affections had pushed some sunlight into my mood. I fed them and myself, checked my phone again and again, for an explanation or anything, finally plugging it into the charger on the foyer table.

My get-out-the-door alarm eventually went off and it was time to get to work. The kittens away, the stove and lights turned off, the phone off the charger and into my pocket, the umbrella retrieved from where it was drying on the porch, and I was out of there, my heart only so much painful mush. I couldn't help but look up and down Ossington to see if I spotted Rage Grrl running along, her car driving up, or a cab dropping her off. Nope. Nada.

The rain seemed to have crushed the spirit of the whole of Bloorcourt. Even car headlights were listless, illuminating nothing in the daylight, but still on as if to say "Yup, we're here, just doing what we were designed to do. Oh well. Ho hum." The few other pedestrians slogged along, beaten down.

This was all ridiculous. It had been raining all of four days and it was like we hadn't seen sunshine in months. This was Toronto, not Vancouver! The rain would leave as quickly as it came and the sun and heat would be back! Tori might not be, but the sun would be. No one waited at the shop with mad urgent map needs, so I unlocked the place, turned everything on, pulled up a chair behind the cash counter, and opened up the Kindle app on my phone. I didn't have the energy to do anything creative, so I read.

Lunchtime rolled around but I wasn't up for the walk home. Truth be told, I wasn't really that hungry and was pretty sure that anything that went in would come back up. I sent a quick text to Tori because if nothing else happened, I wanted closure. Not even an explanation, just to see her face when she said we were done. *We need to talk. Coffee?*

My phone remained silent for forty minutes before it buzzed. *Please don't contact this number again. You are being blocked.* Shit. I guess coffee was out of the question. Likewise with closure. Just to be sure, though, I double-checked the number. It wouldn't be the first time I'd texted a wrong number.

Nope. The number was good, even if her message sucked.

Five-oh-five stumbled up and I was seriously done in. I had no energy to cook, sure as hell didn't have the energy to get a lecture from Aba about what I did or didn't do wrong with Tori, and definitely couldn't face laughter and music at the pub, so I ordered pizza, garlic toast, salad, and three dips through the app on my phone and trudged home.

Soaking wet and not giving a good goddamn, I let the fur-and-claw set out of Shawshank and flopped on the floor just inside the door. They were all over me, despite the puddle of rain around me. Eventually, their hunger won over their love and all five bounced into the kitchen and set up a meow-and-wail session for dinner, lunch, or whatever I was going to feed them since I'd been absent at midday.

They followed me when I ignored them, stripped down, and marched upstairs to towel off and put on clean, dry sweatpants and a t-shirt. I led them back downstairs, although Zwerling and Kerouac tried to trip me on the stairs and kill me. In the kitchen, I hoisted Tuxedo Boy up on the island, fed them all, tossed the rib eyes in the freezer, and poured myself a double rye and Coke. The doorbell rang just as I was savouring the first cold sip. Since all of the kittens were still eating, I scooped up Kerouac and brought him with me. I didn't need him jumping down and getting hurt or stealing food.

It was the Pizza Pizza delivery dude.

"Good evening, sir."

"Hi. Gimme a second to get rid of this wiggly one and grab my wallet."

"Of course, sir."

I put Kerouac in the kitten room, got my wallet off the hall table, stepped out on the porch with him, and took out my debit card. Pizza Dude handed me the portable debit machine—I gotta say I love technology, especially this pay-at-the-door shit—and I settled up, adding a huge tip because he came out in the rain and I didn't have to.

"Thank you, sir." He handed me the box and bag and bolted back to his Corolla.

I opened the door carefully, which was a good thing because Ginsberg was right there, looking for a gap big enough to squeeze through. I tapped him back with my foot and ducked back inside. When I released Kerouac he bolted straight for the kitchen, but I was hot on his heels and grabbed him before he could raid Calliope's half-full or half-empty bowl. I plunked him back on the island at his own dish, and put my food over on the stove, out of his reach. All of this kept me occupied, my brain semi-busy.

I waited until they were all finished before I doled pizza, salad, and bread onto one of my biggest dinner plates and took it to the living room. Holding the food up out of reach in one hand while the kittens scrambled up on the couch, I turned on the big screen and called up Netflix. I wasn't in the mood for funny or romantic, so I settled on the Netflix version of *The Punisher*. It was just the level of darkness I needed to distract me.

I sat, ate, fought off the feline food raiders, and watched Frank Castle take it to the bad guys.

o0o

Friday. Yippee. Since I wasn't expecting to ever hear from Tori again, I turned my phone off as soon as I was out the door to work. The rain was sporadic now, with less serious intent to soak me, as if it had finally figured out I was already beaten down and blue so it really couldn't do much more than women already had. The sun wasn't out, but people were still buying maps before the weekend and three customers each strolled on in.

I loved it when their faces lit up when I asked each of them what they needed their maps for. One was visiting her great-grandparents down near Windsor, one was driving to Boston for a week to see long-lost cousins and watch the Blue Jays beat up the Red Sox at Fenway Park, and the third one was taking her fiancé hiking up near Tobermory on Georgian Bay, three-and-a-half hours north of Toronto. They all sounded like terrific trips and just hearing about them cheered me up, a little bit.

After the last of the three left, I locked up and went home to get kitty love and finish the pizza from the night before. I spent half an hour just watching the five of them bounce around the living room, chasing each other in and out of their boxes.

Back at work the shop actually got busy. I barely had time to restock and tidy between customers let alone mope and whine to myself about the heartbreak of a ten-day relationship going down the toilet.

The flow of customers was so steady that I ended up staying open until 7:00. I didn't mind, really. I had no one to go home to, no plans to go out and about, and the Fabulous Five would be fine for the extra two hours.

The rain was done and puddles were already vanishing as the summer heat reestablished its dominance. I looked forward to dinner. The pizza was finished and I had two luscious rib eyes waiting, one for tonight and one for tomorrow. It was a non-pot-luck weekend so I had my time all to myself.

What Tori did to me hurt, but it was hardly worse than what Michelle did after six years. I'd recover. I lied and told myself it was no big deal. I even strolled up my front walk and onto the porch, whistling *If I Only Had a Brain*, my go-to song for a mindless upbeat mood. Inside the house I was greeted by the quintuplet harmonizing love and welcome... and a little puddle of piss. Someone wasn't happy with the extra two hours after all.

"I have only a couple days left with you sweeties, so let's see if we can't figure out who is 'mispeehaving' and try to change their behaviour, or mine, if that's what it takes." I let them out, cleaned up the tiny puddle, fed them, and retired to the couch with my iPad. I opened the surveillance camera app, but because I hadn't checked it since I recharged and relocated it, I had one long file to go through. Fortunately, there was a fast-forward button and a tracking time stamp.

I sat back, propped the iPad on my lap, and sped through two days of kittens playing, kittens sleeping, me cleaning litter boxes... and Michelle walking into the frame to sit down on the floor in the middle of the kitten room.

"What the *fuck?!*" In the present, the kittens scrambled for cover. I didn't have to squint at the screen or zoom in or anything. It was Michelle. The time stamp was Wednesday afternoon at 2:15. I was at the store and she knew that. I rewound the recording until I saw myself depositing the kittens into the room. I let it play at normal speed, turning up the sound.

"She'll be home tonight, kids. See you in a few hours. Stay out of trouble."

I watched myself leave the room, scooting the little ones back with my bare foot. The door latched shut and a moment later I heard myself off-camera go out the front door and close and lock it behind me. On the far left of the ultra-wide angle view the kittens meowed at the closed door for about thirty seconds, then they split up to do their own things.

Exactly twenty minutes later I could hear a key in the front door. Of course, Michelle still had her key. Technically it was still half her house.

"Hello, my Beauties! Mama is home! Oh my God, you've all grown so much!" Four of the kittens all charged the door, which then opened and Michelle entered to sit on the floor. Her hair was bedraggled and her t-shirt was rain-soaked. But she looked terrific. "Hello! Hello! Hello! Kerouac, it's *me!*"

I could see Kerouac on the bottom level of the big cat tree, staring at Michelle, looking a little pissed off. Good for you, buddy. Don't let her just walk back in and start up where she left off!

It took a couple of moments, but eventually, he hopped down and sauntered over to sniff her hand and then climbed into her lap. She rubbed the top of his head vigorously and that's when I saw the big engagement ring. Damn.

"I missed all of you *so* much. I'm only in town for a few hours. I have to pick up the rest of my stuff and drop off a letter to your papa."

A letter? She couldn't have just mailed it? But I'm glad she was picking up her stuff.

"But first I need a shower. It was a long, gross drive and I need to look presentable for my lawyer."

Her lawyer?

She stood slowly, plucking off kittens who didn't want to let go, unlike Kerouac, who drifted back to the cat tree and Calliope who fled to her box. The other three tried to follow Mish out the door, but she was no rookie and kept them contained. "I'll get you some food after my shower. This place is nice and cool. That air conditioner makes a world of difference. We should have thought of that a lot sooner." Then she was gone, upstairs to shower, I assumed.

Stunned as hell, I just watched the kittens lounge around for twenty minutes before Michelle reappeared wearing just a towel, fresh from the shower. She giggled as the little ones attacked her toes, and then she bent down and freshened their water dishes from the pitcher I kept on the kitchen counter. I could clearly see her in the frame when I heard a key in the front door. I was completely confused.

Michelle turned to the sound. The front door opened and Michelle laughed lightly. "Oh. Hello. Can I help you?"

"Hello... Michelle. It's nice to finally meet you." *Tori?* The time stamp on the recording only said 2:52. Tori was still in Ottawa, training. Her flight wasn't until 6:30.

"Hello. And you are...?"

"Max's girlfriend, Tori."

"His girlfriend? Oh, this *is* awkward, because I'm his fiancée. See. I even have the ring to prove it. Didn't he tell you? He proposed to me just before I flew back to Ottawa."

Yes I did, but she turned me down!

"He said you laughed and turned him down."

"I did no such thing. Oh, I did laugh, because he caught me completely off guard."

"You're in Ottawa."

"I was. Now I'm back. Mom didn't need my kidney after all and the vet clinic I worked at offered me my old job back, with a raise. It's great to be home. You *just* missed Max. He came home for a little lunch and some 'afternoon delight'.

I see he gave you a key, naughty boy."

"Actually, no. I'm renting the basement suite and this is my key. It works on both doors."

"So you just let yourself in here?"

"I... you know what? It doesn't matter why I'm here because I'm leaving. The lying sack of shit is all yours."

"Please leave the key, then."

"No. I'll leave it on the kitchen table downstairs after I've moved my stuff out. I still have the suite for two more weeks, but I'll be gone by the end of today." I could hear a hitch in her voice and it tore my heart out.

"That's probably a good idea. Nice meeting you. Bye."

I heard the door open and slam shut with a thud.

"Ouch. She's a little pissed off, don't you think, kids?" Michelle left the kitten room and I heard her put the security chain in place. "You brats behave while I get dressed and pack up my stuff." I thought I could hear her bare feet pad across the hardwood and upstairs.

For the next half hour, I watched the kittens rush to the door every time Michelle walked near and placed something down on the floor in the entrance-way. They sounded like boxes and maybe a plastic garbage bag of something soft, probably clothes. She made seven trips in all. And the whole time I wanted to throw up and rejoice at the same time. She was moving her shit out, which is what I'd hoped for all along, but she'd also completely ruined my relationship with Tori, just for kicks. What a bitch.

Eventually, I heard the chain being removed, the deadbolt thrown open, and the front door opened. Sounds from the rainy street were now quite clear. Ten minutes later Michelle leaned into the kitten room and addressed the five for the last time. "That's all, babies. I'm off to my lawyer to start the separation from your papa. Tell him there's a letter on his drafting table upstairs, though you probably won't have to tell him because he spends every spare minute up there working on his damned maps so he'll see it sooner rather than later. I hope your forever families love you as much as I do." She made kissing sounds and left, locking up behind her.

I wanted to laugh and scream and dance and punch something. Instead, I found my phone, turned it back on, started the recorder, and called Michelle. She answered on the third ring.

"Hi Max. You got my letter."

"No, not yet. It says whatever it says, but I just wanted to hear why you did what you did to Tori. You're obviously engaged to your dentist so why did you have to pretend you were engaged to me? Have you really become such a bitch?"

"Oh relax, Max. You can do better than that blonde slut. How old is she? Twenty-one? Twenty-two? Really? I'm doing you a favour. Speaking of favours, the letter says it all. I'm letting you have the house. My lawyer is drawing up a Separation Agreement. Of course, you'll have to qualify with the bank for the mortgage all by yourself. Good luck with that, working at that little shop. I have the last of my stuff except for the antique dining set and matching sideboard that's been in my family for over a century. Please take good care of them until I'm back at Thanksgiving with a truck to get them."

"Of course. Just to clarify, though Mish, you and I are not engaged, you're engaged to what's-his-face, and you were just bullshitting Tori because she's too young for me."

"Pretty much. Except that I was bullshitting her because you're a lousy match. She's not too young, she's too *interesting*. She'd be bored with you five years faster than I was. Find a nice librarian and have a good life. Maybe have some babies so you can put your kitty-care talents to human use."

"Thanks, Michelle."

"Of course." She disconnected the call and I needed air. My phone beeped and the voicemail icon showed two messages waiting. They could wait a little longer. I rounded up the kittens and put them back in their room, got a cold beer, and went out to the porch. I downed half the beer before I finally checked the messages.

"Max, it's Kalani. How's Tori doing? Call me." The second message was her again, telling me to call. How the hell did Kalani know what had happened? I checked the time. She should be at work and it would be easier to ask her in person. I finished my beer, went inside to stick the empty bottle in the kitchen, to get my wallet and keys, and to put my sandals on.

The air was still post-storm cool-ish and the short walk was nice. As soon as I walked in the store Kalani rushed over and hugged me, then she slapped me in the arm. "You haven't called me, asshole! I'm worried sick. It's been two days. How's Tori?"

"How's Tori? How about 'How's Max'?"

"You look fine to me, you idiot. *She's* the one that was hit."

I was deeply confused. "What the hell are you talking about, Lani? I never laid a hand on her, and neither did Michelle."

"Michelle? What does Michelle have to do with it? And I never said *you* hit her. You don't even own a car."

I threw my hands up in full-on honest surrender. "I have no bloody idea what you're talking about. Two days ago Michelle showed up at the house to get the rest of her stuff while I was at work. Then Tori came back early from Ottawa and ran into Michelle at the house. Michelle told her Mish and I were engaged and Tori stormed off. Now she's got some guy staying with her at her condo."

Kalani went behind the counter to take care of a couple of customers who looked like they wanted to stay to hear more of my personal soap opera. "I know all that, Max. She told me."

"*Tori* did? When did you talk to her?"

"Not long after she saw Michelle. I was just coming into work and she went running past, the rain not quite hiding her tears. You broke her heart, and I'm pissed at you. I'm also pissed because you didn't tell me you and Michelle are engaged."

"We're *not*. The ring is from the dentist. She's engaged to *him*, not *me*. Where did Tori run off to? She won't answer my calls or texts and has even blocked me."

"If she thought you were engaged to Michelle and had been lying to her, no wonder she blocked your ass. As to where she ran off to, when she left here she ran across at the intersection and got hit by a Lexus."

"Oh shit. Wednesday? Just before three?"

"Yes! You saw it?"

"No, but the police and ambulance went past the shop. I had no idea it was

Tori. Where did they take her?"

"Toronto Western. So you haven't seen her?"

"Of course not! I had no clue. So who is the guy in her condo?"

"I have no idea. Her boss, maybe?"

"That doesn't make sense." I took out my phone, Googled Toronto Western Hospital, and clicked the link, then tapped a couple more on the menu. Nope. "Visiting hours are over, but they start at nine tomorrow. I'll go see her first thing and straighten this mess out. Did you see her at the accident scene? How bad were her injuries?"

"She was unconscious. They strapped her to a spinal board and took her away."

"Shit."

"Yes, shit. And shit that Michelle pulled. I knew that woman had some problems, but who does that to a man's woman when you've already rejected that man and found another one? Really messed up."

"Agreed."

She looked at me and tilted her head as if she was trying to focus on something not quite right. "So where is Michelle now?"

"Back in Ottawa. I just called her."

"If you didn't know the two of them had met and didn't know Tori was in the hospital, how did you know to call Michelle?"

"I have it all on tape. So to speak. Though it's digital, not tape."

A raised eyebrow was her reply.

"You want to see it?"

"I'll take Stupid Questions for a $1000, Alex."

"No problem." I showed her the cat camera footage of the encounter between the two women in my life, and then I played her my phone conversation with Michelle.

"Holy shit! The bitch!"

"That's what I said."

"It's a good thing none of this needs to stand up in court because I'm not sure it was legal to record their conversation."

"I don't need it for court, I just need to show it to Tori and play the phone conversation for her so she knows I never lied to her."

"Then I guess you're off to the hospital first thing. Do you want company? I want to check up on her anyway and can sort of back up your story about not knowing she was there until tonight."

"Yes, please."

"Now go home and get some sleep so you're ready when I pick you up."

"Yes ma'am."

"Don't you *ma'am* me, you old fart." She came around the counter and hugged me hard. "We'll get it sorted out."

"You think so?"

"I hope so. I haven't seen anyone that hurt in a long time, Max. Even though you didn't do anything wrong, you have some long-term repairs to do to regain her trust. She's wonderful and *so* worth the effort."

"I know. Thanks. I'll see you in the morning."

Chapter 17

I was so emotionally and physically exhausted by the time I got home that I skipped the steak, heated up a can of soup, and grilled a cheese sandwich. I didn't bother going to bed. I cleaned up, closed the kittens out of the kitchen and the stairs, and let them sleep on me on the couch. I set the alarm for 7:00, to give me time to shower and try to eat something before Kalani picked me up.

o0o

"You must be Max. Get the hell out of here. Now."

It didn't take a genius to figure out that the big guy blocking my way into Tori's hospital room was the one I'd seen silhouetted at her condo.

"I am, and I'm not leaving until this gets sorted out."

"You broke my little sister's heart. What do you need to sort out?"

"You're her brother?"

"Yes."

"And you're staying in her condo?"

"Just since I came down on Wednesday. How do you know that? Have you been stalking her?"

"No. Not exactly. Look, I get why you're protecting her from me. I admire that, considering the facts as you know them. But everything Tori told you is a lie, except she doesn't know it. Can Kalani go in and visit with her while you and I get a coffee and I show you how this all got so screwed up? Tori was talking to

Kalani just before the accident. They're friends."

Big brother looked at Kalani and seemed satisfied that she was what I said she was. "Tori is asleep, but you can go in and sit with her." He looked at me. "I could use a coffee, so you've got twenty minutes to give me a reason not to have security escort you out."

"I'll take it. Thank you."

He led the way to the Tim Hortons coffee shop in the atrium. We stood in line to order and I paid for both drinks, of course. There were three open tables and he picked one in a corner. "Twenty minutes. Go."

"First of all, what are Tori's injuries? I only know that she was hit by a car."

"She has a mild concussion, a dislocated hip, and swelling around her spine. She has movement and they're sure she'll recover 100% once the swelling goes down, which it almost has. They hope to release her on Monday."

"Okay. That all sounds painful, but I'm glad the prognosis is good. Now, long story short, I foster kittens and have a security camera in the kitten room to monitor them. Michelle my ex was in the kitten room when Tori came into the house. The kitten room has a Dutch door, the bottom half of which is closed during the conversation. I'll play the video right from Michelle's arrival. By the way, she lives in Ottawa and I had no idea she was coming to Toronto this week. She gave me no warning. I had no idea until last night that she was even in the city and certainly had no idea she'd been in the house on Wednesday."

"Fine. Show me."

I did. Then I played the recording of the phone conversation, trying to keep the volume down so other coffee-drinking donut eaters couldn't overhear it. When I was done, Tori's big brother leaned back and sighed. "Wow. Your ex is a nasty piece of work."

"That's the consensus. She isn't usually, but she sure was that day."

"She looks great in that towel, too."

"Yeah, she does. But..." I almost told him that Tori looked much better in a towel, but one, she was his little sister, and two, I wasn't the type of guy who told other guys details about the women I'd been with.

"But?"

"But, she's history. She left me and I'm fine with that, whether Tori comes back to me or not."

"Okay, Max. You get to play all of this for Tori. She'll decide what she decides and we'll all abide by that, but she needs to know the truth and she sure doesn't know it now."

"Thank you."

Tori and Kalani were chatting up a storm when we stepped into the room, but both shut up at the sight of us. My heart dropped down into my gut at the sight of Tori battered and bruised. She was flat on her back with what looked like a horse collar stabilizing her neck and the whole bed tilted up so she could sort of see us. Her arm on top of the blanket was bruised a horrid shade of greenish purple and a smaller bruise on the right side of her face showed where her head had hit whatever it hit. Kalani raised one eyebrow and I nodded. She smiled and nodded back.

"Hi, Tori. You look great."

She didn't smile. "You're a lying piece of shit, Max. Then and now."

Her brother stepped up beside the bed and looked down so she could see his face clearly without straining. "It doesn't happen often, Vicki, but you're wrong about this one. You were scammed by his ex."

"Bullshit. He just fed you some line. I saw the ring. She was half naked in their house, playing with the kittens." Tears trickled out of the corners of her eyes and nearly crushed me. Instead, I started the recording. The three of us listened to it again, and Tori for the first time.

"That proves nothing. Or not much, anyway. I know most of it. I was there. And thanks for telling me there was a recording device in the house, *asshole*."

Big brother gently squeezed her arm. "There's more."

I played the phone conversation. Tori growled when she heard Michelle call her a slut, but when Michelle mentioned the Separation Agreement and admitted what she'd done, Tori's tears flowed in earnest. When it was all done she motioned me over with a pained finger waggle.

"I'm sorry I had so little confidence in our relationship."

"It's been two weeks, Tori, not nearly enough time to build confidence."

"Maybe not, but it's been enough time for me to fall in love with you."

Oh shit. The 'L' word. I guess this was as good a time as any for it to be dropped. "And I love you."

"Kiss me, you fool."

I leaned in and carefully did as I was told.

"That'll do for now. When I'm healed, I'll expect a little more enthusiasm. Oh, and I'll believe that Separation Agreement when I see it. Or when *you* see it, since it's none of my business."

"Me, too. My faith in her has bottomed out. She was never cruel when we were together. This is a whole new side to Michelle. At least I got to see it before we started a family."

"You want kids?"

"Not with *her*. With you, but not with her." Oh shit! What did I just say?! Open mouth, insert foot.

"Really? Me, too, but that's a conversation for much later in our relationship. At least week four."

"Or maybe even week five."

She reached up, took my hand, and squeezed. "Don't you have a shop to open, Map Man?"

"I do."

"Then go, do. And give me a call tonight after work."

"I'll come visit."

"No, you'll play with the kittens. You've got only tonight and tomorrow with them. Give them all the love you can. Eddie is going to hang out with me to keep me from clawing my way out of this rig and going for a smoke. You can visit for an hour or so tomorrow. Maybe bring me one of those rib eyes we were going to cook up."

So her brother's name was Eddie. I don't remember if I knew that or not. "I think I can manage that." I kissed her hand, shook Eddie's, and left with Kalani. The walk to her car was hazy. My foundations had been torn up, bounced around, and then replanted. I was both warm deep down, and a little light-headed. Four days before, Tori and I were just dating, moving forward but not in any great rush. Now, we seemed to have leaped forward past the hesitant goofy stuff and straight into a solid, workable, future-thinking love. We weren't exactly planning the future, but there in the hospital room we had definitely broached the subject, and I was okay with that.

Kalani dropped me at the store with a hug, a kiss on the cheek, and a heartfelt "Are you okay? You look a little wobbly."

"I guess I'm better than I was, not as good as I will be, and just trying to get my head around how fast things can change, for the better or worse."

"So very true. Just don't propose to her in a hotel room surrounded by her friends."

"Why does everyone keep rubbing my nose in that?"

"Because we love you and we want you to know that we may not forget your goofy mistakes, but we also don't hold them against you."

I gave her a last quick hug. "I love you guys, too. Thank you for today."

"Of course." She checked her phone. "It's 10:00. Open up and rock the world of maps, Max. I'm off tonight, so if you need Shannon and me to come over for a bit, we'd be happy to."

"I appreciate the offer. I'll be good, now that it's sorted. Tori and I still have some stuff to work out. She was pretty quick to dump me without even talking to me. Is that kind of knee-jerk reaction what I have to look forward to in the long term?"

"Maybe. Maybe not. But you're right that you need to discuss it. Call if you need me."

"You betcha."

o0o

The day flowed along nicely, with just enough customers before lunch to that I went home whistling again. I stuck with a salad and sandwich and spent most of the time lying on the floor being mauled and trying not to get emotional at their pending departure.

Back at the store, there were six people waiting. "Our realtor told us you have a wonderful map of West End dog parks," one of them explained.

"I do." Leona was getting the word out. I'd have to update the shop's Facebook page, too. "Come on in. We even have a lovely map of the best locations around the city for LGBTQ+ weddings. Parks, accepting churches, Community Halls..."

"That's what *I'm* here for," one person chimed in.

"Me, too."

The customers came and went all afternoon. It was great. I knew it had little to do with anything I'd done so far online and more to do with Leona having her staff pass the word, as well as the end of summer roaring down the asphalt at us and everyone scrambling to get out of town for one last weekend. Tori called in the middle of one such rush, heard the conversations going on and said "Just put me on speaker phone and on a shelf out of the way and I'll listen while you work. Since I can't be there it'll be interesting to hear you."

"Sure. Give me a second."

"I love you."

"I know. I love you, too." I put the phone on speaker, propped it up behind me at the cash counter, and went about helping everyone. I was frankly quite surprised at how many people didn't trust their Google Maps or other phone apps to get them where they needed to be. Most of my clients were over forty and they all seemed to have a story about how trusting their phone got them lost at least once.

It was finally quiet about 3:45 and I took a moment to zip into the bathroom. I'd barely closed the door when I heard a voice in the shop. Everyone was gone and I hadn't heard the door bell, so it was a little creepy. "I'll be right out!" pissed quickly, washed up, and returned to the sales area as fast as I could. There was no one there.

"You forgot about me, didn't you?" It was Tori, on my phone. I *had* forgotten. "Oops. Sorry lover."

"No problem. That was some rush you had there. It was cool to be a fly on the wall. You really know your maps. We need to incorporate your expertise into marketing and get you writing that blog. After I get out of here, of course."

"Yeah, it can wait. I want you healthy and fit."

"Me, too. Mitch just left. He and his wife brought four live flower arrangements that I'm to take home to freshen up the condo."

Right. Her condo. "That was sweet of them."

"It was. By the way, I know I told Michelle that I would have the suite cleared out by Wednesday night, but I'm afraid I didn't."

"You told Michelle, you didn't tell your landlord. I had a chat with him and he's perfectly fine with you finishing out your two weeks, especially if you spend a chunk of that time upstairs with your neighbor."

"He still wants me up there?"

"That's what I heard on the grapevine, through the rumor mill, and down on the corner."

"I was hoping he would. I won't be going back to work for at least a week and then it'll be two weeks of lighter duties and no road trips. Mitch's orders."

"I look forward to finally meeting Mitch in person."

"And he really wants to meet you, too."

The doorbell rang and Flat Earth Robin entered.

Tori must have heard the bells. "I'll let you go, Map Man. I'm going to have another nap and will call you after Eddie goes back to the condo."

"Thanks, Tori. Talk to you later." I hung up and turned to snark at Robin for coming back, but he spoke first.

"I'm sorry." His eyes were red and he looked a little lost so I changed tact.

"What for?"

"Coming back. I really hope you got more... my brother died."

What? "Oh no! I'm sorry, sir."

"Mark. My name is Mark. My brother was Peter."

I wheeled my chair out from behind the counter and pushed it over to him. "Sit. What happened?"

"Heart attack. Yesterday. He wasn't arguing or ranting or trying to convince anyone of anything about the shape of the planet or the moon landing or 9-11,

236 T. G. REYNOLDS

he was just shopping for groceries with his girlfriend and their son. He picked up a bouquet of flowers and was handing them to her when his heart just exploded."

Shit! "That's terrible. Did he suffer?"

"No, Benti said he had this big goofy smile on his face, even after they pronounced him." He coughed, his throat sounding a little dry.

"Can I get you a bottle of water?" I kept a half-dozen in the little fridge for emergencies.

"Water? Sure. Please."

I ducked into the back and returned with a cold bottle. I handed it to him, not knowing what to say.

"Thank you." He opened it, took a couple of sips to test it, and then drained half of it right down. "He liked you, you know. He could tell you didn't agree with his ideas, but you didn't call him stupid or crazy. You respected him enough to listen politely and you told us about the Underground Railroad. He appreciated that. We know our ideas aren't popular and most non-believers don't like being told they're being fooled, but we believe what we believe and have faith in our evidence. I thought Peter was crazy, too, until one day I woke up and it was like I'd taken the red pill and could clearly see the truth. Benti wasn't completely sold on the truth, either, but she loved him with all her heart. They were high school sweethearts but her traditional Indian family wouldn't let them marry."

"So how can *I* help you, Mark?"

"Two things. I really just needed to talk to someone. I don't have many friends." I wasn't surprised by that, unfortunately. "Also, I was hoping you had one copy of the projection tucked away somewhere in the back. I'm putting mine on display at his funeral and want to put one in his coffin with him. I know it sounds stupid."

Yes, I told him that I was all out of them, but it was for his brother's funeral. Crazy or not, the man had just lost the guy who was probably his best friend. "It doesn't sound stupid at all. I do have *one*. On the house. For Peter. Give me a sec." I went to the back, pulled one off the stack, and took it out to him with a tube. I laid it on the center table so he could see it clearly. "How's this? High enough resolution?"

His eyes filled with tears. "It's beautiful. Thank you."

I carefully rolled it up and slipped it into the tube. "It's my honour. Tell me about Peter."

"What do you want to know?"

"Anything. Tell me what you wish the world knew about your big brother."

So he did. I got the whole story about their rural Christian upbringing, how Peter was his protector when they were kids, and their heartache when their parents died when their truck was hit by a drunk hit-and-run driver. I learned about Peter's model train hobby, his online self-education, his love for Benti and their autistic son, and when the Flat Earth theory came into their lives. I learned all of it, and I didn't mind. It was a fascinating peek into the lives of people I would never have hung out with in a million years. Customers came and went and Mark sat quietly leafing through an atlas while I helped them and saw them on their way.

When at last the shop was quiet again, Mark began to tell me about the trip the four of them had planned to England to the site of the original Bedford Level experiment in November when his phone rang.

"Hi, Benti. I did." He picked up the tube. "I have it right here. I'm okay. How about you? I'll be home in a few minutes. Okay. Two percent or one percent? Two it is. See you soon." He hung up. "She's so strong. I don't know how I could handle this without her."

"She sounds amazing. Why don't you bring her by sometime to say hi."

His eyes widened. "You'd let me do that?"

"Sure. We'll just keep the FE conversation to a minimum. I'm sure we can find something else to talk about."

"Thank you. We'll come by. I have to go. She needs milk." He picked up the tubed map. "And thank you so much for this. I promise not to tell anyone where I got it."

"It's my pleasure, Mark. Again, I'm sorry for your loss."

He left and the store was quiet for the first time all day. It wasn't just quiet; a hush seemed to fall over it, but a peaceful one, not a suppressive smothering of sound. A man had lost his brother and best friend, and despite the shop fans blowing, the summer air held on to the memories Mark had shared.

I texted Tori. *I love you.*

Her reply came a minute later. *I love you 2. Everything ok?*

That last customer was Flat Earth Robin whose name is really Mark. His brother died yesterday. A heart attack in the grocery store.

OMG! That's terrible.

Yeah.

Are you ok?

Yup. Just a little shocked. I almost lost you. And now I realized that even two weeks into our relationship I was as sure as I could be that I wanted her in my life forever.

But you didn't. I'm going to be OK. WE are going 2 be okay.

I know. Please come home soon.

I will, Map Man.

I texted back a heart. She texted one back and added *Call me later.*

Ok. I'm sure that part of the reason Michelle moved on was my taking her for granted and not being as romantic as I could be. That wasn't going to happen with Tori.

o0o

The shift finished quietly, which I was more grateful for than I expected. After Mark left with the poster for Peter's coffin, I got to thinking about Mom and Dad a bit, but also about those who were still around. I locked up and walked home, texting my sister as I went. *Hey, kiddo. Just checking in to see how you are all doing. I have a lady I want you to meet soon.* Then I texted Rose. *How is Joe doing? How are you?* Finally, I texted Aba. *Have I got a story for you. I'm home all night. Drop by.*

Rose replied first, just as I was walking across my porch. *He's doing great. Me, too, thanks. You?*

Glad to hear that. I'm okay, thanks. Tori was hit by a car and is in hosp but is expected to recover 100%. Next potluck is going to be an interesting one.

What?!!! Where is she?!

TW. I'm visiting tomorrow. She's home Monday, we hope.

Good. We're in London tomorrow or we'd visit her.

Have a safe trip.

Thumbs up.

I let the kittens out and marched them straight to the kitchen. I fixed us all dinner, which Kerouac ignored in favour of trying to climb onto my plate to get at my spaghetti Bolognese. I blocked his tiny efforts with my palm and lifted him back to his own meal. I was really, really, going to miss him.

Aba's text buzzed my phone right next to Kerouac and the little tuxedo boy jumped straight up with a startled "Mow!"

I'm closing tonight, brother. Can I bring dessert after 9?

Always. See you then.

Aba sent a thumbs up, too, but his was an accurate caricature of himself created with the Memojis on his phone. It was so spot-on with his receding hairline and little goatee it was both great and creepy.

I knew I needed to get the shipwreck map finished, but with so little time remaining with this batch of furry love, I sat with them and did layout work for the desserts map on my iPad. I also caught up on my social media accounts, since Tori was nudging me in that direction for the shop.

The phone rang. Speaking of Rage Grrl..."Hey Handsome. Big brother just left for the condo."

"I'm glad he's there for you, and I'm sorry I wasn't."

"You didn't know, or you would have been. Besides, I'm the one who cut off communications with you; or rather Eddie did, because I was doped up for two days. But I told him to during a moment of semi-lucidity."

"He's a good brother. Speaking of siblings, when you're up for it I want to introduce you to my sister and her family."

"I'd love to meet them. You have the coolest people in your life."

"Yeah, I guess I do, and the ones who've met you are crazy about you."

"How about you?"

I knew what she meant, but I was feeling a little cocky and just *had* to play dumb. "They're crazy about *me*, too."

"You smart ass. How do *you* feel about me? I let Michele get under my skin and between us pretty damned fast."

"True, but she's good at that. She was half naked in my house, wearing a ring, and I told you myself that I'd proposed to her. Your conclusions weren't unreasonable."

"Maybe not, but I could have given you a chance to defend yourself."

"Not really. You were in pain and had to protect your own heart. I would have done the same thing. In fact, I did. When you didn't show up on Wednesday and didn't even reply to my texts—"

"I wasn't conscious."

"I know that now. But that night I walked over to your condo, to see if you were there instead, and I saw Eddie's silhouette on the blinds like an old fifties song. I automatically assumed you had a new guy and I was out on my ass."

"I would never just ghost you."

"But after Michelle left..."

"I understand. We're quite a pair, aren't we, with enough trust and separation issues for a dozen people."

"I'm not going to cheat on you."

"And I'm not going to *leave* you."

"I know."

"Just don't propose to me in an airport hotel room surrounded by your friends."

"Oh for f—." You make one mistake and your friends are all over it. "Deal. I promise."

"Then we're all set. One day at a time."

"Or maybe two."

"I can do two, if you insist."

"I insist on nothing except—". The brass lion pounded on the door and the kittens jumped up from their various sleep spots. "Aba is here with dessert."

"You'd better go...but not before you tell me what one thing you are going to insist on."

I walked the phone to the door and opened it. Aba slipped in while I pushed the kittens away with my feet. "Just that I love you."

"You're so sweet. I love you, too. Now enjoy your visit and I'll see you tomorrow. Goodnight, Map Man."

"Goodnight, Stuntwoman."

"Ouch! I deserve that. Later gator."

"Ciao, Bella." We disconnected and I turned to see Aba watching me with a big-ass smile that went all the way to the twinkle in his eyes.

"You two are so adorable. You told her you loved her. That's *huge*. What's changed?"

I laughed. "Brother, let's get comfortable. Beer, rye, or coffee?"

"Decaf would be nice. We'll need plates." He held up a compostable food container. "*Basbousa*."

"Right this way."

oOo

It took twice as long to tell Aba all that had happened during the week because he kept making me repeat myself so he could get the facts straight to tell Lydia. By the time he left, I was full of Egyptian Basbousa—a delicious almond, coconut, and semolina cake with yogurt—and decaf and ready for bed. The kittens were all sleepy and let me carry them to their room without much fuss. I'd have most of tomorrow with them and needed a night in my own bed, even if it was missing Tori, for now.

oOo

Before I started off for the hospital on Sunday, I called Tori to ask if she really wanted that rib eye and thankfully, she said to save it. While en route I texted the potluck group to tell them that the kittens were going back to the adoption centre first thing the next morning and if they wanted to come by this evening and say goodbye I'd put on a pot of coffee and make sure the Fantabulous Five were on their best behaviour.

By the time I reached the hospital, everyone replied that they'd drop in, though Rose and Joe would be a bit late as they were still two hours away in London, and wouldn't be leaving until after six.

Chapter 18

E DDIE SMILED WARMLY, GOT up, and shook my hand when I entered. It was a nice switch from our first meeting. "Good to see you, Max."

"And you, Eddie." Tori's bruises seemed to have deepened, but her overall colour was better. She certainly didn't look as pale as she had yesterday morning.

"If you tell me I look beautiful I swear I'll punch you in the junk, Map Man."

I waved my hand dismissively at her body. "*This* is all just a shell. It takes shots, gets beat up, ages, but your beauty is in your heart, is in the light behind your eyes, and in the softness of your lips."

"Hallmark Harry has entered the room." She winked at me.

I leaned in and kissed her. She kissed me back, and gently bit my lower lip. "Ouch!"

"Oh don't be a wimp, Max. That didn't hurt. I know *exactly* how much pain you can handle, and *where*."

Eddie raised his hands as if he could fend off her words. "Whoa! TMI, Vicki." I'm going to get a coffee and let you two weirdoes talk dirty at each other." He looked directly at me. "You keep out of her bed. Don't mistake her prone position or flirty words as an invitation. Let my little sister heal before you start doing whatever it is the two of you do behind closed doors."

"Yes, sir."

Tori stuck her tongue out at him. "What makes you think we close the doors?"

"I'm outta here. I'm bringing you both black coffees, whether you want them or not."

"Works for me, Big Bro."

"I'm good with that, too."

Eddie left and I pulled up a chair next to the bed so I could hold Tori's hand. "Do you prefer Tori or Vicki?"

"Tori. Only Eddie gets to call me 'Vicki'. My mother calls me Victoria and Dad calls me Torrible Tori."

"Cute."

"How about you? Maxwell, Max, or Maxi?"

"I answer best to 'Max'. If I upset you, you can hit me with 'Maxwell' like Mom did. Only bullies—passive-aggressive or otherwise—call me 'Maxi'. My sister calls me 'Shithead', so her kids get to call me 'Uncle Shithead', or 'Uncle Max', but never just 'Shithead'."

"I think I'll stick with 'Max'."

"Or 'Map Man', but only from you."

"Thank you."

"So, tell me how Ottawa went, and what the hell you were doing in the house more than five hours ahead of schedule."

"I wanted to surprise you. I was going to do laundry downstairs then come up and make my Oreo cookie no-bake lasagna for dessert, since you'd already bought the steaks. I also wanted to pick up a nice bottle of wine and change into my favourite see-through summer dress and be waiting on the couch with the kittens when you walked in the door."

I was floored. "You flew back early to do all that for me?"

"For us. Every kind or good thing we do for each other benefits us both."

"That's pretty deep."

"I spent two days with Zach and Ashley and saw the effect their love had on their entire outlook on life. I wanted that. *Want* that. With you. I wanted to do something a little crazy, unexpected, and completely from my heart, because you have stolen it."

"I had to because my chest was empty after you stole mine."

"You two are going to make me puke." Eddie stood in the doorway with a cardboard tray and three coffees. "Vicki, do I need to get the doctor to have them examine your head wound, cuz this does not sound like the hardnosed cynic I know and love."

"It's not. I'm not. Well, I still am, but I have to learn to trust sometime, and if I don't start now, I may lose my Map Man."

I squeezed her hand and she squeezed back. "I'm here as long as you want me to be, T. But you and I can do all this lovey-dovey teen talk later. While Eddie is in town I need to hear about what Little Torrible Tori was like growing up."

"Like hell you do!" She squeezed my hand hard and glared at her brother, but he ignored her and I just bore the brief pain in silence.

"Torrible Tori. Or just 'Tori-ble' as our grandmother called her.

"She was a crazy old cow."

"And you loved to push her buttons."

"No, I tried to stay away from her and that wire flyswatter handle that seemed to find my butt when I was least expecting it."

"Anyway, Tori-ble was actually a pretty cool little sister. She was never a whiny brat but instead sucked up whatever punishment me and my friends foisted on her and came back for more. She was tougher than most of the guys I knew, and most of those guys preferred to play hockey without a helmet.

Eddie and I bantered back and forth across prone Tori, teasing her until she took half-hearted swings at us or cursed us out. I learned so much about tough little Type-A Rage Grrl that my love for her deepened with every insight. Eventually, she tired and I took my leave with kisses and mushy words. Eddie walked me out.

"They'll be releasing her after twelve?" I asked.

"That's what they said. It all depends on what her doctor decides when he sees her in the morning and has a chance to look at the MRI she had today. She'll be on some pretty heavy painkillers and anti-inflammatories for about a week, so don't let her drink alcohol, if you can."

"Done. And you'll take her to my place? Or to the condo?"

"Your place, if that's okay. She needs to be waited on a bit and I'd rather she not be too alone for a while. That head injury doesn't look serious but I've heard they can be deceiving."

"I've had a few. They can be. My memory is pretty screwed up."

"That can't be any fun."

"It's not. Anyway, I'd better get home. I've got friends coming over tonight to spend time with the kittens I'm fostering before they go back to the adoption centre tomorrow morning."

"Vicki told me all about that. I think it's cool what you're doing. I'm a puppy man myself, but I'd want to keep them all if I fostered."

"I do with the kittens, too, but especially with this bunch. I've made a commitment to the centre, though, and there are wonderful forever homes waiting for the little beastlettes."

"Nice."

We talked a bit more. I convinced him to bring his family down for a visit when it cooled off a bit in September, and he convinced me to let Tori bring me up for a visit whenever. We parted on much better terms than we'd first met. The bus ride home was quiet and uneventful.

That evening the kittens got so much love from everyone and had so many pictures taken of them that they were passed out cold by the time Joe and Rose left and I bolted the door behind them. I didn't have the heart to put them to bed quite yet, so I sat up for another hour just stroking their little heads, brushing them, and rubbing their bellies. Of course, I didn't do this without shedding a tear or two. Their leaving would be the end of an era of sorts. They were the last batch Michelle and I started fostering together, and when she left they were my lifelines and my strength, despite their diminutive size. A new batch would come in a week or so and they would be the first batch that would be mine alone, with Tori in my life. A new era would begin.

Sensing my upset, the kittens all cuddle closer, draped across my lap or tucked into my hip on the couch. Kerouac, of course, was on the back of the couch behind my head, where I could hear his little high-pitched purr. Eventually, I put them carefully to bed, loaded the dirty coffee cups into the dishwasher, booked a cab for 8:30 am, and called it a night.

o0o

I won't lie. I wept when I let the Magnificent Five out of their room for the last time. And I kept it up as I fed them and ate my toast. Kerouac plodded over on the island to head-butt my hand and I lost it, scooping him up and hugging him close. Normally he would have wiggled out of my grip, but he seemed to sense something was up and so he held still. Calliope and Ginsberg wandered over from their dish and rubbed their heads against my foot, which produced even more tears. When they were fed and watered, I went back to the couch, set the alarm for fifteen minutes, and let them climb all over me. Right then I really wished Tori was there. She'd help me feel less emotional and silly, even though she'd probably be shedding tears of her own. This part of the fostering process was best shared, as I was finding out the hard way.

Ten minutes before the cab was due I corralled the wee ones in their room where it was easier to gather them into the big pet carrier. I put a clean blanket in the box with them and did a piss-poor job of ignoring their little mews of protest.

"I want you to know that I love you all and you will *always* have a huge place in my heart. You're going to find forever homes and will make little boys and girls very happy." I poked my fingers through the cage doors where they nipped and licked my fingertips. "You're always welcome to come back and visit if they let you. You have my number. Call if you ever need anything."

A car horn honked outside and I forced myself to stand up. I already had my wallet and phone in my pockets, so I grabbed the keys off the entry table, pulled a half-used tissue out of my pocket, wiped my eyes and my nose, and then picked up the case by the handle and left.

o0o

I sucked it up and held my tears back at the adoption centre as the kittens were each given a quick examination by the vet who came in on Foster Return Day and then taken into the back. Paperwork was signed, I was congratulated for the good job and thanked for being part of the rescue system. I got hugs from the staff who knew what I was going through because they were fosterers, too. I could hear my little ones' plaintiff little cries as I walked out the door and I lost my shit again. I didn't bother with a cab. I had over half an hour to get to the shop, it was only a twenty-minute walk, and I really needed the air. I put my sunglasses on, and my earbuds in, pulled my Raptors cap down, and made my miserable way to work. The only thing that kept my feet from moving forward at anything resembling a steady pace was the knowledge that Tori would finally be home tonight. My phone buzzed with incoming text after text but I ignored them.

oOo

I splashed a lot of cold water on my face when I finally got to the store, and even though I was ten minutes early I didn't open up early, which I normally would. I took that ten to get a grip on myself. I told myself that they were only kittens, that I'd done this all before and survived, and that I'd forget the five when the next crew checked in for love and care. I didn't believe a word of the shit I was telling myself, but it sort of helped. The cold water helped more, though, and by 10:00 I was mostly ready to face the world.

Despite a steady flow of customers, the morning dragged because I knew that the house was empty and I had no reason to go home for lunch. I went down the street and picked up a sub, returning to the shop to eat it at the desk in the back. I finally opened my phone and checked my messages. There were twenty waiting, and a quick scroll through revealed that they were from the people who loved me most—Tori and the entire potluck gang. There was even one from my sister, and one from the adoption agency formally thanking me for keeping the kittens in such good health.

Tori's text was simply that she'd been released and was now settled on the couch at the house. I yearned to run home and get a hug but knew that I wouldn't be able to leave the house if I got back there. I took a deep breath, texted back a bunch of exes and ohs to her, and then replied to each and every one of the other texts with some short message, which was all I had the energy for. I opened early after lunch and the afternoon dawdled along for about an hour before Leona popped in with cold drinks.

"I remembered that today was your last day with the kittens and I wanted to see how you were doing."

I gave her a half-hearted smile. "Good, thanks. I know they'll go to wonderful homes and be loved. I had the honour of being their first pet-parent, but not their last. That's what fostering is all about."

"Maybe so, but that doesn't mean you can't be sad."

"It sure doesn't."

We sipped our drinks, I helped customers as they came and went, and eventually, Leona had to get to her next appointment.

"Call me if you need anything, Kid."

"Thanks, Boss. Will do."

The remainder of the afternoon cruised on by, my mood improved a little with the chocolatey chill of the drink as I sipped it and did my best not to get brain freeze again. I locked up right at 5:05 and made my way home, ready to start the next phase of my life.

I clomped up the steps and was met at the door by Tori. She moved slowly, favouring one leg and arm. "Hey, girl. I'm willing to bet that doctor told you to take it easy."

"He did. I'm only here to give you a hug and welcome you home. Anything more strenuous or intimate will have to wait a few days, at least." She opened her arms and I stepped into them, careful not to squeeze her too hard. She eventually pulled back and planted a deep, passionate kiss right on target. I returned the passion and depth and finally started to feel my heart beating at a normal pace again.

"That's for all the kisses I wanted to give you at the hospital but couldn't because Eddie was there."

"It was worth the wait."

She took me by the hand and led me into the cool of the house. I kicked off my sandals and let her guide me to the kitchen. "How about a cold beer, my Map Man?"

"How about you sit your ass down and let me get it myself?"

"Fine." She sat, but the look she gave me was odd. Like I was missing something really obvious, or like she had a secret that she couldn't wait to tell me. She didn't say a word as I fetched a cold beer from the fridge. "Would you like a juice or a pop?"

"A juice would be nice, thank you."

Kerouac called at me from the kitten room and I realized that in my excitement to see Tori, I forgot to spring the kidlettes from kitty prison. Then I remembered there were no kittens. It was just my imagination. Just a weird memory in a brain that had a shitty memory.

He called again. I was sure of it. "Did you hear that? It sounds like Kerouac."

Tori shook her head. "No. I don't hear a thing." There was something odd about the light in her eyes. She wasn't being honest. Or was I just so damned tired that I was imagining things?

"Mew."

"There it is again." I put my beer down and walked back to the kitten room, certain I was losing my mind.

"Mew."

"Mew."

There were two voices? I *was* losing my mind. I looked over the bottom half of the door into the now empty and lonely kitten room, except that it wasn't empty. Kerouac and Calliope both stood at the bottom of the door, begging to be let out.

"What the every living...?"

Tori came up behind me and slipped her arms around my chest, wincing with the pain. "I couldn't let them go. The ladies at the adoption centre said that it's common for foster homes to have permanent resident cats and it can actually help kittens to have older cats around as they adjust."

"You adopted these two?" My heart did a flip and grew two sizes, as if I'd just learned the true meaning of Christmas.

"*We* adopted these two. This is now their forever home."

I kissed her. And kissed her. And kissed her again. "I can't do it alone."

"Why, what on earth are you suggesting, Mister Maxwell?"

"I do believe, Miss Victoria, that I'm suggesting you make this *your* forever home, too."

"I really like that idea. And you didn't even ask me in a hotel room surrounded by your friends."

"Oh for... but I didn't ask... Oh. I guess I just did. Are you going to laugh at me?"

"Not a chance, Map Man. Only *with* you." We kissed, but the kittens grabbed our attention again and we had to let them out. It seemed like the right thing to do.

"Welcome to your forever home, you cute little brats."

o0o

Thursday rolled around in no time at all and we both knew the time had come. Now or never. It was strange to make the rounds at the club and introduce Tori to everyone. They'd all met Michelle, but she was withdrawn and not entirely comfortable there, so it seemed more like a chore than a pleasure. With Tori, it was all joy. She immediately got along with absolutely everyone and somehow we ended up sitting with J'Neece, Patty, and Normal, instead of huddling at the back like I usually did. My old patterns were falling by the wayside, one by one.

Benny swung by the table to say hi and simply raised an eyebrow at me when we made eye contact. I smiled back and nodded, his eyes went wide, and that was that. Twenty minutes later the lights went off, the stage lit up, and Benny opened the show. He warmed up the audience with a little stand-up, a hilarious story about his toddler great-niece and his first exposure to dirty diapers, a quick, punchy poem of his own, and finally an introduction I'd waited a long time to hear.

"Strangers are just friends you haven't met yet. Friends, I have a special treat for y'all. A rare moment, a moment we'll all cherish as much as he does. Please welcome up onto our humble little stage for his first slam EV-er, taking the bullet for everyone else tonight, my friend, the Cat Man himself, Max-Well *Wal*-Den!"

There were only thirty people in the place, but they made the noise of a hundred as I made my way up to the stage, my folded-small poem tucked tight in my sweaty hand.

I'd love to tell you that *What I Know About Women* went perfectly and that I didn't make a single miss-beat, but I can't because I don't remember a damned thing. It is a complete freaking *blank*. But Tori recorded it all on her phone and it sure looks like I rocked the room.

About the Author

According to CBC Radio, Tim Reynolds is "Canada's modern-day Aesop".

That's great praise he struggles to live up to, but what he *will* admit to is being a prize-winning, award-nominated Canadian with stories to tell. He's also a romantic at heart.

Based out of Calgary, Alberta, Tim grew up in Toronto, earning first a B.A. and then a B.Ed. from the University of Western Ontario.

He currently remains trapped in his house, a willing indentured servant to his animals.

Find out what Tim is working on now at www.TGMReynolds.com

Also By Tim Reynolds

Stand Up & Succeed

The Cynglish Beat

The Broken Shield

The Death of God

Waking Anastasia

The Sisterhood of the Black Dragonfly

The Gravity of Guilt